The Wizard

and the

White House

by

Mike Maggio

LITTLE FEATHER BOOKS, INC.
NEW YORK

Also By Mike Maggio

FICTION

Sifting Through the Madness

The Keepers

POETRY

Your Secret Is Safe With Me

Oranges From Palestine

deMockracy

Haunted Garden
(forthcoming)

LITTLE FEATHER BOOKS, INC.

Library of Congress Cataloging-in-Publication data on file.

ISBN 978-0-9913329-7-7

Cover Design: LFB Studios
Cover Images: ©Kirsty Pargeter and ©Vicgmyr, Fotolia
The LFB logo is a trademark of Little Feather Books, Inc.

Dedication

To all those who believe the world can be a better place;
let's continue to believe, to hope, and to strive.

.

The Wizard

and the

White House

Chapter 1

ONE DAY—and it was a most inauspicious day, with dark clouds looming in the distance and a lone black bird circling portentously above the White House grounds—President Gerald Wellington Thorne woke up in his dreadfully uncomfortable bed, from a disturbing dream he could no longer remember, and found, quite by chance, that he no longer had a mouth.

It was a bright, tranquil morning, apart from the impending clouds—a Sunday in the early days of spring—when life was meant to be lazy and quiet, just as God had intended. As President Thorne awakened, he peeked out his bedroom window, ruffling the dark, heavy drapes, and noted the groundskeepers, already tending to the White House gardens, not a worry on their minds except for trimming the roses and pulling the weeds and making sure the gardens looked perfectly square and uniform.

"Wouldn't it be nice," he thought to himself for a very brief moment, "to be like them—simple and—well, not to be simple—I mean, they are simple and… Gardeners are a simple people!" he concluded in exasperation.

He pondered this thought for another brief moment, perched in the presidential bedroom, then continued with his ruminations.

"Wouldn't it be nice to be able to take a quiet stroll through the grounds with the First Lady at my side," (the First Lady was, at that very moment, sound asleep, dreaming of a very private getaway in Europe, so private that even he was not included), "or to take a leisurely drive in the country, just the two of us. No Secret Service. No pool of reporters trailing behind us."

And then:

"Wouldn't it be nice to get away from the tedium facing me each day as president—I mean, it's a tedious job, filled with—tedium."

President Thorne stopped himself again. Feeling the weight of guilt hanging heavily over him like a huge stone—he did, after all, take his responsibilities to the nation seriously—he forced these thoughts out of his mind and, looking up at the sky, noticed an odd-looking cloud— black and strangely shaped—hovering high above the city, a cloud, he thought, with a shudder, that could portend nothing but evil.

Now, President Thorne was a very religious man, so he recited a silent prayer and, gazing over his shoulder wistfully at his wife, who remained in the warm arms of sleep, wished he was back in Texas, back on his ranch or anywhere other than in the confines of a house where he had not been able to get one good night's rest since the day he had moved in.

"The beds are too stiff," he had complained to the staff when he first arrived, as they rolled their eyes and walked away. "Too old and too musty is where the problem is."

But what he would not tell them, or anyone else, especially his worrisome wife, was how he would hear strange sounds during the night—creaking boards and the peculiar comings and goings of footsteps, and indiscernible voices that seemed to come from within the very walls.

"This house is haunted," he concluded, but only to himself. Then, he added, almost as an afterthought, and with an odd smile on his perpetually bewildered face: "Haunted with the histrionics of our nation."

And he was pleased with himself. Pleased with his understanding of the nations' history, of his fearless grip on the English language.

So on the day that our story begins, President Thorne carefully returned the heavy drapes to their original position, making sure they were exactly as they had been so the housekeepers would not complain, and softly tiptoed across the room to mitigate the sounds that emanated from the wooden floor (for he did not wish to wake the First Lady who could be cranky in the early morning) and stepped onto the cold bathroom tiles, in the same bathroom, he noted each morning, where former presidents had done their business before assuming their duties for the day. He imagined Lincoln, sitting on the throne, contemplating the Gettysburg Address. And Teddy Roosevelt lathering up a shaving brush and preparing to wield his very big stick. And because they were heroes to him, (all except for the one who had preceded him, that one, he insisted as he flushed the toilet, had brought nothing but shame and ignominy on the White House), because he had admired them all as a child, he often found it hard to believe that he was now one of them, a member of a very special club that only the very privileged could join.

President Thorne stood before the bathroom mirror in preparation for his morning shave and attempted to formulate his thoughts for the emergency cabinet meeting that had been called—had they no consideration that this was a Sunday? he wondered—and longed once again for his Texas ranch, where he could chop wood or ride his horse, Dolphin, or do anything besides deal with the constant crises that seemed to arise out of nowhere. And then, looking into the mirror, he was faced with a situation that would forever change his life, for he discovered that where once were situated the thin lips from which he would constantly proclaim his infamous one-line solutions to the nation's problems, there now stood nothing but a flat swath of tough, white skin.

Now, this was a totally unexpected situation, an abrupt state of affairs with absolutely no forewarnings—no pre-indications, no symptoms that could be diagnosed early on and preventatively treated. Instead, it came of a sudden, and it was especially disturbing to President Thorne (who was not one to dawdle, who refused to let things fester until they spiraled out of control) because he had to make a major policy address that evening (something that terrified him under the best of circumstances)—and now he was uncertain (even more than he had been prior to this disturbing event) how and whether he would be able to deliver his carefully scripted speech. Besides, it made his already expressionless countenance—which often appeared to have the look of utter confusion—seem even more dubious.

This must be the work of terrorists, he concluded (though this time without the help of his senior advisors). Or maybe it was the Chinese, or perhaps, even, his political enemies who struggled daily to portray his administration as an utter failure.

Turning on his heels, President Gerald Willington Thorne rushed out of the bathroom, across the hard, wooden floor and approached his wife, who was in the midst of a very pleasant dream—for the First Lady reveled in every moment that allowed her to escape from the tiresome events that took place each day at the White House—and said, "This is very disturbing,"—or at least he tried to, for all he could manage was to twitch uncontrollably like a muzzled dog and groan from the inner depths of his very peculiar-looking lack of a mouth.

"Not to worry," the First Lady mumbled in her carefree way, turning over in her bed and resuming her reverie, for she knew every nook and cranny of her husband's mind, so much so that she had no need to actually listen to a word he said. "Something will come up between now and then," she said, yawning. "One of your staff will find a solution. They always do."

"I guess you're right," he attempted. And then, remembering his religious convictions, he added, unintelligibly: "The good Lord will see me through this."

Relieved by the First Lady's good counsel and proud of her skillful way of smoothing things out, President Thorne leaned over to kiss her, but quickly realized that he was unable to pucker his lips—for he no longer had any—and, instead, he buried his round, expressionless face deep under the covers, as he had often done as a child, hoping and praying that a firm resolution would soon come to light.

Meanwhile, on the other side of town, in a section of Southeast Washington where President Thorne had never stepped foot, Larry White, a tall, burly man who worked as a janitor at Union Station, whose handsome appearance was known for always attracting the women, who was notorious for carousing with the menfolk on many a summer's evening and who now, in the midst of a severe hangover, was busy shaving the heavy growth on his ebony face, opened his bleary eyes in shock and awe, and stared in bewilderment into the mirror, which had a long, sinuous crack running down its center, a splintery fracture that had been there since the day he and his wife had moved into their rundown apartment.

Wiping the white lather off his weary face, Larry moved this way and that, trying to find a spot in the fractured glass where he could get a clearer look, then, in exasperation, called out in a high-pitched voice to his wife who was sitting in the next room, quietly reading her Bible.

"Larry. Why you calling me like that, now," she scolded, running quickly into the room, "like you seen a ghost?"

Larry covered his face with his big, solid hands and turned slowly toward his loving wife with a deep groan that made her jump back in fear.

"Larry White!" she exclaimed. "What you up to this time? You trying to get outta going to church again? Lord have mercy, Larry! When you gonna stop that drinking? When you gonna see that the only true path in life is the one that leads to the Lord!"

Dismissing his wife's needling—for she always seemed to find an excuse to scold him for his lack of faith—Larry removed his hands from his face and lifted his aching head for her to plainly see.

"Pearl, baby" he exclaimed. "Tell me it's not true. Tell me I'm still drunk. Tell me I'm in the middle of a bad dream. Tell me, baby. Please!"

Pearl stared at her husband in disbelief and shouted the Lord's name, once, then twice, then in loud, fervent waves, begging for mercy and praying for her husband's swift deliverance from evil, for there on Larry's face, spaced evenly one above the other, were two mouths, one that blended in harmoniously with his features and complexion, the other as white and mismatched as the chipped tiles on the bathroom wall.

Larry turned back to the mirror and took another long, desperate look, squinting his eyes to focus better. He traced the lines of his own mouth with the tip of his finger. Then he pressed tentatively against the other and let out a loud cry, for from the mouth that had suddenly attached itself to his once-evenly sculpted face—a colorless, expressionless maw of two lips that seemed to have a life of their own—now rose a moan that sent shivers running up and down his sturdy spine.

"Lord have mercy, Larry White!" Pearl proclaimed, jumping back in fear. "What devil has gotten inside of you? Didn't I tell you to stay away from drink? The Devil's milk, didn't I say? And now look what's become of you."

"*This is quite disturbing*," came the sudden response in a voice that bore no resemblance to Larry's deep Washington drawl.

Pearl leaned forward tenuously and stared at her husband as if he were a demon who had just materialized and was about to cause her harm. A sudden sadness overcame her, for she was weary of the life she had carved out with her husband, and though she loved him as much as she had when they first met, she wanted, more than ever, for him to change his ways and seek out the way of the Lord.

"Larry," she said, at last, "we got to rush to church. We got to pray to the Lord to make you well."

"*I guess you're right*," came the unexpected words from Larry's new mouth. "*The good Lord will see me through this*."

Now, Larry White was not a religious man, though he could sometimes be coerced into attending Sunday services. So when Pearl heard her husband's unexpected response, she opened her eyes wide and struggled to hold back tears of joy. This strange transformation, she thought, observing her husband's monstrous face, was a blessing in disguise. It was God's way of bringing her man back to the fold.

"Larry," Pearl shouted joyously, "I believe you have been delivered. Praise the Lord! Larry," she persisted, "this is a sign from God to mend your ways and follow the true path. The Lord works in strange ways, Larry. Hallelujah!"

"Pearl," Larry shouted, in his own loud, coarse voice. "Call the doctor. Call 911. I need someone to help get this goddamn thing off of me!"

"No, Larry White," Pearl declared. "I will not call the doctor. I will call Reverend Willis. He'll know what to do. He understands the meaning of the Lord's ways."

Pearl White jumped for joy. Not since she had been a young woman, dreaming of finding a man to wed, a partner to have children with, had she felt so happy. She was giddy, like a child whose dream had just come true, or like a young woman who had suddenly, helplessly fallen in love.

Pearl rushed blissfully out of the bathroom, humming a hymn and praising the Lord, leaving Larry trembling and perplexed, half-shaven and double-mouthed and quite disconcerted as to how events were taking shape on this ill-fated Sunday, on what was supposed to be his one true day of rest.

Down along the Potomac, around the Tidal Basin where the morning sun was slowly rising and the cherry blossoms were in full, glorious bloom, Fuzzaluddin Choudry, a Pakistani immigrant who had settled in northern Virginia, where he owned a humble butcher shop that catered mostly to the Muslim community, who was known as Fuzzy to the few American acquaintances he boasted, who constantly praised Allah and thanked his lucky stars for the good life he had been able to make in his newly-adopted country, was taking an early morning stroll and enjoying the peace and quiet that comes only at this early hour of the day, when there came a sudden rumbling from the middle of the bay.

Choudry turned his freshly shaven face (for he did not believe in long, scruffy beards as a measure of religious fervor and desperately wanted to blend in with the non-Muslims around him) toward the bay where he witnessed a large waterspout rise up and heard what he thought was a loud voice calling out his name.

"*Allahu akbar!*" he exclaimed.

He looked around to see who might be calling him but, to his surprise, the park was completely empty and the only sound he could distinguish was a gentle breeze blowing through the blossom-laden trees.

"Fuzzaluddin Choudry," came the deep, hollow voice once again.

Choudry turned his glance back toward the basin where the huge waterspout, illuminated by the morning sun's brilliant rays, hovered magically just above the water. Seeing no one around, he fell to his knees in fear and prostrated himself, shouting God's name and praying to be delivered from the clutches of what he believed could only be an evil *jinn*.

"Fuzzaluddin Choudry," the voice said again. "You have been chosen."

"*Allahu akbar*," Choudry shouted, prostrating himself over and over. "*Allahu akbar.*"

"The president of the United States is in grave danger. You must go to him immediately."

"But, but—" was all Choudry could manage to say.

"You have been chosen, Fuzzaluddin Choudry, to carry out this mission. You must do everything in your power to protect him."

Choudry raised his head to get a better view, but was blinded by the bright light burning in the bay. Closing his eyes, he gathered up his courage, took a deep breath and shouted: "Who are you?"

"Do what I ask," the voice responded, "and I will guide you."

And then, as quickly as it had appeared, the waterspout vanished and the bay went as flat and calm as it had been prior to Choudry's strange, inexplicable vision.

Choudry was trembling like a lone tent in the middle of a violent windstorm. Slowly, he stood up and looked around and found that the park was as empty as it had been when he had first arrived. As fast as his overgrown belly would allow, he ran off to his old rattletrap of a Chevrolet and jumped inside, gunning the engine and taking off with a screech of its threadbare tires.

When he reached home, Choudry hastily parked his car beside the withered remains of an olive tree which had not made it through the winter. Rushing inside his house, he sat down on an old camel's saddle he had brought from his ancestral village on the outskirts of Lahore, and threw his head down in fear, panting breathlessly and repeating God's ninety-nine names.

"Is that you, Choudry?" his wife shouted from the kitchen, calling him by the name she had used since the day he had taken her on their wedding bed. "Breakfast is almost ready," she said, entering the foyer. Then, taking one look at her husband, she shouted: "Choudry, what is wrong? Are you ill? Did you not take your medication? Didn't I tell you you need to lose weight?"

Dressed in a traditional *salwar kameez* and with a headscarf draped loosely around her neck, ready to deploy in case of sudden visitors, Choudry's faithful wife eyed her husband, fearful his health was finally catching up with him. She knew his careless ways—eating poorly, never exercising, never remembering to take his medication on time— and she wondered now if it was all about to catch up with him, if, perhaps, it was already past time for her to call an ambulance.

"Choudry!" she shouted. "Talk to me. Tell me what's wrong. Shall I make you a hot water bottle? Shall I call the doctor?"

"Amina," Choudry said at last, struggling to catch his breath. His droopy eyes were filled with panic and the look on his face was that of a man who was staring into the gaping door of death. "Pack our suitcases," he said. "We've got to go."

"Go?" Amina questioned.

"Go," he responded. "Immediately."

Amina looked at her husband as if she had just stepped on a stone, a look exhibiting more annoyance than pain, more impatience than anger.

"Just like that?" she asked. "Go? Don't we need to make plans first? Don't we need to tell our children? Don't we need to decide where we're going?"

"Anywhere," Choudry responded. "We'll go to Pakistan and visit our relatives. We'll go to Saudi Arabia. We can go to Mecca and make *umra*. We just need to get away from here. As quickly as possible."

Amina looked at her husband, her impatience turning to concern. She was beginning to understand. After being married all these years, she knew her husband as well as the recipes she prepared for him each day. And she concluded, instinctively, that he had done something wrong, something that would reflect badly on him and the entire family.

"Choudry. What has happened? Are you in trouble? Have you been giving to those charities again? How many times do I have to tell you not to give to those charities? Give to the people in the street, give to the mosque, to the church even, but not to those charities. It will only get us in trouble. Did I not tell you that?"

"Amina, please," Choudry broke in to halt his wife's incessant chatter, "I have not given to the charities."

"Then what have you done, Choudry? These are dangerous times. We must be careful. We must not let the world think that we are terrorists. We could be arrested. Removed from our house and thrown to the—to the wolves."

"Amina," Choudry said wearily, letting out a sigh. "There are no wolves in Arlington."

"You know what I mean, Choudry. This is not a laughing matter. I don't see why you have to make so light of it."

Choudry gazed blankly at his wife and wondered what had possessed him to marry her thirty years back. It was something in her eyes, he recalled, though his memory had since dulled, something, it seemed, now through the haze of time, about the way she had applied henna to her palms the day he had gone to her family's house to ask for her hand.

He took her puffy hands in his and patted them, as he always did when she was agitated, noting the wrinkles that now stood out as boldly as the henna she had applied back then and the small, stubby fingers he had come to know so well, then held them up to his face and covered his eyes with them.

"Amina," he said when she had at last quieted down, "you must listen to me. What I have to say is very—extraordinary. Very—" he paused, trying to search for the right word, "unbelievable."

Choudry looked up at Amina and saw that her lips had started to tremble, a sign, he knew, after all these years, that she was ready to listen.

"Amina," he said in a soft, breathy whisper. "Allah has spoken to me."

"*Allahu akbar!*," Amina shouted, pulling her hands back and catapulting them high over her head in shock. *"Allahu akbar!"*

"While I was walking in the park," Choudry persisted. "He appeared to me and spoke."

He struggled with the words, as he had struggled when they had read *alfatiha* the day they had become engaged, pronouncing each one slowly and carefully, while trying to suppress his emotions.

"Amina," he said at last, wiping a tear from his eye with her hand, "I'm afraid."

Amina didn't know how to respond. She had heard many strange things from her husband over the years, things he dreamed about, wishful thinking about things that would never come true, but mainly what she recalled hearing from him was a lot of nonsense. Utterances, she had finally concluded after years of listening to him, that wives were simply supposed to put up with. But this was too much. This was something she could not remain silent about.

"Choudry," she said, "this is blasphemy. God does not appear to just anyone, especially to a poor butcher like you who does not even attend the mosque. Have you been drinking? What will become of us now? Think of your family, Choudry. Think of your children."

"Amina, please. For once in your life, please listen to me."

"Listen? You want me to listen to such nonsense? No, Choudry. I have listened to you all my life. I listened when I left my family to go with you to that awful house in Lahore. I listened to you when we came here to America. And look where that has gotten us. I have had nothing but listening, Choudry, and I am tired of it."

Choudry abandoned his wife to her chatter as he tried to formulate what his next step would be. He could sell the butcher shop. That would be easy enough to do. Then the house. Then they would leave for Pakistan. He would build a villa there with the money and still have enough to open a business. His children were grown. They could stay or they could come with them, as they liked. And if his wife wanted to stay behind with them, that would be fine too.

Having formulated his thoughts, he let out a big sigh of relief that caught Amina off guard and caused the pitch of her voice to rise even further. He felt better now that he had a plan. He would begin first thing Monday morning.

"Amina," he said, standing up and walking calmly toward the dining room, "I am ready for breakfast."

"Choudry," his wife shouted, "are you listening to me?"

"Yes, Amina," he answered. "I can wait. I will wash up in the meantime."

Somewhere in the Hindu Kush mountains, in a cave hidden away in a narrow pass deep within a secret gorge that only local guides knew about, lived an evil old wizard named Sharir whose mastery of sorcery had not been seen since the days of Merlin. So potent were his potions and so infamous his evil ways that the sound of his name caused those who knew of him to buckle at the knees and fall trembling to the ground.

Stroking his long grey beard and squinting his small, beady eyes, Sharir would pore through his books, devising new ways to wreak havoc and devastation on anyone he saw fit. With a flick of his magic wand, he could shake the mountains. With a pinch of asphodel or the incantation of a spell, he could cast an epidemic on an entire region, or cause the most benign of leaders to plague the world with death and destruction.

So, on this most consequential day, when the president of the United States had awakened to find that he had lost his mouth, when a poor janitor from a working-class neighborhood in Washington, DC had found himself suddenly sporting a second orifice on his weary, unshaven face, when a simple Pakistani butcher discovered that he had been chosen to save his newfound country from an unspecified disaster, Sharir glared into his crystal ball, with a slight curl of his hairy lips, and rose up from his cobweb-covered chair, letting out a wild laugh that echoed through the mountain pass outside his secret citadel and caused his unwilling apprentice to awaken suddenly from his sleep.

"Akram!" he called out, in his deep, coarse voice. "Come! We have work to do!"

Chapter 2

CHARLOTTE WENTFORTH MELLONCOURT THORNE was a Southern belle. A Texas Southern belle. With short, wavy brown hair and pecan eyes that looked out hazily on the world and reflected her deep Southern roots the way a puddle of rain mirrors the clouds it came from.

She had been born in Louisiana, to a privileged family, into a sheltered life where everything she wanted fell into her lap instantly like manna from heaven. And though she had grown up on the Texas plains, far from the plantation her father had abandoned in order to seek his riches in oil, she managed to maintain her antebellum charms and her penchant for the pleasures in life that are the absolute right of every Southern belle. Whether it was a particular confection in a fancy storefront display or the latest outfit modeled in an upscale magazine, her every desire had always been fulfilled. Denial was a word she had never come to know.

Not that she was spoiled. Pampered would be a more appropriate description. And having been pampered, she never worried about navigating life's challenges or seeking solutions to even the most mundane of problems. Life had been handed to her on a delicately-patterned silver platter shimmering fiercely under the Texas sun, blinding her to the plain realities of everyday life.

So now, rushing down a private flight of stairs that led to the offices where her husband's staff—the *president's* staff, she reminded herself—went about their daily business, she held back a doleful tear, having been forced to face a situation that was not particularly pleasant, and wondered how she had ended up in its tiresome clutches to begin with.

She had never, after all, asked to be the First Lady, or even, for that matter, to marry the man she now found herself painfully bound to. It had all just happened: quickly, almost without her noticing it, like when, on a quiet summer's day, a sudden storm appears and you frantically seek shelter and find yourself safe and dry but in the most unpleasant of places. A barn, perhaps. Or (she shuddered) a chicken coop.

Now, in the midst of this strangest, this fiercest of tempests, she searched the hallways, not quite knowing where she was going, seeking shelter from the one person she knew might be able to resolve this most unpleasant of situations: Mark Drove, her husband's loyal chief of staff.

As if lost in a frightening dream, she knocked on darkened doorways and peeked through curtained windows and tried to remember which office Drove occupied. And she wondered when this particular storm might pass, when she might be able to run back out, out of this horrid shelter, back to her lazy-daisy, rose-colored dreams, back to a place where she could coil up like an innocent child and once again feel warm and secure.

For the First Lady loathed the White House. She detested politics and she hated the individuals whose lives it consumed. And she readily acknowledged to anyone who might listen that she put up with her insufferable husband and his dubious career only for the perks it offered: the overseas trips to exotic places where she could aspire to happiness, the bright, sparkling limelight, where she could show off her impeccable taste in clothing and jewels, the fancy dinners she could host without actually having to do the work. What more, she concluded, when she found herself suddenly ensconced in a life that had just appeared—like a horrid little genie from a tarnished lantern—could a Texas girl ask for?

What more was something she could never have imagined back then, when she was young, back when she was simply Charlotte Wentforth Melloncourt, dreaming of glamour and excitement. For now, after years of tedious marriage to a man whose appearance had seemed unconvincing from the start, came this horrible affliction, this mysterious palsy which had appeared suddenly on her husband's face and made him seem even more unappealing than he actually was. It was too much for a Southern belle to bear, and she knew instinctively that, just as the June bug appears like clockwork during the early days of summer, the weeks ahead would be even more miserable than all those that had meandered by. She pictured her veranda early in the morning, covered with dying June bugs, a few clinging to life with a flip of the wing, and shuddered again.

At last, she stumbled upon Mark Drove's office and, having now done her duty as wife and First Lady (having, that is, fetched her husband's closest advisor and confidante), Charlotte Wentforth Melloncourt Thorne walked the endless halls back to her room, retraced her steps in self pity and shame, accompanied by the one man she believed could right whatever wrong had been committed. She did not speak a word as she made her way through the quiet hallways, had not spoken since she had abruptly and incoherently broken the news to him ("My husband," she had begun as she entered his office, in a shower of tears, "the president," trying not to say it, as if saying it would make it suddenly real, "has turned into a—a monster.").

Drove had not understood a word she said, had chalked it all up to the hysterics of a woman who was known for being temperamental, who was prone to acting erratically and, at times, irrationally. The First Lady, after all, had a reputation and, as far as he was concerned, she was simply doing her best to live up to it.

But as he opened the door to the presidential suite, her words instantly shed their veil of vagueness, for he found the president gesticulating like a crazed monkey in front of the bedroom mirror, nervously twitching his face and moving his jaws back and forth, as if he had suddenly lost his mind. And what was even more disturbing was the accuracy with which the First Lady had described his appearance, for the president's face, which resembled that of a pitched bird under ordinary circumstances, had been transformed into an unrecognizably horrid façade.

Mark Drove was a robust, rotund man with a shock of wavy, gray hair and a big, jovial smile that tended to conceal the somber, serious way he dealt with the president's affairs. And while he always strove to be politically correct, he managed, just the same, to be as truthful and forthcoming as circumstances would allow. So now, as he stared incredulously at the president, like a scientist examining a rare and strange-looking creature, he coldly assessed the situation and surveyed the room, as was his habit, to make sure no one was around, closed the door and carefully locked it to ensure privacy.

"Mr. President," he said, calmly and without emotion. "You have indeed outdone yourself this time."

And then, when there was no response, when his wry attempt at humor to calm the situation fell on unresponsive ears, he quickly added, "I will summon your doctor at once. And I will ask the vice president to come as quickly as possible."

President Thorne responded by moving his jaws in curious ways and poking his tongue against the tough wad of skin that prevented him from uttering even the simplest of sounds.

"Mr. President," Drove said, calmly, holding out a pad and pencil. "May I suggest that you use these until we find a solution?"

President Thorne stared at his chief of staff with a baffled look on his blank face and wondered how he managed to remain calm even in the worst situations. He admired this quality in Drove, had noticed it immediately when they had first met, wished now he could make it his own. He took a deep breath and held it tight, trying to settle himself down, but his eyes simply bulged and his face turned red and looked as if it was about to explode. Then, suddenly and with no intention on his part, he let out a sudden sound that seemed to emanate from his nostrils and that bore a slight resemblance to what one might call speech.

"Sir?" Drove responded, unflinching.

Encouraged, President Thorne inhaled deeply again and with all his might, forced the air through his nostrils: "What the...?" This was followed by a long series of incomprehensible syllable-like utterances until Drove was finally able to make out the following: "Is this some kind of practical joke? Cause it'd be a heckuva lot easier if it were."

"Mr. President," Drove responded as if nothing out of the ordinary had occurred. "No one plays practical jokes on the president." And then, to lighten the mood, "tampering with government property is a serious violation." And then, "I will ask the CIA to look into possible international connections. The FBI will investigate domestically."

"I have a speech to give tonight," President Thorne snorted, his nostrils quivering like those of a raging bull. "What is the FBI going to do about that? One of my hardest jobs is figuring out what they're going to do about that. Are they going to deliver the speech for me? There'd better not be any goof-ups, or heads will roll."

President Thorne huffed and puffed angrily and turned to the First Lady for comfort. Taken aback by his sudden anger and the way it manifested itself ("he was like a raging animal," she would later recall, "a horrible, frightening, vicious animal"), she flinched, then took hold of his hand and declared, in her sweet Southern drawl: "I told you we should've gone away for the weekend."

Raising her eyes, she stared off past him, dreamily, off into the distance, imagining a quiet place by a river where life was calm and birds sang peacefully and the world's troubles—*her* troubles—dropped like leaves and lazily zig-zagged their way down to the ground where they magically disappeared. Then, looking back at her husband, she let out a loud gasp as she realized just how awful her marriage had actually become, for as bad as it had been, she could now no longer bear to even look at him.

Charlotte Wentworth Melloncourt Thorne took a deep breath. She squinched her eyes to better bring into focus the man she had lived with for the past twenty-odd years, and tried to imagine how her life might have been had she decided to follow her initial impulse to refuse his marriage proposal. She had put up with much throughout their marriage—sacrifices for his career and attacks on his skills and abilities, which ultimately reflected on her. And while she had never found him all that attractive, she had never imagined that, one day, the man she had decided, almost on a whim, to spend her life with would turn into such a horrible specter. She clenched her tear-streaked face, let out a deep sigh of anguish and said, quietly and unconvincingly, "Camp David is so lovely this time of year."

Then, with lips trembling, she quickly added, almost as an aside, in the way she always did when she could no longer face reality, "Well, not to worry. This will pass. Just like all the other crises we've had since moving here. Just like all the other crises we've had since we've been married. They always pass."

The First Lady covered her face with her hands.

"It's all right, Charlie," President Thorne snorted as gently as he could.

He put his arms around her and pulled her close against him.

"We'll go to Camp David as soon as this is over. I promise."

He tried to smile, tried, unsuccessfully, to muster up an expression of comfort, but each of these attempts ended in failure and resulted in making him look even more horrid than he already did.

Charlotte Wentworth Melloncourt Thorne turned her eyes toward her husband, toward the man she now knew for certain she had chosen by mistake, and immediately pushed him away in revulsion.

"Drove," President Thorne commanded, taken aback. "Give us some privacy. And get the First Lady some breakfast!"

"Yes, Mr. President."

"And gather my cabinets together immediately. This is an emergency!"

The Blazing Path of Light Ebenezer Baptist Church, LLC was a small, storefront operation in Southeast Washington, ministered by the Reverend CJ Willis, whose skills at inspiring the faithful and admonishing the unbelievers were renowned. In what was once a shabby grocery store on an otherwise deserted street, the church boasted a following of one hundred and three regulars (Reverend Willis based this on the number of admission tickets he collected each week at the door), plus the fifty or more passers-through who flocked to his sermons by word of mouth or upon seeing the faded gold-emblazoned cross that clung tenuously to the grimy window display where it had been originally placed. In less than two months, the church had become so popular that the good Reverend Willis, never one to turn God's needy children away, broke city code and tore through the back wall to make room for additional seating (folding chairs he had borrowed from the friendly imam at a nearby mosque) to accommodate those in spiritual need.

Having taken a three-week mail-order course, and having become duly and legally certificated, and having been inspired by the preachers of his childhood (for the good reverend, being an orphan, had been brought up properly by his maternal aunt and was severely beaten on those Sundays when he sneaked out of services as she succumbed to the spirit and he to the call of youthful vices), the Reverend Willis could deliver a fiery sermon that would bring everyone to their knees, after which they would rise up and testify, glorifying the Lord and raising their voices in song and rapture, while opening their wallets to barter away their sins.

"Jesus loves you," he would shout in his deep, euphonic voice, and the congregation would respond with full-voiced choruses of "Hallelujah" and "Amen."

So, on this most unusual of Sundays (for he had awakened from a strange dream—there were horrid creatures whose features continually transmogrified and flames which voraciously licked the flesh of the living—and had spent the night contemplating its meaning), the Reverend CJ Willis sat bleary-eyed in his makeshift office, in the basement of The Blazing Path of Light Ebenezer Baptist Church, LLC, putting the final touches on the day's sermon and estimating, unwittingly, the amount of donations he would bring in that day, when there came a loud knocking on the door that jolted him right out of his rickety chair.

Reverend Willis quickly regained his demeanor, walked across the cluttered room, unlocked the door and stared in shock as a horrible-looking demon materialized from his dreams and looked him straight in the eye.

"Reverend Willis?"

Unskilled at appeasing evil spirits and fearful of antagonizing the double-mouthed devil that now stood before him like an omen, Reverend Willis reluctantly turned his attention to the heavenly voice that seemed to float from beyond this ghastly creature.

"It's me," the voice said. "Pearl White. From the congregation."

Pearl nudged her husband out of the way, poked her head inside the doorway and smiled.

"Pearl?" Reverend Willis repeated as if in a trance, returning his gaze fearfully back to the monstrous creature standing beside her.

"Pearl," she repeated. "I received the spirit last Sunday. Remember? This is my husband, Larry."

"Larry."

Reverend Willis looked from Pearl to Larry and then back to Pearl, not sure whether he should cry out for help or abandon his fate to the hands of God.

"Reverend Willis," Pearl continued, "the most amazing thing has happened. Larry has been delivered."

"Pearl, baby," Larry muttered in a deep, hoarse voice that caused the hair on the Reverend's back to stand up. "I told you I want to go to a doctor."

"Larry White," Pearl scolded, sternly. "Hold your tongue. You are in the presence of the Reverend CJ Willis. He will know how to save you. Now you just stand there and hush up. Reverend Willis," she said, turning to the preacher and modulating her voice, "couldn't we just come in?"

"Certainly," he answered, getting a grip on himself, for he reasoned that, if this woman, whom he vaguely recalled seeing in his congregation, wasn't afraid of the horrible looking creature standing before him in the doorway, then neither should he.

"Please. Come in. Have a seat."

Pearl and Larry stepped into the tiny office, stuffed with old furniture and odds and ends that had been salvaged during the church's expansion, and sat down in front of Reverend Willis' cluttered desk.

"Now," he said, "how can I help you... uh..."

"Pearl."

"Pearl," he repeated. "And—?"

"Larry," Pearl said.

"Larry. How can I help you today? I am a little short of time—you know—Pearl. Services are going to start shortly."

"Yes, I know," Pearl said. "Well, you see, Reverend Willis, my husband, God be praised, has had a transformation."

"A transformation?"

Reverend Willis glanced at Larry with a look of wonder on his weary face.

"Yes. And—"

"Goddammit, Pearl," Larry shouted, slamming his fist on the good reverend's desk. "Get to the point, woman. I have exactly till tomorrow morning to get my face put back like it was before or I won't be able to show it at work."

"Larry White," Pearl began, exasperated by her husband's behavior. "Reverend Willis is here to help you."

"*There'd better not be any goof-ups*," Larry shouted in a voice that took Pearl by surprise, "*or heads will roll.*"

Reverend Willis' eyes bulged as he watched Larry speak in a voice that sounded like it had just emerged from hell. His hands began to tremble and he wondered if what he was witnessing had been discussed in any of the books he had received during his training.

"I'm sorry," he said, at last, "—Larry, right? I don't do exorcisms. You'd do better going to a Catholic church. There's one not too far from here."

"But Reverend Willis," Pearl protested.

"Much as I'd like to help," he said, fumbling for his watch, "services are going to begin shortly."

"Can we come back after services?"

"Yes," he said. "Later—this afternoon, that is. In the meantime, try the Catholic church. Yes, they'd surely be able to help you."

"Pearl," Larry said, standing up and grabbing his wife's hand, "let's get the hell out of here. I told you we should have gone to the hospital." And then, in a hellish voice, *"This is an emergency."*

"Now, Larry," Pearl responded, as she pulled her husband toward the door. "Reverend Willis is a very busy man. You'll see. He'll help you later. He would never turn down a man who's been delivered. Isn't that so, Reverend?"

"Yes, of course," Reverend Willis answered as he pored over his papers. "See you later, then."

Back in Pakistan, Choudry mused, sitting quietly in his living room, fingering a string of prayer beads and drinking a glass of over-sweetened dark tea, things would be quite different. Back there, he would simply call one of his relatives to take over the shop. There was always a cousin or two begging for a piece of bread, a distant relation who would happily abandon his village and come to the city to help out for nothing more than a room and a plate of rice and meat. That failing, he could pack up everything and sneak away, in the middle of the night, leaving no word of his whereabouts. Some corrupt party member would eventually appear, no doubt, willing to help for a price, making sure that whatever debts he owed would be wiped out one way or another.

It was like that over there. Someone was always willing to help.

But here in America, things were different. Here, the landlord was a huge company—an anonymous corporation or a fancy LLC—not an individual who could be easily identified, persuaded, bribed. Here, everything was registered: the county, the state, the federal government. He could not just close up shop and leave without a trace. There would be consequences when the rent was not paid. There would be a price to pay when bills were not settled, when loans were not settled. And it would affect everyone he left behind. As for more unconventional means—an accidental fire, perhaps, or a break-in that left the place in utter ruins—it would be hard to get away with anything like that these days with so much focus on his community.

In this land of the free, where he had indeed been presented with such opportunity, Choudry found his hands utterly tied.

Then there was Amina. He could not just abandon her. Who would she go to? Their son? A two-bit big-shot. A so-called businessman. His lifestyle did not include taking in family members. MBA, indeed! Whoever heard of such nonsense? And he had practically abandoned his religion, shunned anything that even vaguely smelled of his background. No, he certainly could not depend on him. And their daughter, Fatwa; much as she would jump to help, she had her own problems. Three kids and a lazy husband whose religious views were extreme, to say the least. Besides, she had no room for her mother who, at any rate, would refuse to stay there.

Choudry took another mouthful of his sugary tea, swished it around in his mouth and glanced impatiently at his imitation Rolex watch. He leaned back deep into the faux-French couch he had purchased at some garage sale he had once stumbled upon, and looked around the room, numb from the clatter of pots and pans originating from the kitchen, and the incessant mutterings of Amina, who had not yet gotten over the shock of his encounter with God. He tried to focus on the *sura* hanging crooked on the wall, the only ornament in the room except for the dusty, silk rose hastily placed in a plastic blue vase on the wobbly end table, but his attention was distracted by Amina's grating voice, and he shut his eyes and tried to imagine a life where wives were complacent and life's problems were resolved in quick, simple ways.

"Wait till your children hear about his, Choudry!"

Amina's voice nudged its way back into his consciousness like the loud blast of a trumpet, over the pots and pans, over the sizzling of something frying and the hissing of a pressure cooker, through the kitchen door and straight into the room where he sat. "You know, Choudry, if my mother and father were still alive, Allah rest them, I would return to Pakistan. But where to go? Now where are the spices? Choudry, I need spices to cook your meat. Choudry! Choudry! How can you sleep at a time like this?"

Choudry opened his eyes and observed his wife hovering over him like an irritated bee.

"Amina," he said, calmly with a sigh, "I was thinking."

"Thinking? Hasn't that gotten us into enough trouble? I need spices, Choudry."

"Yes, Amina."

"Cardamom. Chili powder. Fenugreek."

"Yes, Amina."

"Now. Before they arrive."

"Yes, Amina."

"Have you taken your medicine yet?"

"Yes, Amina."

Choudry hoisted himself up off the couch. He hurried out of the room and into the foyer, where the old camel saddle from his youth beckoned him with memories of a simpler life.

"And whatever you do," Amina said, rushing after him, "please don't tell anyone about this. Especially the children. I beg you."

"Yes, Amina."

She glared at him with angry eyes, hardened from years of bitterness and neglect. Then her face softened and she wiped a lone tear with her headscarf which lay loosely wrapped around her neck.

"You know, Choudry," she said. "Sometimes I feel just like a stone. A hard, cold stone in the middle of the road."

Choudry waved his hands in the air.

"You and your feelings!" he said, opening the front door. "You and your metaphors!"

"You just wait, Fuzzaluddin Choudry," Amina called out after him, wagging her finger like a weapon. "One of these days, I'm not going to sit here so complacent. You won't be able to ignore me anymore."

Choudry got into his car and slammed the door shut. Putting the key in the ignition, he cursed his wife under his breath and vowed to leave her once and for all, swearing to God that he would not put up with her abuse for one more day.

The engine grated to a start, and Choudry pulled the sputtering car out of the driveway and onto the street. Wishing he had never gotten out of bed that day, he invoked the wrath of God on the cherry blossoms, whose serenity and splendor had enticed him, like a seductive woman, into going to the Tidal Basin in the first place. He gunned the engine and steered the car toward his butcher shop, a humble storefront in a small strip mall in a part of town he had driven to so many times for the last twenty or more years that he had no need to even think about where he was going. The ride was so habitual that he often joked how his old rust-bucket of a car, its faded yellow paint chipping around the edges, could get there on its own.

Choudry drove absentmindedly, the events of that morning repeating themselves over and over in his mind like an old movie. He wondered what he had done to deserve this fate—a God who had requested an impossible task from him and a wife who refused to believe in what had happened—and, once again, he cursed the cherry blossoms and prayed for a blight to destroy them, or an unexpected frost that would make them wither up and die.

Choudry smiled as he pictured the stricken cherry trees shedding their shriveled blooms. Then, the sound of a horn woke him from his reverie and he saw that his car was headed in the wrong direction, east toward the city rather than west toward his shop. As he approached the next intersection, he put on his signal and slowed down to make a U-turn, but, strangely, the steering wheel refused to move. He screwed up his chubby face and exerted as much force as he could muster but, no matter how hard he tried, it would not budge and the car remained on the same precarious path toward the District.

Choudry slammed on the brakes. Fearful that some mechanical failure was about to take his life, he invoked the Koran and recited prayers for his safety, but, the car continued to move on its own, despite the screeching that grated from the brakes, entering I-66 and heading stubbornly toward the city. By the time Choudry reached the Roosevelt Bridge, he was so convinced that he was going to die that he forgave Amina all her trespasses and promised Allah he would never abandon her, no matter what.

At last, Choudry's rattletrap of a car came to an abrupt stop— beside the guard gate at the first checkpoint to the White House—and Choudry slumped over the steering wheel and let out a deep sigh of relief.

"*Alhamdulillah*," he cried out loud, thanking God for saving him from what he thought would be a certain death. "*Alhamdulillah*."

Then, he sat back and turned his head and took one look at the mean-looking guard pointing a semi-automatic right into his face and prepared himself for death.

"This is government property!" the guard shouted. "State your business!"

Choudry looked at the guard through his droopy eyes, his sallow face begging for mercy and his voice dry and silenced from fear.

"State your business," the guard repeated curtly, "or remove your vehicle at once!"

"I have come to see the president."

The words came out on their own, in long clear syllables embellished with Choudry's lilting accent, and they shocked him as much as they did the worn-out guard whose long night shift, which was about to come to an end, made this seedy-looking individual sitting before him in his broken-down car seem like the remnants of a bad dream.

"Sir!"

The guard trained his weary, bloodshot eyes on Choudry, noting his blubbery lips and his overall unseemly appearance. Bristling for the worst, he tensed his muscles and tried to recall the techniques they had discussed in the terrorist training he had recently received.

"This is government property," the guard shouted. "Remove your vehicle immediately or I will be forced to take action."

"Young man," Choudry said. "I have come to see the president. This is a matter of national security."

Choudry spoke calmly and clearly, the lilting words flowing from his mouth as if he were reciting poetry.

Fearing the worst, the guard sounded the alarm and, within seconds, Choudry's car was surrounded by armed soldiers who trained their weapons directly at him and prepared to fire.

"Out of the car!" the guard shouted. "And keep your hands in the air!"

"But—"

"Now, or we'll shoot."

Choudry opened the door, grabbed on to the frame and heaved himself out of the car.

"I have come to see the president and I will see the president," he said. "It is my right. I am an American citizen. Now put that gun down."

Without thinking, Choudry reached for the gun that was pointed directly in his face. A barrage of gunshots immediately went off. The shooting lasted for what seemed like a minute but, miraculously, Choudry did not receive even a scratch and the guards, who kept firing their weapons, watched in amazement until someone tackled him from behind, brought him to the ground and handcuffed him.

"You're under arrest," the guard shouted.

Sharir's bellowing voice came echoing through the hollow, underground caverns. Akram cowered in the corner and trembled. He wondered how he had ended up here, how, being the only son of a simple peasant whose existence was dedicated to raising goats and sheep, he had become the apprentice of a sorcerer whose great skills were dedicated only to evil.

Many nights, as he lay awake in his straw bed, he dreamed of escaping. Many times, as he tossed and turned, he schemed and plotted. How he would sneak out, while his master was sleeping. How he would hike through the mountains, through the snow and wind and bitter cold, until he would reach a place in an even more obscure area than the one he was in now, where he could hide. But he knew he would be found. He knew he could not hide from the all-powerful Sharir.

Sometimes, he even considered killing him. Poison would be the only way. Or some potion that would let him sleep eternally. But that took skill, and the only way he could gain those skills would be to continue serving him.

Sharir bellowed again, this time more loudly. He called Akram's name three times, and his deep, piercing voice reverberated through the caverns where he was hiding. He curled himself up into a ball and concealed himself in the mouth of a little cave, struggling to hold back his tears.

He thought longingly of his mother, a simple, hardworking woman who toiled in the fields and tended to her flock of eight children as best she could. His sisters were kept under close watch, staying close to her as she worked the crops, singing the songs she had learned from her mother, teaching her daughters as they would one day teach theirs.

And at night, when they were all gathered in the little hut that overlooked the great sprawling valley, the hut that had been in their father's family for generations, the girls would sit by their mother's side and learn to cook or, by the light of a kerosene lamp, sew the simple clothes that covered their bodies, that kept them modest according to their traditions and protected them from the hot summer's sun and from winter's relentless cold.

The boys were left on their own. When they were not out with their father, who traveled often to bring supplies, they were off tending the herds of sheep and cattle that provided them with sustenance throughout the year. Young and innocent, they soon learned to protect their flocks from wolves and other predators, learned quickly how to recognize kindness in passing strangers or danger in their small stealthy eyes. Soon their innocence molted like the sheep they took care of, and they learned to defend themselves and those who depended on them, became bold and cunning, learning skills that would become essential in their adult years.

"Akram! Where are you? Skulking like the lazy boy that you are! I should punish your father for your indolence. Put a blight on his flock. Akram! Come here at once!"

All except Akram, whose youthful dreams clung to him like a just-slaughtered lamb desperately clings to its quickly ebbing life. Fond of his brothers and in awe of his towering father, he struggled to learn their ways while refusing to abandon the fantasies of his youth. Where they boldly faced the challenges each day brought, he sat wistfully dreaming of quiet summer nights, of love and the girl he might someday marry. And where they easily recognized danger and could spot a thief like a falcon spots her prey, he trusted each passing stranger as if he were a distant, long-awaited cousin returning from a long journey.

Which is how he got in trouble in the first place. Which is how, on a clear summer's night as he gazed up at the stars, he had encountered Sharir. Innocently. Unknowingly. Then, when it was too late and he was under Sharir's unyielding grip, and his father knew there was no way he could free him, the two men struck a deal. And now here he was: a slave, a prisoner, possessed body and soul with no possible hope for salvation in this world or the next.

"AKRAM!"

The earth shook. The stalactites swayed precariously overhead. The ground felt as if it would open its giant maw and swallow him up.

"Yes, master," Akram called, giving in as he knew he must.

He stood up, reluctant and frightened, made his way slowly through the dark, dank tunnels, and skulked into his master's library like a child expecting to be beaten for some unfathomed prank, known only to his elder. He tiptoed quietly up to his master's ancient table and silently waited, sticking his hands in his pocket and bowing his head, sullen, to the floor.

"Akram," Sharir called out.

"Yes, master," Akram answered sullenly.

"Ah, so that's where you're hiding," Sharir said. "Put a log in the fire. And go down to the caves and get me some wart's root. We've got plans to arrange and destinies to set."

Sharir peered into his crystal ball and watched the White House guards drag Choudry away, delighted, like a little boy whose toys respond just as they are supposed to.

"It's wonderful, don't you think? To watch them in action. Thinking they control everything they do. We will show them something new about themselves, Akram. And in the end, we shall be their masters."

Akram stood in his spot, staring silently at the ground and waiting for his master to dismiss him.

"Why do you stand there? We will do this together. And you will inherit my skills. Now go. Do as I say."

Akram ran off at his master's command, stopping at the entrance to the caves to still his heart and harden his resolve to do what he could to someday defeat this curse on him and his family.

Chapter 3

IT WAS ALL A PUZZLEMENT, these last several hours, these puzzling events that had suddenly intruded on his simple, carefully planned, well-intentioned life, and President Thorne was—well, puzzled.

"The thing is, is things like this just don't happen," he said, but just to himself, for no other creature on earth could hear him. "Not in the real world. Not in reality, at least. Well, I reckon they do. Cause they did. Cause this is reality, I guess. As real as the nose on my—"

He was sitting in the Oval Office, thinking. To himself.

"But not to presidents. Not to leaders of the free world. I mean, this is the free world. And that means things are free to do what they want—to happen as they do—freely—but—"

Alone and thinking all by himself.

"But that doesn't mean they're free to do things like this. That's why there's laws. They don't call it laws for nothing."

He pondered this last thought, thought about it until his head ached, until his eyes throbbed, until his throat smarted and he felt a moan starting up inside.

Though there must be similar things that have happened. Over time. Some occurrences. In history, that is.

"I'm sure there are."

He tried to think of some.

"Assassinations. Yes, that was one. And illnesses. Some presidents even went lame. They call them lame ducks."

But those were different, he thought. Those were to be expected. And ducks was not what the problem was here. And besides, they could still rule. Lamely, maybe. But they could still execute things from the Executive Office. After all, they were all Executives.

"But *I'm* speechless," he said in his own muted way. "I mean, I do hear voices. Inside. I just can't get to them."

Yes, it was all a mystery. An impossible mystery. A veritable whodunit. One that could not be solved. Seemingly.

He recalled the strange voices he heard at night and wondered if there was any relationship, wondered if the ghosts of history had decided to snatch away his mouth, in the middle of the night, take it away to some invisible place, while he was tossing and turning in that dreadful bed, had torn it off and run away with it into the darkness, without his even knowing.

He scratched the sudden itch that manifested itself around the spot where his mouth had been (*oh, how I miss my mouth!* he pined. *oh, how I would give anything to get it back, reunite it to my own self in such a way that it would never disappear again*), scratched and itched and pinched and rubbed until he was all tuckered out and red in the face and said, at last, forlornly:

"They didn't tell it like this in the history books. And history tells the truth. That's why it's called history. Hiz-tory."

And he squeezed his face into a ball of perplexity, tried to picture himself, flat-faced and mouthless, on a page in an elementary school textbook, thought and itched and scratched some more.

And cogitated. Tried to fathom what was supposed to be and what wasn't, what was in the history books and what was left out, what would be and what wouldn't, until his head ached further and his skin reddened some more and his mind felt like it would expand and explode.

"Did Lincoln," he wondered, stopping himself, "ever have such a day?"

It was a legitimate question, after all, one, he wondered, if those damn historians had every contemplated, investigated.

"What about Washington? I mean he didn't just wake up one morning and find a wooden tooth growing in his mouth."

Maybe he just needed to read more. Maybe his childhood teachers had left something out. Something terribly important. Or maybe he had slept through that particular lesson, as he had done in many a class.

"I've got myself to blame, I reckon," he said to himself at last. "And God's shoulder to cry on."

And he sighed and stared off vacantly into space and waited anxiously for his cabinet members to arrive.

And at ten o'clock, they did. Began to file in, one by one, long-faced and grumpy and—well—annoyed, it seemed. Or perhaps it was disturbed. Nervous. Apprehensive. President Thorne couldn't tell, but he collected his thoughts and set them aside, watched each individual enter the room, observed, solemnly, how they each tried to hide their shock at his odd appearance, attempted to conceal their obvious feelings of revulsion, avert his eyes with swift, nervous glances. All carefully hidden, it seemed, all disguised under a thin gauze of profound gravity. And he stared at them, trying to gauge their profundity, and their eyes darted to and fro, as he struggled to ascertain who would remain faithful and who would bolt.

Soon, Mark Drove appeared, marched into the room with his steady, even keel, strode in, a mask of resolve on his stalwart face, his demeanor as calm and officious as if he were about to conduct their regular daily briefing. President Thorne watched him take his seat, watched as he collected his papers into a neat pile as he always did before proceeding, and wondered if he would be able to once again work his magic and rescue him from this most extraordinary, this most unpredictable, this most disastrous of situations.

Drove scrutinized the dour, perplexed faces sitting around the room without blinking an eye. Knowing full well that loyalty was the most crucial element needed at this critical time, he rested his elbows on the table, leaned forward, and carefully studied each individual, trying to calculate the odds that they could be fully trusted.

"Gentlemen," he began grimly, and he rested his hazel, quartz-like eyes on Candice Brice, the lone woman on President Thorne's team, without flinching at this apparent *faux pas*. Undaunted, she returned his stare with a cold, relentless smile and curled her lips up with rigid determination. She was used to standing out, was used to being treated differently from the rest, and so she let this statement of Drove's pass by like a sudden, cold wind that she was forced often enough to brave.

"I don't believe I need to explain why we're here," Drove continued.

President Thorne attempted to hide his embarrassment, but he flushed red and his face waxed into a look of utter bewilderment as all eyes in the room turned toward him.

"It's the Iraqis, by God," the Secretary of Defense shouted, breaking the silence. He pounded his fist on the table as if to emphasize his point.

"Mr. Secretary," Drove said calmly. "It's too early to lay blame. We've asked for an intelligence assessment and are waiting for an update. What we need now," he continued, looking at the others, "is, to put it bluntly, damage control."

Everyone began talking at once, and Drove picked up a spoon and tapped it against the table to get their attention.

"If we could have just one person at a time, please," he said, raising his voice above the din and trying to quell his impatience. "Yes, Mr. Vice President."

"Well, Mark. It seems to me we need to be truthful, as we have been all along during this administration, with the American people. We need to make a simple statement to the press that the president has had a personal emergency that he's been forced to attend to. We'll emphasize that he is in no danger, and we'll assure the public that he'll return to the White House just as soon as he can. I believe that sums it up nicely without supplying all the details and without concocting some cock-and-bull story that will surely unravel."

"That's all well and good," the Secretary of the Interior retorted, "but you know as well as I do how the press will run with that. Give them an inch of the truth and they'll want the whole nine yards. And when we don't give it to them, they'll find out soon enough. Bet your damn last dollar they'll surely find out."

He cleared his throat and grimaced as he said these last words, and his lips quivered nervously as he looked around the room and waited for their response.

"Then we must swear secrecy," the attorney general interjected. "No press conferences. No leaks. That should be easy enough to manage. No one outside this small circle has seen the president's condition."

"If I may interrupt," Drove said. "The president has a major speech to give tonight. People—party loyalists—have paid thousands of dollars to hear him speak. What do we tell them? Surely we need to explain in more detail why he cannot be there. What kind of personal emergency? How long will he be away? How will that impact the government? Security? Foreign relations? The stock market? And even if it were to hold water, what do we do about the president's physical condition? That's the real problem that has to be resolved."

Another burst of chatter ensued, and president Thorne squirmed in his chair as his advisors argued incessantly as if he weren't present, as he tried, unsuccessfully, to break in, to respond to their comments and counter their concerns. His body jerked and his face contorted into indescribable expressions as he tried to communicate. Unable to get their attention, he tried once again to speak through his nose as he had done earlier that morning. He huffed and puffed like an angry beast but was unable to force even the simplest syllable through his stubborn nostrils. Finally, in a last attempt to make his presence known, he took off his right shoe and banged it loudly on the table, causing the room to fall rapidly into utter silence.

"Really, Mr. President," the Secretary of Defense said through the sudden hush. "There's no need to behave like a Bolshevik."

President Thorne glared at his cabinet members. His body began to shake uncontrollably and his throat trembled from the force exerted on his vocal chords. Then, unable to bear the pressure any longer, he stood up, took a deep breath and growled, "Dammit! I hired you to see me through this administration. Now put your sorry heads together and come up with a solution. Or, as the Lord is my witness, I will fire each and every one of you."

A painful silence erupted that even the direst crises of the past couple of months had not produced. Though they each well knew why they had been called here this morning, though they had now seen, firsthand, the president's disturbing, unmistakable condition, the gravity of the situation suddenly became as clear as crystal as they witnessed their leader grunting through his nose like a feral pig.

"If I may make a suggestion," Candice Brice said at last, interrupting the silence.

She leaned forward with just a touch of haughtiness and stared them all down with her piercing brown eyes and a steady look that contrasted sharply with their rampant, sophomoric behavior. A woman of impeccable thinking—an African-American who had learned early on not to speak until she had fully assessed all the facts—she was known for her surgical insights and her calm, cool resolve to stick to her conclusions once they had been reached.

"Go on, Miss Brice," Drove said.

"Plastic surgery."

It was all she said, and an embarrassing quiet took hold of the room, as if they had silently, telepathically agreed that what she had just suggested was so ridiculous that it was not even worthy of consideration.

"Miss Brice?" Drove said.

"Plastic surgery," she repeated.

The expression on her face conveyed what little regard she held for their feeble intellects, and she leaned forward further and smiled.

"We need to have the president's face reconstructed," she explained, pronouncing each syllable carefully, as if she were laying out building blocks one by one for them to play with.

It took some time for her words to settle into their rigid minds, but the simplicity of the solution gradually revealed itself like a springtime flower with all its feminine brilliancy.

"We'll tell the public," she continued, pointedly enunciating each word, "that the president has to go in for surgery. We'll call it minor surgery, so no one gets alarmed, and not specify the nature of the procedure. We'll make it seem like this is something he's known about for quite some time, something he's been postponing because he's been preoccupied with the nation's business. Meanwhile, we'll hunt down the best plastic surgeon in the country and the job will be done. Simple and easy."

Candice Brice folded her arms and rested her case. As her words filtered slowly through their minds, the sense of crisis that had gripped the room began to lift like a dense fog, and a look of calm soon began to settle over the taut topography of each face in the room. Even President Thorne attempted a smile.

Mark Drove looked around the room to determine the level of concurrence. "Does anyone have any disagreements with Miss Brice's suggestion?" he asked.

When no one answered, he asked, "Are we all in consensus?"

Then, after another short silence, he said: "Very well. We'll go with this plan. We'll need to come up with a statement for the press. And we'll need to locate a plastic surgeon. We'll leave that to the surgeon general. Any questions?"

"I do have one question," the Secretary of Interior said, breaking in with a loud, grating harrumph. "Do you think the president will ever be able to speak again?"

The Reverend CJ Willis was in the middle of his Sunday sermon at The Blazing Path of Light Ebenezer Baptist Church, LLC, ("drink," he was exclaiming, in his loud, resonant voice, pounding his fist on the pulpit for emphasis, "must be drowned in the drain") when Pearl slipped quietly into the church hall, dragging her reluctant, weary, conspicuous husband by the hand, who ranted with one mouth and raved with the other. Having been told at the Catholic church that exorcisms were not performed on Sundays and that, regardless of the day of the week or the fact that Mass was at that very moment being said (and why, they were asked, were they not in attendance?), they would need to travel to Baltimore to seek advice from the Archbishop, whose specialty was confronting devils of all shapes and colors and battling demons no matter their purpose, no matter their source, no matter the individual they had taken up residence in. "We are," the monsignor had concluded, smiling self-contentedly as if to emphasize that his church was in tune with the times, "an equal opportunity religion."

Disappointed at the monsignor's casual response and worried that Larry would take things into his own hands and miss his one golden opportunity at salvation, Pearl rushed back to The Blazing Path of Light Ebenezer Baptist Church, LLC against her husband's wishes, while Larry, who was unwilling to waste any more time, especially if it involved traveling to Baltimore, railed on about the hypocrisy of the religious and the stupidity of their ways.

"What I need, woman," he kept saying in a deep, raspy voice, "is a damn good doctor. A really damn good doctor."

"And woman*izing*," the good reverend shouted, emphasizing the last two syllables and casting his fiery gaze on two elderly men who were sitting innocently at the front of the humble congregation, "womanizing, that wantonly wicked way of the flesh, must be whipped into submission and conquered, as we must conquer all that is evil in this world. It is the way of the Devil, and we must defeat the Devil and embrace the way of the Lord. Praise God!"

"Praise God," the congregation shouted back.

"And now," Reverend Willis asked, pausing to survey his congregation, "who among you will testify to the ways of the Lord?"

Silence filled the church hall. Then, through the hushed silence, a middle-aged woman—a Mrs. Wattleby, to be exact, who was one of the mainstays of the neighborhood congregation—stood up and made her way meekly up the aisle. Wearing a yellow spring bonnet with a giant blue bow in front and dressed in her Sunday best, she turned to the congregation, lifted her arms into the air and began to shout in a voice that reverberated throughout the packed church hall.

"Oh, Lord," she lamented, "I have sinned. Forgive me, oh Lord, and give me strength."

"And what have you done, sister?" Reverend Willis asked.

"Oh, Lord, I am a weak, wicked woman. I have cheated on my husband in ways that shame me."

"Confess your ways, sister, and the Lord will forgive you, for the Lord loves those who ask for forgiveness."

"Oh, Lord," Mrs. Wattleby intoned, "when there was bread, I said there was none. And when there was meat, I lied and gave him beans. And when my child, my only, my innocent child, cried for his lunch, I told him there wasn't enough money when there was. Oh, Lord, forgive me."

"And what did you do with that money, sister?"

"I spent it on myself, Lord forgive me. Here is the hat I bought with that wicked money."

Mrs. Wattleby grabbed the bonnet from her head and threw it into the aisle.

"And here is the wig I purchased for my own vanity," she said, tearing the wig off her balding head and flinging it down beside the bonnet. "Here is the bracelet, here is the ring, and here are the fancy earrings. Oh, Lord, forgive me," she shouted.

And Mrs. Wattleby began to cry. Loudly. Spontaneously. Weeping vociferously, she fell to her knees and shouted supplications between gasps of tears and beseechments for forgiveness.

"The Lord loves you, sister," Reverend Willis shouted.

"Hallelujah!" Mrs. Wattleby cried, her body starting to tremble.

"The Lord is a loving God!"

"Praise God," she bellowed as she began to writhe on the floor.

"Praise the Lord, sister, and He will forgive you."

"Praise God! Praise the Lord! Hallelujah! Hallelujah!"

Reverend Willis scanned the congregation from his pulpit like a shepherd overlooking his flock as the euphoric Mrs. Wattleby thrashed about on the floor in jubilation, producing unintelligible sounds that filled the worshippers with awe and humility.

"The Lord," Reverend Willis said, raising his hands in prayer, "loves those who ask for forgiveness as He loves those who help support his church. Our sister has repented and, God willing, has been forgiven. Let us pray for all those who sin against the Lord. Let us dig deep into our hearts as we dig deep into our pockets. Praise the Lord!"

"Amen," the congregation shouted.

And while the congregation stomped their feet and waved their hands ecstatically in the air, two men gently escorted Mrs. Wattleby back to her seat, then passed baskets around for the obligatory collection.

"Who next will come forward and ask for God's forgiveness?" Reverend Willis asked as the congregation settled down.

"Larry," Pearl whispered, nudging her husband in encouragement.

Larry glared at his wife with a look that would have frightened the Devil had he been in attendance.

"I'm telling you Pearl," he said in a voice as subdued as he could muster, "I need to get outta here. Your Reverend can't solve my problem—"

"Hush, Larry," Pearl interrupted, trying to keep her composure as the members of the congregation twisted around in their seats.

"Who will come forward and testify to the Lord?" Reverend Willis repeated.

Quiet whispers filled the hall as news of a monstrous presence spread from one parishioner to another until, gradually, the entire congregation had turned toward Larry.

Then, as if possessed by the Spirit, as if the invitation of the good Reverend Willis had stirred something inside, as if the gazes of all those staring at him, horrified, had created a sudden need to break the ice, Larry began to tremble. Standing up, he looked contemptuously around the church and spoke from his newly acquired mouth.

"*The Lord is my witness*," he said with a stunned look that mirrored the shock of the parishioners as they witnessed his grotesque face.

Reverend Willis, who until now had not noticed that Pearl and Larry had returned, suddenly realized what the commotion was about and gazed fearfully at Larry.

"Go on," Pearl whispered gently, prodding her husband with her elbow.

Larry stepped into the aisle and walked slowly toward the front of the church, fueled by anger and frustration, motivated by the embarrassment that now streamed through his body as the crowd stared at him in horror and pity. He looked up at Reverend Willis, who stood trembling at the altar, and gazed at him with a mix of disdain and respect as his two mouths nervously opened and closed in unsynchronized fashion, giving him the appearance of a horrible, ferocious beast.

"*The Lord is my witness*," he said with one mouth.

"God," he cried with the other, "get me the hell outta here!"

"*The Lord will see me through this.*"

"I just want to wake up, goddammit!"

"*I've got God's shoulder to cry on.*"

"Goddammit! I need a doctor. Someone please get me a goddamn doctor."

Larry mesmerized the crowd as he spoke like one possessed, shifting between two mouths, switching between dual voices and two personalities that somehow seemed to mesh into one.

"Oh, Lord," Reverend Willis bellowed, startling the congregation, "forgive us and save us from this wretch that stands before us."

"Somebody help me," Larry shouted, tears falling from his eyes, "Somebody please help me."

Larry's body began to tremble. Unable to control his emotions, he fell suddenly to his knees, lifted his arms in the air and continued to plead for help.

As Reverend Willis witnessed this transformation, he had a sudden, miraculous epiphany. His fear started to fade and his heart began to soften. Calculating the effect Larry's appearance would have on his following and anticipating the fame that would follow and the thousands, maybe millions, more parishioners that would flock to his sermons, once this was made public, he seized the opportunity, stepped down from his pulpit and approached Larry like a prophet ready to heal a leper.

"The Lord loves you, my son," he said with a gentle smile. "The Lord will forgive you if you ask Him."

"I just want to be normal again," Larry cried. "Goddammit, I will do anything. Just please help me. Lord, please help me."

"Hallelujah!" Pearl shouted, jumping up with tears in her eyes. "Praise be to God! The Lord has saved my husband."

"Hallelujah," shouted the parishioners, and one by one they rose and stomped their feet, and shouted and clapped and praised the Lord.

"The Lord loves you, my children," Reverend Willis bellowed as rapture filled his church. Turning toward his congregation and shouting over their deafening cries of joy, he said "Come forward, my children, and ask the Lord for forgiveness. You will be saved as this wretch here has been saved. Let us pray for all those who sin against the Lord. Let us dig deep into our hearts as we dig deep into our pockets. Praise the Lord!"

And Larry, confused by the commotion that surrounded him, trembled emotionally and shouted fervently, from one of his mouths: "Praise the Lord!"

Back at the Choudry residence, Amina sat in the living room drinking her dark, sweetened tea and wiping tears from her eyes with the hem of her orange headscarf. Between sips and sniffles, she recounted the events that had transpired earlier that day, carefully avoiding the worst revelation regarding her shameless husband and lamenting the fact that, several hours after he had left the house to go to his shop, he had still not returned.

"Spices," she cried, nearly tipping over her tea glass as she threw up her hands in despair. "I send him out for spices so I can cook his meat and he does not return. Why do you think your father does this to me, Fatwa?"

Fatwa wiped her mouth on her long, baggy, black sleeve. She observed her mother through her droopy eyes and wondered to herself what would become of them if her father did not return.

"Amir will find him, Mama," she said at last. Her tone was more tentative than convincing, and she reached over for a biscuit with a puzzled, nervous look.

"*Insha'llah*," Kazi interjected in a sharp, reprimanding tone. "God willing," he said in English to emphasize his point. "Amir will find him, *insha'llah*."

He set his small, burning eyes on his wife, looked sternly at her with his thin, narrow face, and slowly stroked his long, graying beard.

Fatwa glared angrily at her overzealous husband. Settled precariously beside her mother on the faux-French couch, she whispered a few supplications to restrain her tongue from lashing out at the man she had mistakenly married in an arrangement her parents had set up soon after her birth. And though she had been given the choice, on the night of her engagement, the decision had caused her so much consternation that she could not clearly articulate the nebulous feelings that had overwhelmed her that night. Marriage had been something constantly instilled in her as a God-given requirement, and Kazi, she had been told, was the one whose name had been written in Allah's enormous book as the man she should spend her life with.

"*Insha'llah*," she mumbled at last, and she turned away from him and bit down hard on the stale biscuit.

Smiling, Kazi watched his obedient wife and silently stroked his long, unkempt beard, content that he had done his duty to keep her in line with Allah's commands.

"I told him so many times," Amina continued, swallowing her tea and placing the glass on the worn coffee table. "'Please Choudry,' I said, 'do not give to those charities. It will only get us in trouble.' And do you think he listens to me? No, he gives to the charities. He keeps the charity boxes in his store. He asks the good people who come to his shop to donate to those charities. What do you expect? Do you think America will ignore his foolishness? And now he's gone. Snatched up by vultures, for all I know."

She paused to wipe her eyes with a balled-up tissue and took another loud sip of tea. Adept at telling stories, she knew when to pause, which words to emphasize, and what tone to use to create the best affect. Looking over to her son-in-law, who, despite his faults (he was too strict, she had always said, too rigid in his narrow thinking), was good to her daughter, made sure she was always fed and well taken care of, she cleared her throat and reached out for her empty glass. Kazi jumped up immediately and poured fresh tea from the steaming metal teapot.

"Auntie," Kazi said, holding out his mother-in-law's freshly filled glass across the scratched coffee table. "Do not worry about this. A man who gives to charity will be blessed by Allah. Do not fear America. It is Allah we must fear."

"But he has committed blasphemy, Kazi," Amina countered in a hushed voice, her tears suddenly dried up and her vow to keep this one last secret suddenly loosening its rigid grip on her tongue. "He told me when he came back from his walk this morning. 'Amina,' he said, 'Allah has spoken to me. He appeared to me in the lake,' he said."

"*Allahu akbar!*" Kazi shouted in shock. "*Allahu akbar!*"

"Just like that," she continued. "He did not even question whether this was possible. He did not even ask for God's forgiveness. No. Amina: God has spoken to me. How is a wife to feel after all these years when she suddenly finds her husband is—is—oh, I can't say it, Allah forgive me."

Amina burst into another tempest of tears as naturally and spontaneously as a sudden summer storm.

"Mama," Fatwa said, thumping her hand against her chest. "Is this true?"

"Yes, my daughter," Amina answered, interrupting her sobbing. "It's true."

Fatwa let out a wail that shot through the house like a death call. Now that her mother had confirmed this startling revelation, she joined wholeheartedly in her lamentations, holding her face between her hands and emitting a cry so shrill that the children came rushing up from the basement where they were playing and ran into the room to see what calamity had befallen their family.

Kazi watched helplessly, dismayed by their laments and appalled by his mother-in-law's startling story. In a loud voice, he beseeched God to forgive them all and invoked the wrath of Allah on his father-in-law whom he had always suspected of holding less than orthodox beliefs.

In the middle of this commotion, Amir arrived from his unsuccessful search for his missing father. Hearing their cries and screams from the driveway as he carefully parked his red convertible and fearing that some new disaster had occurred during his short absence, he rushed into the house, entered the living room, and stared, with a slight feeling of shame, at his mother and sister, both dressed as if they had just arrived from the village, and at his brother-in-law, whose scruffy beard swayed back and forth in rhythm to his furious supplications.

Standing in the doorway, dressed in a casual suit jacket, a tight black tee-shirt and a pair of neatly pressed jeans, Amir absently felt his smoothly shaven chin with his manicured fingers and wondered how a perfectly good Sunday afternoon, which he could have been spending with the woman he had just met the previous night, could have so swiftly taken a nosedive to hell.

"Has someone died or something?" he asked, breaking through the din.

"*Wa aleikum salaam!*" Kazi reprimanded, interrupting his supplications. "Is that how you enter a room of Muslims? Where are you salaams?"

"Kazi," Amina scolded, ceasing her wailing at the sound of her son's voice and flashing an angry look at her son-in-law. "Amir, have you found your father?"

"No, Mama," Amir responded. "No one at the shop has seen him."

"*Allahu akbar*," Amina cried. "Why am I blessed with such a foolish husband?"

"Mama, it'll be all right," Fatwa said, wiping the tears on her scarf and laying her fat, flabby arms on her mother's to comfort her.

"But Fatwa. He said he was going to leave the country. *Allahu akbar*," she wailed. "My husband has abandoned me."

"Amir," Fatwa said, "maybe we should call the police."

"Police?" Amina shouted. "Police? Your father is in enough trouble. No. No police. Allah, what will become of us?"

Fatwa and Amina plunged into a new storm of lamentations when the front door opened and Choudry entered, appearing as if he had just been in a scuffle. Limping toward the aged armchair that was always left empty for him, he collapsed into its frayed, comforting arms and, running his hand through his tousled hair, stared blankly in front of him as if he had just awoken from a terrible nightmare.

"Papa," Fatwa cried, jumping out of her seat and rushing over to her father. "What has happened? Kazi," she cried, turning to her husband. "Maybe we should call a doctor."

Kazi fingered his long beard with one hand and his prayer beads with the other when Amina abruptly interrupted her howling and shouted, "Choudry. Where have you been? What has become of you? Where are my spices?"

"Amina," he replied wearily, casting his eye at his unruly family as they stared incredulously at him. "There's no time for dinner."

"No time for dinner?" Amina replied, her wailing now put on hold. "Are we to sit here and starve while you run around town like a lunatic? Look at you Choudry. Your clothes are ripped. Your hair is a lumpy mess. You look like you've been wrestling with the Devil himself. What has become of you, Choudry?"

Amina mustered up another round of tears, raising her voice yet another octave, rocking back and forth in her chair and lifting her hands in the air. Frightened by the ghastly sight of their grandfather and the frantic reaction of their grandmother, the children joined in, and the room was quickly filled with wails and cries that not even their mother could stop.

Wishing he had not answered the phone earlier that morning, Amir watched this dramatic display of emotions with a pained, embarrassed look on his face. Then, trying to calm the situation, he said, casually, "Dad. Where've you been?"

Choudry looked from his wife, to his daughter, to his son-in-law, to his son. He glanced at his grandchildren, now suddenly quiet, sitting by their mother like frightened sheep. As he had done so many times in the past, he tried once again to understand them, to comprehend each one's mismatched personality, to figure out how they had all ended up in the puzzle that his life had become. He examined each one cautiously like he examined the carcasses that arrived at his shop each day, looking for imperfections, trying to make sure he had not been cheated as he sometimes was. His wife, while bad-tempered, had been faithful to him; of this, he was sure. But she was rigid in her thinking, could never entertain anything that strayed even a centimeter outside her tiny, insulated universe. His daughter, who had always been affectionate, was the model of obedience, even more so since her ill-fated marriage. His son, on the other hand, had always been defiant, until now; he rejected the values Choudry had tried to instill in him. And his son-in-law? A real disappointment. He had no mind for this world, was too preoccupied with his rhetoric and his prayers to be attentive to anything of importance around him. So how could he expect them to be understanding of what he had been through today? How could he expect them to accept that God had appeared to him, that he had been mysteriously driven to the White House where, after being shot at, after intense interrogations, he had been just as mysteriously released when the men, who had been grilling him in an underground cell, suddenly smiled, shook his hand and told him how nice it had been to meet him. How could they possibly understand that any of this was happening? How could they believe him when he, himself, barely believed anything that had taken place today?

At best, they would think him insane. At worst, his son would call him crazy while the rest would brand him a heretic.

"Amina," Choudry said at last, breaking the silence and letting out a heavy sigh. "I will go to the shop now and get what you need."

"Go?" she said. "Looking like this? Go, like you did this morning? Maybe never to come back? Maybe this time to leave the country?"

Amina once again wiped her eyes on the hem of her thin, orange scarf.

"Choudry. What have I done to deserve this? Haven't I been a good wife to you all these years? Look at your children, Choudry. Your grandchildren. Think about your family, Choudry. What you are doing to them?"

Choudry looked at his wife as if he were looking through a dense piece of gauze. She seemed, somehow, not of this world, not of the world he had suddenly been thrown into for reasons he could not comprehend.

"Amina," he said, as everyone in the room watched him, waiting to hear his response. "I will not leave the country. I will not leave the city. Allah wants it that way."

"*Allahu akbar*," Kazi shouted.

Choudry stared coldly at his son-in-law, as every negative feeling he had ever felt for him now surfaced in his mind.

"Kazi," he said, calmly and resolutely. "For eight years now, I have tolerated your intolerance. I have sat here and listened to you mumble about America. Rant about Christians and Jews. Enough is enough. God asks us each to serve Him in our own way. And today he has shown me what I must do."

"May Allah forgive you for this blasphemy," Kazi answered.

"*If* it is blasphemy," Choudry said, raising his voice, "then it is blasphemy. But it is what I must do. Now, this is my house. If you want to behave as a civilized man, you may stay. Otherwise—"

"Choudry," Amina interrupted. "How can you talk to your family like this?"

"Amina," Choudry responded angrily. "Do not interfere."

Amina looked at him through her swollen eyes. He had never spoken to her like this before, had never raised his voice, had never said a bad word to anyone. Now, suddenly, he had become strong and forceful, spoke with a voice of authority that shocked her so much she knew she would need to relearn how to interact with him.

"Now. Amir," Choudry said to his son, "go to the shop and get what your mother needs."

"But Dad?"

"You heard what I said. Fatwa, go help your mother in the kitchen."

"Yes, Papa," his daughter answered dutifully.

"And Kazi. Go make your ablutions. We will pray together for God's guidance."

With a thin wan smile carved into his gaunt face like a jagged scar, Sharir peered through the sparks and flames that spat out from the huge hearth. A ghostly image of Choudry and his family wavered above the blaze as Sharir cast herbs into the hungry fire.

"Ablutions," he said, mimicking Choudry with a feigned laugh. "Make your ablutions my friends. None of your prayers can help you now."

He fed more herbs into the crackling flames, then waved his arms to and fro, manipulating his victims like a master puppeteer. Then, with a flick of his finger, the image of Choudry and his family disappeared, and Larry materialized, his face contorted, his hands and arms moving chaotically in the air like those of a frenzied dancer.

Standing beside Sharir, Akram watched, at once rapt and horrified, as Sharir performed his magic and Larry withered onto the floor of the church then rose up like a marionette, babbling from both of his mouths as if a sudden, inexplicable throbbing had risen from his soul and had forcibly overtaken his body. His eyes turned and twisted as if he were possessed by the Devil and his two voices cried out with an evil, unintelligent moan that Akram could not recall ever having heard.

Sharir waved his hand furiously in the air. He tossed more herbs into the flames, then mumbled an incomprehensible incantation, and President Thorne's figure emerged from the flames, snorting at his cabinet members like a rabid pig as they looked on in consternation and struggled to deal with the crisis that was unfolding before their very eyes.

"Excellent," Sharir said.

Turning toward his apprentice, he eyed Akram through his pinched eyes. He was young, he thought, examining him like a prize pheasant. Young and innocent and with much to learn. Lazy, perhaps. But he could be prodded. He could easily be molded. Easily be made to learn his ways and bend to his will.

"Why do you stand there staring like that?" Sharir shouted. "Don't you know that I am the greatest wizard that has ever lived?"

His voice echoed through the cavernous chamber, and Akram stared down at the cold, stone ground, silent and fearful.

"They think they have such control over their lives," Sharir continued, turning his scornful gaze back to the fireplace "But I will show them otherwise. *We* shall show them otherwise. Together. You and me."

Sharir turned toward his table and scooped up a stone mortar into his arms. With a large, twisted pestle, he slowly stirred its vaporous contents, then lifted the dripping rod up over the flames and mumbled an incantation.

Akram watched as Sharir's face darkened and waxed into a black ball of fury. He wanted to run to his bed and hide his head as deep as he could into the musty straw, but he knew he couldn't. He knew he had to stay until he was dismissed, had to listen to his master's wicked spell and witness the terror he was inflicting on his innocent victims, whose images blazed among the furious flames as if they were burning in hell. So he stared silently, listened reluctantly to the evil words seeping from Sharir's mouth like a poison gas.

"Go now," Sharir said at last, turning to his apprentice. "Go and rest. There's much to be done, my little friend. But when we are finished, you and I shall rule the earth. And no one shall stop us. No one."

Sharir flung his arms into the air and gazed upwards.

"No one," he shouted into the air. "Do you hear that, Goro? No one can stop us."

Chapter 4

THE NEXT MORNING, President Thorne awoke with a sharp pain in his lower back. Cursing the creaky, eighteenth-century bed (how, he thought, had those people gotten any sleep?) and the White House housekeepers who had refused to replace it, he gently massaged his sore muscles, flexed his throbbing back, and struggled to get his mind off the pain, trying to focus his attention instead on a small, brown spider meandering indiscriminately along the shadowy filigree of the moonlit wallpaper.

What had he done to deserve this, he wondered. What sin against God had he unwittingly committed? As the pain in his back began to subside, as the little brown spider scurried quickly up the wall, he remembered his mouth—remembered, rather, that he no longer had a mouth—for a raw, scratchy feeling suddenly emerged deep inside his throat and he could do nothing to soothe the abrasive stinging that manifested itself each time he tried to swallow. As he winced in pain, he felt his flat, expressionless face crinkle and stretch like a taut balloon.

President Thorne cried out in fear, a futile whimper that emerged from the depths of his being as a mere, muffled moan. Unable to produce a clearly articulated sound, unable to express the most basic expression of existence, he jumped up in a panic, sending a sharp pain racing along his lower back, causing the bed to rock and the First Lady to rouse from the comfort of a very pleasant dream.

Detecting her husband's garbled moans, the First Lady turned on her side and decided they were simply the distant howls of a stray animal or the elusive echoes one encounters in the folds of sleep, and she fell back into a heavy slumber and resumed the exotic dream that had so thoroughly consumed her (she was lying on a mysterious island in the middle of the South Pacific, and there were miles and miles of white, empty beach and palm trees waving in a gentle breeze, and the soothing waves lured her deeper and deeper to a place where wild animals and tedious husbands and other unwelcome intrusions into her sheltered life would not be able to break in).

Incensed by his wife's lack of concern, President Thorne gently eased himself back down onto the bed and watched the lonesome spider haphazardly loop its delicate web.

Meanwhile, the citizens of the greater metropolis gradually began to awaken from their restless slumbers. One by one, bedroom windows lit like a series of synchronized lights, and the city slowly began to resume its regular routine: the rush-hour swelled to exasperating intensity, the daily toll of fender benders and broken down vehicles accumulated like litter on the region's highways, and swarms of weary commuters flocked hypnotically, like pilgrims on a mandatory mission, toward the center of world power.

Amidst it all, a new and ominous aura settled upon the unsuspecting populace like a thick, choking fog, and despite signs that things were not quite right, no one as yet, including the anguished and unsuspecting President Thorne, who lay squirming in stunned silence in his lumpy bed, understood that a national crisis was rapidly in the works.

For, as the sun began its slow ascent into an azure sky, an unexpected combination of news announced itself like the blast of a tempestuous trumpet. ATTEMPTED BREACH AT WHITE HOUSE (SUSPECTED TERRORIST ESCAPES UNCHARGED) read the lead story in *The Washington Post*. Beside this stark headline, in equally bold letters, was a similarly alarming headline: PRESIDENT THORNE ANNOUNCES UNEXPECTED SURGERY, CANCELS ALL APPEARANCES. Meanwhile, on the front page of one of the lesser known DC papers, a local weekly produced in a downtown warehouse, the following caption appeared: MAN SPEAKS IN MOUTHS, FINDS SALVATION AT SOUTHEAST HOUSE OF WORSHIP.

While the news quickly spread in a flurry of media frenzy that had TV anchors chattering like garrulous geese, a sudden and mysterious outbreak of head colds spread like a raging wildfire across the entire metropolitan region. People sneezed, people coughed, people blew their relentless noses. This outburst of symptoms led to a rush on the region's pharmacies as large crowds gathered in panic, desperate to get their hands on cold medicines, cough syrup, nose sprays and hand sanitizer. By eleven a.m., when the city should have been thoroughly settled into its monotonous morning routine, the mobs at the pharmaceutical outlets had grown so uncontrollable and the supply of cold remedies had dwindled so rapidly that the news industry, in time for its late morning edition, was able to sum it up neatly in just one word: PANDEMIC!

When Mark Drove awoke to the rash of news blaring on his TV, he jumped out of bed and immediately summoned President Thorne's cabinet members to the White House.

"Nothing we can't handle," he assured each one of them in between sniffles and sneezes. "Nothing that the best minds in the world can't resolve," he promised President Thorne before abruptly hanging up and scratching his head with a look of wonder.

Unrested and unable to breathe, President Thorne extracted himself from his bed with the assistance of the First Lady, who, having reached a point in her dream where the call of wild animals had become too frightening to bear had awakened with a sudden start to the squirms and whimpers of her husband.

"Really," she declared. "We just have to get away from this place or I'll go completely mad."

She shook her head as if she were shaking off an unwanted speck of lint, sat down on the edge of the bed, and wiped a tear from her sleepy, unmade face. President Thorne attempted a look of encouragement, a look that filled his face with such horror that the First Lady's quiet whimpers quickly erupted into a full bout of wailing.

"I promise you," he tried to say. "As soon as I locate my mouth and put it where it belongs, I'll make it up to you."

But President Thorne's inability to convey his thoughts made him appear even more like a savage beast, and his attempts at communicating manifested themselves as a horrid snarl. Mrs. Thorne watched in horror as her wailing crescendoed into a full frenzy of cries and tears.

When President Thorne arrived at the Oval Office, one hand clutching his back, the other a box of Kleenex, he quietly took his seat behind his desk and stared blankly at his weary aides as they entered the room, glum and silent except for their persistent sneezing. As the last cabinet member shuffled through the door, Drove surveyed the room like an eagle assessing its territory and called the meeting to order.

"Gentlemen," he began, his eye resting on Brice, "the nation is in a state of crisis."

It was said matter-of-factly, said as if this was just another challenge that he had somehow to fix.

Not only, he continued, had a pandemic suddenly appeared with no apparent warning, but the story of the president's surgery had somehow been leaked. They now had to come to grips with the fact that the nation was facing an unprecedented test of its collective will.

"An historic challenge," he said emphatically, "unparalleled to anything the nation has ever witnessed."

Moreover, he continued, there was, it seemed, a mole among them, someone who had exposed their carefully planned narrative, a narrative, he stressed, that they had put together in the interest of national security. If they did not get a handle on these challenges, he concluded, everything would quickly unravel.

"And I mean everything," he said, stopping to gaze at each and every one of them, as if to ascertain which of them it might be.

"In short, lady and gentlemen," he concluded, "we have a national emergency on our hands."

Everyone spoke at once. Everyone, that is, except for President Thorne who tried his best to pay attention, who was, after all, under the weather, who, he quickly reminded himself, as he attempted to focus on what was being said, was a victim of extraordinary circumstances, a mouthless specter of a political figure unable to participate even if he wanted to. Still, he endeavored to concentrate on the words that emerged from their mouths (words, he thought, that sounded hazy through the miasma of congestion and political wrangling), and he did his best to focus his blurry vision on his aides who seemed like so many disembodied ghosts. He tried to grasp their gist, to fathom the meaning behind their intentions. At last, he squinted his swollen eyes until he could barely see, crumpled back into his chair, frustrated and angry, and folded his arms like a schoolchild lost in the details of the class discussion.

"Who was the intruder at the White House gate? And why in God's name was he allowed to leave?"

"It seems to have been some immigrant. Undocumented, no doubt. Illegal. Fresh off the boat. Without papers. However you want to describe him."

"Who leaked the president's surgery? We were supposed to announce that this morning. We need to find the mole and squelch him."

"Why on earth do we suddenly have a pandemic on our hands?"

President Thorne listened to the strings of words, to the fragments and phrases that sounded as if they were emerging from deep under water, that seeped through his mind like a slow, annoying leak as the voices of his aides ebbed and flowed through his consciousness like muffled, murky waves. A dense cloud had engulfed him, and though he tried his best to muster up his full attention, he could not get a grasp on the simplest words, could not understand even the shortest of sentences.

All he could think about was finding his mouth. Whether it was under a pillow or hidden on the White House lawn like an Easter egg or stored away in a box deep within some obscure closet, his sole purpose now was to reunite himself with this lost fragment of his body. And not until it was located and reattached to his face and he could once again speak freely would he allow his aides to ramble on as they were doing, without one thought or care for his state of affairs.

Perhaps it was the lack of sleep or the severe head cold that had manifested itself. Or maybe it was the fact that the conversation in the room had become loud and unruly. Whatever the reason, President Thorne felt a sudden urge to scream at the tops of his lungs. He wanted to tell everyone to shut up, to stop their prattling about national security, their blathering about epidemics and all the other drivel they were spouting and to focus instead on his condition. Was that all they could talk about: intrusions, leaks, damage control? What were they going to do about him? Why were they so worried that a poorly concocted story had gotten out while they were doing absolutely nothing to locate the surgeon who would restore his face back to normal?

But President Thorne immediately found that his tenuous attempts at speaking through his nose were now completely thwarted. And so he sat there, silent, his blood pressure slowly building, his anger starting to boil over.

In the midst of President Thorne's cogitations, the surgeon general stood up and tried to quell the commotion that had overtaken the room. Though not an especially successful physician, he was considered a wise, circumspect man, well respected among political circles. And while he had not prepared either himself or the nation for an outbreak of this proportion, he had learned throughout his long, tedious years in the industry that fighting a head cold simply called for lots of bed rest and the consumption of large quantities of fluids. And so he now came to the conclusion that the most efficient solution to the current health crisis facing the nation was really quite simple: everyone, he believed, should be ordered to stay home and the government should distribute massive amounts of bottled water to all affected areas. FEMA, he thought, would have the necessary resources, and the surrounding jurisdictions, where the pandemic had manifested itself, would have the authority to declare a state of emergency and order everyone to stay in bed.

So the wise surgeon general, who finally managed to get everyone's attention by rubbing his watery eyes with one hand and waving the other frantically in the air, was about to prescribe his solution to the current health crisis facing the nation, when President Thorne stood up suddenly and banged his fist on the desk as loudly as he could.

The room went silent.

"Sir?" Drove asked, breaking through the quiet.

President Thorne stared angrily at them as his body started to shake. His eyes bulged and the welt of skin that covered his mouth swelled as if it would suddenly explode.

And then, without warning, President Thorne sneezed, a sneeze so loud and copious that it stunned everyone in the room and was heard well beyond the closed doors of the Oval Office. And beyond the shock that it created among his aides and the sense of disgust which they tried their best to hide, it left him with a sense of power he had never before experienced, for not until now had he ever gotten such a quick reaction from his staff.

He glared at his cabinet members as they hastily reached for something to wipe their faces, and he sized up the sense of abhorrence they could no longer conceal. And then, just as suddenly, he braced himself for another irrepressible sneeze and watched each of them as they instinctively covered their faces and turned away, stunned and disgusted.

When everyone had had a chance to recover from the shock, they wiped their faces as discreetly as they possibly could and pretended to proceed as normal. Watching them with a sense of triumph, President Thorne understood then what he had not fully comprehended all along: that despite his title, despite the respect they each showed him whenever he entered the room or convened a meeting or requested information on a particular subject, despite the fact that he led the nation through its failures and successes, through its tragedies and joys, he was really just a meaningless puppet. A classic political pawn, like those he had read about in the history books. Only those individuals usually presided over some overseas dictatorship in some obscure country whose political legitimacy was in name only. He, on the other hand, was the head of a genuine democracy, had been duly and legally elected.

Whether he had a mouth or not, President Thorne concluded, in a fit of clarity, did not matter. Whether he could speak was of no consequence. Whether his appearance was comely, his ways diplomatic or his words well chosen and well spoken held no sway. What mattered was what was forced upon him, however subtly, by powers beyond his control, what he, knowingly or unknowingly, ultimately succumbed to. Even the decisions he made on a daily basis—which bills to sign, which policies to authorize, which clandestine operations to put his stamp of approval on—decisions he seemed to make with relative ease and independence—these actions, he now realized, were not really his. Never had been and never would be.

This revelation was both a relief and a new source of anger, for while it now seemed to liberate him as he had never been before, it left him with a distinct and rather bitter taste of humiliation on his tongue, a tongue he had no way of setting free.

President Thorne observed his aides as they scrambled for the box of Kleenex on his desk. He watched with a secret sense of joy as they each jostled for a tissue with an outward semblance of respect and tried to hide their desperation behind a façade of politeness. And then, when they each began to sneeze, one after the other and in no particular order, and Candice Brice called out to Drove in her cool, measured voice to send for an extra carton of Kleenex, he felt that, as powerless as he might be in their eyes, he was, at this very moment, more powerful than anyone of them could possibly imagine. And he concluded that not having a mouth was, indeed, a blessing in disguise, for no matter what he thought, no matter how ridiculous the person sitting before him might be, how pompous, how utterly distasteful, his feelings for that person would never be revealed.

"I am truly at peace now," he said to himself. "I'm a peaceful man." And President Thorne smiled serenely to himself (it was an internal smile, of course, though the skin that covered the spot where his mouth had been did move somewhat in an upwards fashion), and he sat back quietly in his executive chair and watched, content, as his aides sneezed and honked and sputtered and spewed.

In the meantime, the Reverend CJ Willis, who had promptly alerted the press of the miracle that had come to pass in his humble inner-city church (for it *was* a miracle, he repeated again and again to himself, had all the markings as detailed in his trusty textbooks) sat enthralled and starry-eyed in his cramped, stuffy office, one moment making note of the paint peeling along the broken molding on the wall, another lost in the glittering future that beckoned him like a distant pot of glittering gold. Twirling a dull pencil between his trembling fingers, he reran in his mind the scene of Larry's sudden rapture and contemplated the meaning of this wondrous, telling sign.

This specter of an individual, whom he had never before seen, this horrid-looking creature, who possessed two mouths and spoke in tones at once horrid and graceful, had somehow stumbled upon his church, *his* house of worship, praise the Lord, had suddenly and spontaneously embraced the word of God. And right before the members of his very own congregation. Yes, he thought, a big smile beaming across his flushed face, his gold tooth cap gleaming like an auspicious star, it was a miracle, praise God, and he had witnesses to prove it, eager, willing witnesses, just in case there were any Doubting Thomases to challenge his word.

At last, it seemed, all his training, all his hard work was beginning to come to fruition, all his hopes and dreams were about to be realized. His name would become known across the nation. He would be the new Billy Graham. Presidents would summon him, ask for his advice. World leaders would seek him out. And all because of an unsightly individual who had serendipitously stumbled into his church to seek God's mercy.

The Reverend CJ Willis—the reputable Reverend CJ Willis, the righteous, the compassionate, the loving Reverend CJ Willis—sat behind his desk, in his cramped basement office, in The Blazing Path of Light Ebenezer Baptist Church, LLC, surveying his lowly surroundings, observing how small and undeserving his establishment really was, how inadequate, how unbefitting the current circumstances, and decided that soon, very soon, he would need to expand yet again, though where and how he did not know, for the building would not accommodate the required growth, nor would the street where it was located, nor would the neighborhood.

So Reverend Willis dreamed on of his glorious future while the phone rang off the hook. He wrapped himself up in deep contemplation. He mulled over his next move, deliberated on where his new church should be located (for it had to be in just the right place if it was going to be in the national spotlight) while a loud knocking on the front door echoed relentlessly throughout the building. Jolted back to the present by the bothersome commotion, he remembered Larry, locked away in his church, convinced more than ever that he could not let this wondrous creature get away. For if the nation was to benefit from his guidance and counsel, Larry's presence in his esteemed house of worship was an utmost necessity.

While Reverend Willis wrestled with the trials and tribulations of being the nation's foremost preacher, Larry sat silent and despondent beside Pearl in the apse of the church chamber (a former showroom, filled with folding chairs neatly lined against the walls, its windows covered with thin layers of fading vinyl stained glass), and wondered what would become of him. He could not escape, for the church entrance has been bolted shut (merely to protect him, Reverend Willis had assured him, from the swarm of reporters who had parked themselves outside the door of the ministry, anxious to catch a glimpse of the creature whose story of transformation had spread like wildfire). Nor would he have wanted to, even if he had not been locked up like a prisoner. For where would he go? Where could a person like himself, a revolting individual with two mouths, venture in this world without being persecuted, without being looked upon as a freak? He would be made fun of, needled in public, shunned by his friends and endlessly stared at by strangers.

Covering his eyes with his hands, he rested his head in Pearl's arms, convinced that his debauched life had been the cause of this miserable, impossible situation. Looking up at the vinyl stained glass window through which the sun's rays shone with its promise of revelation and tranquility, he cursed the day he had ever put liquor to his mouth. These circumstances, he reasoned, could only have been caused by overindulgence, by one too many bouts of stone drunkenness, by the effects of hangover after hangover, the last of which had been so severe that whatever hallucination it had created had seemingly become real. Looking back at his dissolute life, he now concluded that his body had been so unable to deal with the amount of drink he poured down his miserable throat that it had had no choice but to develop a second orifice to allow for this volume.

As Larry swooned in misery, Pearl—the woman who had rescued him from the gutter, the woman who lavished him with love and rebuked him whenever he went astray—held him close, wrapped him safely in her arms like a mother comforting a frightened child. She gazed lovingly at him, as he focused his weary eyes on her smiling face, seeking her reassurance, for she, above anyone else, had loved him unconditionally, had accepted him, even at his worst. As he buried his face in her bosom, she stroked his head with a look of serene bliss and thanked the Lord for delivering her man.

Having grown up in poverty, Pearl had learned early on never to expect a great deal from the world, had come to understand over the years that happiness was something that visited very rarely and then up and ran just as quickly as it had arrived.

As a child, she had hopscotched her way through life, trying to ignore the desperation that surrounded her, trying to forget the father who had abandoned her at an early age, hoping and praying that he would one day return. Then, in her early twenties, after a short bout of abandonment, she discovered God and her world changed dramatically, so that when Larry came into the picture like a stray animal, at a party where he tried to get her drunk so he could take advantage of her, she knew that she had found her man *and* her mission in life, all wrapped up in one hard-to-resist, attractive individual. With the utmost fortitude, she had defied his moves, had been so strong and so righteous that she had been able to overcome his overtures and, in a twist that shocked him as much as it did her, had instead seduced him into entering into marriage and leading a faithful though somewhat checkered life. And though he had never fully accepted the word of God, they soon settled down into a life that was the envy of her closest friends, though she often secretly had to retrieve him from the gutter whenever he strayed.

And now, through God's mysterious and merciful ways, her man had been delivered, here in this church, where they now sat together in reverence, here in this mission that was ministered by the Reverend CJ Willis, here in this place of worship that she had recently discovered when the one she regularly attended had folded into bankruptcy, with the man she believed to be the pillar in her life, his head nuzzled in her bosom, her face emitting joy and tranquility like a gentle flame radiating warmth and light.

"Larry," she said in a voice that was so angelic it echoed ever so faintly in the church chamber and seemed to originate from the heavens. "We are blessed, you and I. Doubly blessed."

Larry started at these last words, but Pearl calmed him down again with a gentle pat on his head.

"God has bestowed His grace on us," she said. "First, He saved me. And now you."

Larry closed his weary eyes and ran his finger softly along his face. Slowly, he traced the shape of each of his two mouths: the original one as familiar as ever, the new one seemingly with a life of its own. He wondered if he could control it, tried now to move its muscles, to smile with it, to grimace, but he seemed to have no power over it. Instead, it somehow possessed him, and he gave up his attempts at mastering it and unwillingly let out a sigh of resignation as tenuous as the words that followed:

"I am truly at peace now."

The words surprised him but the look on Pearl's face, which now beamed even more strongly at him as he opened his eyes in shock, provided him comfort. He watched her skin burnish under the soft sunlight that filtered through the rosy vinyl glued to the window above the make-shift altar, thought he saw the shape of an arc appear just above her head, and felt a sudden source of calm and repose take hold of him.

Perhaps, he thought, two mouths would do him just fine once he got the hang of it, for it certainly appeared to have a calming effect on his wife, as horrible as it seemed to him. And as long as it made her happy, kept her from nagging him as she was prone to do, his life would be better. Besides, he said to himself, his mood suddenly changing, he'd be able to kiss her twice as much when they made love.

"Pearl, baby," Larry said, in his deep, rich voice, sitting up and putting his arm around her.

He looked around the room to make sure they were alone and kissed her, slowly and passionately. Then, finding he could not coordinate his two mouths against her one, he became so discombobulated that he pushed himself back with a look of anger and frustration on his face.

Pearl beamed at him, blushing like a girl on her fist date.

"Larry," she whispered. "Maybe now, we'll have our baby. Maybe God will see fit to bless us just one more time."

"Baby?' he said, shocked into reality. Then, remembering how much she had wanted a child, he smiled, broadly and doubly, with the knowledge that Pearl, the woman who had seen him through the most wretched years of his life and now fully accepted his grotesque condition, was still willing to make love to him, was willing, even now, to risk having a child, one that might even turn out deformed.

"Baby," he said, putting his arm around her and pulling her close. He tried kissing her again, but as he puckered up his four lips, he felt her vanish from between his arms and, looking up, he saw that she was no longer beside him.

"What the…" he said, looking around the room. "Pearl," he shouted. "Where you at? Why you always playing games with me?"

"Larry," Pearl called, in a voice ethereal and distant.

Larry lifted his head and watched Pearl rise slowly into the air, her face beaming with joy.

"Whatchu doing up there, woman?"

Pearl hovered beside the vinyl-covered window and looked down at him with a look of peace and tranquility.

"Larry," she said, in a voice that now seemed not her own. "We're going to have a baby. I feel it. God will see to it. Through His miraculous ways, we will conceive. Like Mary conceived. Purely. Through the miracle of love. And you will be my Joseph. You will be the father of our miraculous child."

Pearl smiled down at him, an arc of light radiating brightly around her head.

"Woman," Larry shouted, "come down here right now."

"God has called me, Larry. I need to heed His word."

"You leaving me, baby?"

"Trust me, Larry. Trust me."

"Pearl, baby, where you going? Please, baby, please don't leave me."

Then, like a ghost, Pearl passed through the glowing window pane, her figure illuminated in the rose-colored sunshine, and disappeared.

"Come back here, woman," Larry shouted into the air.

But it was too late, and Larry rested his back against the wall, confused and frightened, and wondered whether, after everything that had happened, after all was said and done, he would still be considered a man.

While the city awakened to the startling news regarding the state of the nation, while the early aurora dimly lit up the skies, Amina quietly finished up her morning prayer. Turning her head from her right shoulder to her left, she intoned her last salaams and wiped her face piously with her hands as she did each time she completed her obligations to Allah.

How, she thought to herself, resting quietly now on her prayer rug and glancing over at her husband who refused to wake up for *fajr* prayer, who remained snug in his bed, curled up in sleep, snoring peacefully as if he had done nothing wrong—how could a man who had just committed blasphemy, who, God forgive him, persisted in saying he had seen God, who had, out of the blue, driven to the White House and demanded to see the president—how could such a man sleep so soundly? How could he just lie there, oblivious to her, insensitive to her feelings, unconcerned for the very safety of their family after having suddenly disrupted their comfortable, ordinary, inconspicuous lives? Would the police not come knocking on their door at any minute? Would the FBI not investigate? Would the government not suspect them of being terrorists? Throw them in jail? Lock them up forever, never to see again the light of day?

"Choudry," she called, her voice breaking the morning silence.

Choudry's peaceful snoring broke into an abrupt staccato at the strident sound of his wife's voice, then quelled back into a steady rhythm as he turned over and resumed his restful sleep.

Grumbling at his insensitivity to her concerns, Amina returned to her thoughts, her supplications, her fears of what would become of them, when she heard a faint rustling in the garden just outside her window. It was something like footsteps, though lighter, less substantial, something like the whoosh of leaves, as if the giant oak tree in her yard was being shaken by a gentle breeze or by the movement of some nocturnal creature.

She listened for a moment, her back taught and tense, then, passing it off as a small animal—a squirrel, she concluded, quickly reassuring herself, scampering along the branches, or maybe, she thought, letting her mind get away with itself, a wolf treading stealthily through her vegetable patch, searching for chickens or squab or some other delicacy he could steal. But she did not have chickens and squab, she reminded herself, trying to calm herself. And there were no wolves in Arlington. Hadn't Choudry promised her? Assured her? Hadn't he scolded her for having such naïve thoughts?

A streak of embarrassment gently crossed her face, and she settled back onto her soft, comforting prayer rug, blushing ever so briefly at her own gullibility, and raised her hands in supplication, praying for her foolish husband who always managed to bring havoc into their small, unassuming lives.

How could I have married such a man? she wondered, now angry, now filled with pride and love for the only man she had ever known. Always dreaming. Always trying to do things he had no business doing. Always finding a way to get himself into trouble. Hadn't he any shame? Hadn't he any sense of decency to think of his family before acting so rashly?

But he was a good husband, she thought, quickly chiding herself. Despite his strange ways. Hadn't he always been kind to her? Hadn't he always provided for her and her children? And, in all these years, he had never lifted a hand to her, had never mistreated her in any way. There was always food on the table. Everyone always had the proper clothing. And while their home was not a palace—their dishes were cracked and chipped, she remembered now with a sudden frown, their furniture, handcrafted by some distant relative when they were first married, now showed the signs that time and the toll of moving had taken on them. No, it was not a palace. Not by any means. Still, it was a place that provided all the comforts that were necessary in this life. Yes, she thought to herself, satisfied, it was a place, not a palace—and she smiled now at this little twist—a place that was at the very heart of her existence. And he had worked very hard to make it that way.

No, he was not a lazy man, not her Choudry, except when it came to his prayers. He worked very hard at his shop, selling his meat, peddling his produce, promoting the items he imported from Pakistan, things that would not otherwise be available here in America. But he was, at times, a little—well, she didn't want to criticize him, not when he was sleeping, not when she was making her morning prayers—but, truth be told, he was not exactly an honest man. Charging more than he should, Allah forgive him. Manipulating the scales so that people paid for more than they got. And Allah only knew what he did with the money in those charity boxes! Still, he could be generous, would never hesitate to help a person in need.

And then there was his dreaming! Amina, he would tell her, a big smile on his chubby face, one day we will live like royalty. One day we will travel the world. One day, one day... *Oh, how could I have married such a dreamer!* she said to herself, raising her hands in frustration. But she was criticizing him again, and there he was, sleeping peacefully with not a care in the world. Still, she wished he would be more practical, would stop this wishful thinking of his. That's what always got them into trouble. And now—

"Choudry," Amina shouted, sweeping the thought from her mind. "Get up, Choudry. You will miss your prayer."

Amina raised her hands in supplication again, entreating God to get them through this crisis, to deliver her husband from his tomfoolery and the trouble he had now gotten himself into.

"How," she said out loud in exasperation, "how does God appear to a man who does not even say his morning prayers? Choudry!"

Amina pushed herself up from the floor and folded her gold-trimmed prayer-rug in half in one smooth motion that had been repeated five times a day, year after year. She laid it gently in the corner beside the little wooden stand that cradled her Koran when she heard another sound in the garden, this time louder and more distinct. Trying to make as little noise as possible, she tiptoed to the window and gently pushed the curtain aside, peeking through the blinds, lifting one of the slats just enough to get a view.

"*Allahu akbar*," she intoned, for though she could clearly hear a loud rustling, she could not see anything moving in her yard. "Choudry," she whispered fearfully, "Choudry, come here quickly."

Now, even in the midst of a very deep sleep, Choudry could clearly distinguish Amina's ceaseless chiding from a moment of genuine crisis, so hearing her startled voice, his eyes immediately snapped open and he popped up like a jack-in-the-box and sat upright on his bed.

"Amina," he said. "What is it? Why do you wake me when I am having such a pleasant dream?"

"Quickly, Choudry," she said, clutching her headscarf. "Come here. There's someone in the garden."

Terrified, Amina began beating her breast rapidly.

Choudry took one look at his wife, whose face was now as pale as a ghost's, and rushed over to the window, carelessly parting the blinds to see what it was that had so easily frightened her. Peering through the window and squinting to get a clearer view, he gazed in disbelief at what looked like a woman, hovering among the branches and leaves—and there—well, he could not be sure, could not tell if he were still in the midst of a dream or if it was just the sunrise, if it was merely the way the rays of early morning light slanted through the leaves—but it seemed as if there was an arc of light floating just above her head, illuminating her dark, shimmering complexion.

"*Allahu akbar*," he said in disbelief.

"Choudry," Amina said. "What is it? Who's there? *Allahu akbar!* What will become of us?"

Amina fell down to the floor in a swoon of fear. Rocking back and forth and beating her hand against her breast, she shouted supplications to God and begged for their safety.

Choudry looked out the window again, blinking his eyes to make sure he was awake, but the mysterious woman remained, suspended magically among the leaves and branches of the tree. She had a kind, peaceful look about her, and smiled gently at him, beckoning him with her hand to follow her. Then she turned her back to him, and slowly began to float away, out of the garden and off to the east.

"Wait!" Choudry shouted.

"Choudry," Amina said, interrupting her frantic gesticulations. "Who's there?"

"Did you not see it, Amina? Did you not see that ghost in the trees?"

"Ghost? Choudry. Have you gone completely mad? What is wrong with you? First you say God has appeared to you. And now you see a ghost? Choudry. Talk to me. I'm your wife."

"Amina," Choudry insisted. "Come. See for yourself."

Amina stood up and hesitatingly peered out the window to see only the sunrise extending its warm, golden glow over her garden.

"Choudry," she scolded. "You should be ashamed of yourself."

"But Amina. She was there. I swear to God."

Choudry took another look out the window but saw nothing.

"She's gone," he said.

"She!" Amina shouted. "She! Choudry. Is there another woman in your life?"

"I've got to find her."

Choudry let the blinds fall down with a tinny crash and walked briskly out of the bedroom and down the stairs.

"Choudry," Amina called, running after him. "Where are you going? Come back here. Chasing after another woman right before my own eyes! Choudry! Choudry!"

"She wants me to follow her," Choudry said, rushing into the foyer.

Stopping abruptly at the front door, he turned to his wife

"Don't you see, Amina?" he said. "This is part of God's plan."

"God's plan," Amina answered sarcastically. "To leave your wife and chase after another woman? And in your pajamas? Have you no shame, Choudry? Have some mercy on your wife who has sacrificed her whole life for you."

"Amina," he said, looking at her with a slight look of pity—for she was a simple woman, he realized, could not possibly see beyond the simple limits of her ordinary life. "You will see."

Choudry opened the door and rushed toward his car. Amina called out after him but was overcome by a fateful fit of sneezing that prevented her from saying yet another deprecating word.

"Choudry! Choudry!"

Sharir burst into laughter, bellowing with a force that sent the mice scampering back to their nests, as Amina's words, punctuated by the fitful rhythm of her sneezing, repeated with the hollow sound of an old gramophone. Gazing into his crystal ball, he grinned greedily from his thick hairy lips, satiated with the mischief he had so far created, and wondered what other havoc he could devise, wondered how else he could influence the lives of these vain, insignificant individuals who were mere specks, so easily influenced, so easily duped. They were like insects, he thought, though less essential, instinctively wandering about, blindly, with wide-opened eyes, yet so unaware, so small in their outlook they could not possibly notice the giant foot ready to crush them until they found themselves suddenly trapped, unable to escape, unable even to lift their feet to scamper back to safety. Such naive creatures, he thought. So gullible. So self-assured. So certain they were in control of their lives.

Sharir wearily approached the massive fireplace and listened to the flames crackle beneath the cauldron where he was preparing a new and highly potent potion. Controlling the world was not an easy job, he thought, amused with himself. It took time and skill. It took planning and preparation. It required strategy to keep one step ahead of those whose lives he was trying to influence. He could not afford to make mistakes. He had a reputation to maintain. He was, after all, Sharir. The evil one. The one who made the villagers quake. The one who inspired fear in the hearts of men and loyalty in their breasts. They knew he would skewer their children if they turned on him. They knew their villages would burn if they made one false move against him, defied his wishes.

Soon, he would have the world at his feet. In just a short while, the most powerful leaders would beg him for mercy, come crawling to him with just one wish: to be released from the misery of his perfect grip. And then he would have his revenge. Then he would avenge the atrocities his family had been subjected to, centuries ago, by one arrogant, callous king.

Sharir's face turned angry at the thought, and he quickly focused his bloodshot eyes on the cauldron that boiled with his sinister brew. He watched the thick bubbling concoction, trying to forget how his people had been chased from their homes, imprisoned, tortured. Spying a large, hairy spider crawling on the worn arm of the chair beside the fireplace, he grabbed it furiously with his long, bony fingers, plucked off two of its legs and tossed them into the ancient pot with an incantation that seemed to make the ground shake, crushing, as he did so, the squirming spider with the tip of his toe.

At his feet, Akram slept restlessly by the warmth of the fire, coiled up like a snake. Having gathered all the ingredients Sharir required for his potion, he had become drowsy, almost against his will, as if the herbs he had harvested had somehow cursed him. Sharir watched him, considered him as a shepherd would inspect a lamb before its slaughter. He could kill him right there, add his liver to the brew, preserve his kidneys, his spleen, the bile in his gallbladder for future spells. But he had bigger plans for this child. He would train him, give him the skills to become a powerful and feared wizard and then, when the time was right, he would perform his greatest feat: cloning him with a magic potion so strong that no force on earth could stop its wicked effects. There would be thousands of him, and they would swarm out, armies of evil warlocks, ready to do his bidding.

But he first had to create the right formula. He first needed to gather all the elements that would combine perfectly and complete his wicked scheme.

Akram stirred on the cold, hard stone floor, as Sharir turned to the cauldron and began adding aconite, bicorn horns, mandrake, asphodel. The brew bubbled over and sparks crackled and flew. Akram's arms flinched and his face grimaced as he struggled in his sleep. A heavy plume of fog coiled its way up from the cauldron and slowly snaked its way over the boy, winding itself sinuously around him. Sharir peered into the thick smoke, mumbled an incantation and watched as Amina appeared, sitting now in her living room, trying to soothe herself with a glass of tea as she struggled with her tears and wrestled with her sneezes. He gazed at Choudry wandering off in his pajamas into the city with no idea of where he was going, following Pearl as she hovered in the air beckoning for him to follow. He observed President Thorne, dumbfounded and perplexed, examining himself helplessly in the mirror, twitching his face from one side to the other, contemplating his blank visage and wondering what was in store for his future. And he laughed as Larry, who had started to make love to Pearl on the church floor, then sat up startled, finding himself unexpectedly alone, wondering where his wife had suddenly disappeared to.

Sharir smiled. He was content, and he sat down in his armchair and allowed himself to fall asleep.

Chapter 5

PRESIDENT THORNE was locked in his room. Like a prisoner. "Like that prisoner of—" President Thorne thought. "That prisoner of… of Zambia."

His mind was struggling, like a wild animal futilely resisting the river's currents, his mouth was pulsing, pulsing and throbbing, and he sulked like a child and stared vacuously at the IV the surgeon general had tethered to his arm, watched it drip, drip, drip away like a leaky faucet as the clear, soothing solution slowly filled his veins.

Now that he was medicated, his face—a small, expressionless mug with a flat, triangular nose and fanning, oval ears—had taken cn a new depth of bewilderment: his smallish eyes were swollen and droopy, his dimwitted expression had grown as blank as a failed computer's monitor, and his mind had turned dazed, his thoughts evasive as the sluggish trickle of the IV took him further and further into a fog of confusion.

Though the cold symptoms gradually diminished—the fits of sneezing slowly subsiding, the endless sniffles gradually diminishing, the muffled coughing, each lingering bout causing a plosive swell between his puffed-up cheeks, steadily decreasing in intensity—a sense of stupor now began to take hold, an unmistakable vagueness of thought, an inability to formulate coherent sentences, an unmistakable feeling that he was no longer in control.

"I can't grasp a hold of my own thoughts," he said to himself. And he held his head tightly between his two hands, as if he were trying to keep it from snapping off and rolling away. "I think—I can't think, I think. What is this thinking thing anyhow?"

And then, suddenly, he stopped and recalled his wife's startled overreaction before running out of the room, remembered now, as he stared at his flimsy reflection in the mirror, how she had looked at him in horror and shouted—what was the exact word?—appalling. Yes, that was it.

"Appalling!"

He could still hear her voice echoing inside his head like a loud, hollow bell, ringing with a muffled thud as if the sound were trapped and could not get free, just like his voice. She had covered her eyes, he remembered, had cried hysterically, turned her face away and stared coldly at the floor to avoid looking straight at him. And then, with a cry of despair, in between violent sobs, and to no one in particular, she threw her hands up in despair and said, "My husband…" stopping, trying to calm herself, "how… how embarrassing! How… inconsiderate!"

Then, brushing aside her remaining tears, when all her words had dried up, when what remained of her hysterics had shriveled up like an untended flower, she dropped onto the bed, unrelenting, inconsolable, and then, only then, plunged her haggard face into her lace-lined pillow and whimpered.

And like a fool, he said, "It's all right, Charlie," trying to calm her. "It's just a… a mouthpiece," attempting to make the best out of an awkward situation. "And mouthpieces," he added, "have always been… well… misoverestimated."

But he knew it wasn't all right, knew, when she looked up at him in disgust, understood, when she resumed weeping uncontrollably into the soft folds of the bedding, that she could not hear a word he was saying. How could he have forgotten? And then she stood up, took one last appalled look at him—yes, she was appalled, he could see it clearly now—and fled the room as if she had just encountered a common street thug.

President Thorne pressed down hard against the pulsating wad of skin that remained of his mouth. He wanted to stop the rhythmic throbbing, make the irritating sensation go away. Only then, he was convinced, would things start to take a turn for the better. But the throbbing became worse, the maddening pulsing only made him feel more anxious, and he gave up, with a look on his face that would have melted even the hardest of hearts, had any been present, and stared pathetically at his ghastly figure in the gold-filigreed mirror hanging above the dark marble mantle. Squinting, he tried to focus his weary eyes on his reflection, to force the stubborn image into something he could recognize, but he stared back at himself with a look that was merely blank and nondescript.

"Misoverestimated," he repeated soberly. "Or is it..." and he put his finger to his scalp, "overunderestimated?"

Perplexed, he sat down in the antique armchair facing the fire-place, focused, through the fog of medication, on the droning of the TV at the other end of the room, and forced himself to be comforted by its mesmerizing rhythms.

A news commentator's voice wafted in and out, prattled on and on, it seemed, about pandemics, chattered unnecessarily about the apparent ineffectiveness of the season's flu shot, about panic in the streets and uncertainty in the public sector, about how to deal with this sudden health crisis that loomed over the nation.

President Thorne tried to listen, tried his very best to concentrate, to make sense of all this endless blathering. The TV flashed at him like a broken street light, and then a man appeared, a stodgy individual in a black suit and tie, a spokesman, the news anchor announced, from the Association of Pharmaceutical Executives. With a long, drawn face and brazen blue eyes, he stared unflinchingly into the camera and staunchly insisted on the benefits of getting the yearly flu vaccination despite the fact that it did not appear to be working.

"The flu shot," came his raspy voice, like a distant sound on the wind, as he wiped his nose and cleared his throat, "is an easy and essential element for staying healthy," he said.

"But what about the—" the news anchor countered. She was a querulous individual, it seemed, a woman with bloodshot eyes and a smokers-like cough, and President Thorne felt an immediate dislike for her.

"There are no buts, Nancy," he insisted. And then, as if to emphasize his point, the APE representative wiped his red nose with a crumpled-up handkerchief and looked straight into the camera: "Just get it and forget it," he stated as emphatically as he could given the heavy symptoms he was experiencing.

Now, Nancy was a news anchor who had apparently worked hard to get to where she was, and she was not about to sit there and accept his word without a challenge, so she proceeded to question him vigorously, grilling him on this point and disputing him on that. The APE spokesman responded as carefully as he could, as truthfully as circumstances would allow, that is ("We are in a crisis," he stated bluntly. "There's no use in creating a panic," though panic was already filling the streets), coughing and sneezing and wiping his chapped nose as he formulated his responses. At last, having said everything that needed to be said, having done, that is, his very best to convince listeners and viewers to heed his word ("It's a small price to pay, a token, really, to assure your own wellbeing and the wellbeing of those around you."), he thanked everyone kindly for their time and patience during this terrible, unavoidable emergency and abruptly disappeared.

Reaching into her box of tissues, the news anchor wrapped up her segment, carefully summing up the main points for her viewers and imploring them to get their inoculations as soon as they could—as soon as a new supply could be made available, that was.

President Thorne listened to the voices drift in and out, tried to grasp them like one would grasp a hollow echo, then turned his face away from the TV. Looking up into the mirror again, he was immediately reminded of his own untreatable condition—one for which no inoculation was available—and he stomped his foot against the polished hardwood floor like an angry child.

"Damn! Damn! Damn!" he cried.

He could feel the words forming inside, bouncing against his cheeks, trying to release themselves into the cold, uncaring world. Tears formed in his eyes, and a barely audible whimpering rose up from within. He took a deep breath, puffed up his cheeks and tried to release the energy.

Though he had never thought much about it before, his mouth now took on a new significance as he gazed into the mirror. Before, it had just existed. He spoke with it, ate with it. Used it to breath sometimes, to kiss his wife, or even, despite her protests, to lick the stamps for the Christmas cards they wrote each year. Nor had he given much thought to the gift of speech, how his tongue darted about willy-nilly when he spoke, how his lips came together to produce sounds. Intelligible sounds. Meaningless sounds. A cough. A gurgle. Or even a rush of air as he breathed in deeply after a hearty meal.

And then President Thorne remembered food. He had not eaten since the banquet they had given two nights before for that Haitian president whose name he could never pronounce ("those damn French," he scowled, "never did know how to pronounce a word completely"). And despite the nourishment he was getting from the IV, he now sensed a sudden pang of hunger race through his stomach.

"This must be how the poor and needy feel", he thought. "Poor and needy."

Suddenly, President Thorne jumped up from his chair. He paced the room like a madman, tugging the IV carelessly behind him, stopping only to fidget with the tube which kept tangling from his movements as a new reality began to set in.

How, he thought, was he going to survive? Forget his position as the leader of the free world. Forget the deals that came his way, the transactions that occurred as a result of his office (everything legal, of course, nothing shady, nothing no one else wouldn't do if they were in his place). This was now a matter of life and death. Food was essential. Water was necessary for life. It was the right of every living creature. Of every man, woman and—

He stopped short and sat down. He was beginning to sound like the opposition. And, what was worse, he was beginning to feel…compassionate. Conflicted.

His face turned red and beads of sweat appeared on his brow. A feeling erupted inside, intense and uncontrollable, a sudden realization that manifested itself for the very first time in his long and privileged life: survival, it seemed—the instinct to do anything to sustain one's existence—was an essential part of one's nature. And while he had never before experienced this basic impulse until now, he suddenly realized how compelling a drive it actually was.

Maybe, things weren't black and white after all. Maybe there were different hues in between: shades of gray he had never before noticed.

"Life is a mix of colors," he said to himself. "And colors is what makes... the world is a much more colorful... a beautifuller place. It just makes the world beautiful."

He stopped himself again. But for some strange, incomprehensible reason, he felt relieved, felt more alive than he had ever felt in his life. It was a remarkable feeling. A sensation that made him feel suddenly free.

President Thorne slowly approached the bookshelf at the other end of the room. It was filled with old dusty books he had never read, volumes with perplexing titles by men whose names he had heard: Smith, Hamilton, Madison, Rousseau. He examined the aged spines looking for something to stop his mind from racing out of control, opened up one book after another, scanned the indexes, hoping to find a word or phrase that would lead to a page that would help explain the odd things that were happening to him, the strange thoughts and feelings that now possessed him. He needed an explanation. He needed someone to assure him that these unorthodox feelings were normal, something that would soon pass.

The sound of the TV caught his attention again, and he abandoned the books and stared hypnotically as the newscaster described the fear that had overtaken the city. On the screen, crowds of people, their faces covered with medical masks and handkerchiefs, stormed neighborhood drug stores as an invisible voice described how the pharmaceutical companies had formed an emergency alliance with a promise to come up with an immediate remedy.

Then, a picture of a man appeared on the screen, a man he barely recognized. He listened as the newscaster read a statement about the sudden medical procedure he needed to undergo, nothing serious, she emphasized, nothing to interfere with his ability to continue leading the nation. And then he realized she was talking about him, and he bristled as she explained how he would be absent from the White House for several days, grimaced, to the best of his ability, when she mentioned how the vice president would be in charge.

President Thorne switched off the TV and threw the remote control aside. He stood up again, yanked the IV angrily behind him, and walked in circles like a mad dog chasing his tail.

Then, the most lucid revelation he had ever had occurred: he wanted out. Pure and simple.

"The hell with the nation," he said. "The hell with the White House. The hell with politics."

And though he could not hear himself, though no sound emanated from inside, the words resounded more loudly than anything else he had ever proclaimed. And he understood that, more than anything else, he wanted to be free. He wanted to live his life like an ordinary man. Mouth or no mouth, he wanted to breathe deep and easy, he wanted to be done with the likes of Drove and Brice and all the others he had surrounded himself with all his political life. Who cared, he thought, about oil in the Middle East? Who cared about all the tea in China? All that really mattered right now was freedom. *His* freedom.

"If I'm the president," he declared, "then I'm the decider."

And just like that, he decided he would leave. Take just what he needed and disappear. But where, he wondered, would he go? How could someone like himself, he thought, someone nationally known, someone unmistakably recognizable, simply disappear and not be spotted and, well, recognized?

President Thorne looked into the mirror, examined his face, distorted and alien and, for the first time in two days, he felt relieved. Surely this would be the perfect disguise. Surely, this dreadful, unmistakable condition was the path to his salvation.

And President Thorne smiled, a smile that emanated from deep inside though it could not manifest itself physically. He breathed a huge sigh of relief, muffled though it was, and felt suddenly light until the TV mysteriously switched itself back on, and he found himself staring in disbelief at a curious-looking woman, surrounded in white mist and beckoning him with a long, slender finger.

He grabbed the remote and fumbled with the power button, but the TV remained stubbornly on as if it possessed a life of its own. He tried changing the channel, but the woman refused to disappear. He wanted to call out for help, to summon his staff and demand that they come up with an explanation, but instead, he stared mesmerized at the mystifying woman whose calming presence took hold of him and gave him a strange sense of peace.

Before his very eyes, she emerged from the TV screen, materialized, miraculously, live and whole, engulfed in a white cloud and an aura of luminous tranquility, smiling peacefully and instilling in him a feeling of calm he had not experienced for a long time.

"Follow me," she said, in a voice quiet and ethereal.

And she turned and walked away, passed through the wall and disappeared. And just as mysteriously, President Thorne followed after her, tugging his IV behind him like a little child, and vanished into nowhere.

"Damn! Damn! Damn!"

Larry awoke with a start, with a dazed look on his incomprehensible face. He tried to remember where he was. His head was pounding and his eyes felt like they would shatter. He stared at the faded, vinyl stained-glass in the window above, his face bathed in the hazy sunlight that filtered down like a soft spotlight, and wondered if he was in the midst of an irrepressible hangover.

"Damn!"

His voice echoed. Long. Drawn-out. Deep and groggy. The sound he always had when he woke up after a long night of drinking, only it seemed hollow this time. Not completely his own. Uncharacteristically loud.

He closed his eyes and tried to think. Then he remembered: it was Monday morning. He was supposed to be at work. Making his rounds. Checking to make sure that the restrooms were clean. That the lobby was spotless. That the litter, scattered here and there by passengers rushing off to catch their morning trains, was immediately disposed of. That the mess the porters were always creating as they ran off after their clients—luggage tags scattered here and there, random papers tossed willy-nilly—was quickly picked up.

Damn those porters! Damn their souls! Damn their carelessness! Always making a mess. Always creating more work for him. Especially on Mondays, when what he really needed was a goddamn quiet day to recover from the weekend.

"Damn!" he shouted. Then: "*Damn! Damn! Damn!*"

And then he remembered as he opened his eyes and looked around suspiciously. Remembered, suddenly and clearly: he was in church. And that damn preacher was lurking around somewhere. And Pearl—

"Pearl, baby," he cried out.

Where the hell was that woman anyways? Up and disappearing on him like that. With no damn good reason! Vanishing right into thin air. Through the window like a damn ghost. Just like that! Like she was practicing some sort of black magic. And right after she had told him she was going to have a baby!

Larry rested his aching head against the wall.

Just like a woman, he thought. Getting his hopes up and then letting the air out. Things like this just didn't happen. Not to him. An ordinary Joe. A black man trying to get by in a white man's world. And black men had better things to do than to worry about than ghosts and black magic. And crazy ol' preachers.

"Hogwash!"

The word echoed through the empty room. Larry wondered if he was dreaming, wondered if, perhaps, he was stone drunk again. He forced his eyes wide open, slowly surveyed the church chamber. He scratched his head and tried to make sense of everything that was happening to him: the sudden appearance of a second mouth, the strange disappearance of his woman, the unmistakable feeling that something in his life had gone terribly wrong and that there was nothing he could do about it.

Larry slapped both his hands against his drawn, sallow cheeks, hoping that he might wake up from what could only be a very bad dream, when the back door of the church chamber opened with a loud, hollow echo and Reverend Willis hurried toward him with a crazed look about him. And then he knew that this was no dream, knew that what he was seeing and hearing and feeling was as real as the unmistakable second mouth that had appeared on his unshaven face, but he continued slapping himself as the frenzied preacher stopped at his feet and towered above him.

After much contemplation and a bit of prayer, Reverend CJ Willis had come to the firm conclusion that the glorious future of The Blazing Path of Light Ebenezer Baptist Church, LLC depended solely on Larry's presence and on the wondrous and miraculous manifestation of his strange-looking mouth. How better to demonstrate to the world the power of salvation? What better way to illustrate the supremacy of the Lord and the mercy He bestowed on all His creatures? How else, he decided, than to display, right here in this very building, this monstrous-looking individual who had fully repented right before his congregation? Here was his chance to demonstrate God's power and glory to the world and to claim his rightful place in the annals of evangelical history. But to accomplish this, he needed to make sure that this blessed creature, whose wretched appearance had brought a fortuitous ray of light upon his humble mission, did not simply get up and run away.

As the Revered Willis looked down at Larry, who sat on the floor and slapped himself like a madman, jerking his body about as if he were possessed, the expression on his face transformed from panic to relief, and he raised his hands in the air, turned his eyes to the flimsy cross hanging on the wall and mumbled a pious prayer of thanks.

Larry ceased his self-flagellations and eyed Reverend Willis cautiously as the wily preacher turned his gaze toward him once again, the gleam in his eyes sparkling furiously like those of a man greedily coveting his secret treasure. And as the good reverend looked down upon him, his arms held out, his face beaming with joy, Larry's mistrust in this man of the cloth reached its peak, and he jumped up on his feet and shouted in a deep, groggy voice:

"Get the hell away from me!"

The words caused Reverend Willis to quake in his shoes, as he stared and wondered what evil powers Larry might possess.

"I need to get the hell out of here. *The hell with the world!*"

Larry's face swelled with resentment and his two mismatched mouths, one puckered in sadness, the other raging with anger, convulsed furiously. Looming before Reverend Willis, Larry's eyes bulged as he tried to grapple with a whirl of emotions that rose up inside and confused and paralyzed him. He yearned for comfort, even from someone he did not fully trust, yearned for someone to tell him everything would be all right, and he held out his trembling arms and stepped forward like a zombie. Reverend Willis, fearful for his life, immediately jumped back and raised his hands in prayer.

Larry watched Reverend Willis cringe with revulsion, and he understood now just how horrible he must actually be. Unable to accept that his once handsome face had suddenly been transformed overnight into something ugly and grotesque, he opened both his monstrous mouths and screamed as loud as he could, filling the church with the desperate sounds of one whose soul had been irretrievably lost

Reverend Willis blanched. The hair on the back of his neck bristled. Believing that the sounds he had just heard had come straight from the depths of hell, he covered his ears and waited for his fate to reveal itself.

"The Lord is my Savior!" he shouted. "I take refuge in His mercy!"

Falling to his knees, he squirmed like a dying snake, and Larry wondered whether this preacher, who groveled shamelessly before him like a beggar, should be pitied more than him, for seeing him plead for mercy from a god he had put all his trust in only demonstrated how weak a man he really was.

Then, without understanding why, Larry knelt down before him. It was as if his spirit had suddenly surrendered, as if his entire being had somehow become transformed, as if he were now ready to confess his worst sins and repent. Looking into Reverend Willis' eyes, he cried. "She's gone."

He tried to hold back his tears, but his body trembled, and a mournful moaning rose up from deep inside as every ounce of his being channeled itself into a single eruption of emotion.

Reverend Willis was so petrified he could not move, and he watched Larry with a look on his face as if the end of his days had come.

"Pearl, baby!" Larry cried out. "Where are you? Come back to me."

Raising his head, he looked up toward the window where he had last seen his woman hovering in the air like a voodoo doll, stared as the rose-colored light filtered softly down around him. With his hands stretched up as if in prayer, he called out again, hoping she would rematerialize as mysteriously as she had vanished, but his cries were answered only by a rush of dust in the bright, still light.

When he turned his face back down, it had become totally transformed, and Reverend Willis stared in wonder, his mouth hung wide open in shock. Perhaps it was the way the sunlight slanted through the vinyl stained-glass or the particular angle of his vision, but one thing he could say for sure was that Larry's skin, which was once a rich, deep brown, was now pale and gray, and his eyes, which had been brown and lustrous, had turned a light shade of blue though they sparkled with a hint of red under the rose-colored rays of light. And the look of desperation, which had cut deep across Larry's face, had changed to one of sullen resignation as his two mouths curled down simultaneously into sadness.

"*A mouthpiece,*" Larry said. "*It's only a… a mouthpiece.*"

Resting his eyes on Reverend Willis, he added, in his own deep Washington drawl, "Did I say that?"

Then he began to speak from both mouths at once, slowly at first, then rapidly as each mouth moved independently. "Vanished. *Misoverestimated*. Like a ghost. *The hell with the nation*. The hell I will! *Damn!* Damn! *Damn!* Damn! *Overunderestimated*. Damn! *Damn!* DAMN! "

Reverend Willis watched Larry transform miraculously right before his eyes, watched as his skin flickered like a dying light bulb, as his two mouths spoke simultaneously, as his duo of voices merged into one steady stream of speech. Mesmerized, his body began to tremble and his heart quickened, shifting from fear to disbelief to utter awe. Clearly, he thought, this creature must be speaking in tongues. Clearly, he had been touched by the Lord. Clearly, if God could embrace him— if God could transform him in this manner—then he, as His instrument here on earth, must certainly embrace him as well.

"Right through the window," Larry continued. *"This is very disturbing."*

Reverend Willis' face softened and his trembling fingers stilled themselves. Recalling his mission and remembering his dreams, he reminded himself of the role Larry played in their realization and he leaned forward with a new sense of purpose.

"Larry," he said. "You must have faith in the Lord."

"You are responsible," Larry responded, wagging his finger in Reverend Willis' face. *"Heads will roll."*

Reverend Willis did not flinch. Instead, filled with resolve, he felt his faith rise up like a gathering tide, and he thought back to his training manuals and recalled a chapter on how to counsel those who were in spiritual need. Here was his chance, he thought, to hone his skills. Here was his opportunity to save this wretched creature from eternal damnation and propel his humble church into everlasting fame.

"Larry," he said, his voice quiet and ministerial. "Pearl is in the Lord's hands now. We must have faith in Him. Only He can see us through these dark, uncertain days."

He smiled gently and placed his hands on Larry's forehead.

"We must pray, my son."

Larry folded his fingers tightly over the Reverend's hands and squeezed his eyes shut to control his emotions.

"The Lord will see me through this."

"Yes, Larry," Reverend Willis responded, his voice getting stronger. "The Lord will see you through this. We must pray to Him. We must pray for healing. We must ask for God's forgiveness."

"Lord forgive me for what I've done!"

But suddenly, Larry pulled his hands back and looked at Reverend Willis, startled and confused.

"Forgiveness?" Forgiveness! I ain't done nothing wrong."

"Forgiveness, Larry. God loves those who ask for forgiveness."

"But I want my Pearl back."

"She'll return, Larry. If God wills, she'll return. In the meantime, you must remain here. With me. We will work through this together. For God. And for Pearl."

"No," Larry responded. "I can't stay here. I got to go find her. Now."

Larry jumped to his feet and rushed toward the church door.

'No, Larry," Reverend Willis shouted, hurrying after him. "You can't leave. You've got to put your trust in the Lord. The Lord is our Savior, Larry. You must believe in Him. Dammit, Larry! You can't leave!"

Ignoring Reverend Willis' pleas, Larry unbolted the church door and threw it wide open. The bright sunlight rushed in and blinded him, and his skin ceased flickering and reverted to its normal hue. He stopped and squinted, closed his eyes and covered his face with his hands. The sounds of sneezing and coughing punctuated the hushed silence and caught his attention, and he knew he wasn't alone. Slowly, he uncovered his face, gradually opened his eyes and witnessed a crowd of people standing before him, staring at him in wonder and disbelief.

"*I am the president of the United States,*" he announced in a loud, clear voice.

Cameras went off, and a swarm of reporters rushed forward and shouted questions at him. Startled, Larry stepped back into the church, back inside to the cool, soothing darkness where his skin once again began to flicker like a Christmas tree.

Reverend Willis slammed the door shut and locked it.

"You see," he said, "how dangerous it is out there? You see how safe it is here? With me?"

And he carefully engaged the deadbolt, thanked the Lord silently for this fortuitous turn of events, stared into Larry's strange, blue twinkling eyes and watched in disbelief as his skin shimmered magically in the darkness, then reverted to its former hue.

Back at the Choudry residence, Amina sat motionless on the faux-French couch, clutching a glass of hot tea against her chest and staring off wistfully into space, lamenting over the callous behavior of her reckless husband.

"Chasing after another woman," she cried, wiping her swollen eyes with the edge of her headscarf.

Fatwa poured another glass of tea for her anguished mother and tried once again to comfort her.

"It's not like Papa to look at other women," she said. "He's always been so faithful. He always told me, 'Fatwa. God has allowed me to have four wives but, *alhamdulillah*, after your mother, I could never even imagine marrying another woman.'"

"But Fatwa. I saw it with my own eyes. There she was. A woman standing in the garden—"

"Mama," Fatwa said, interrupting, "you told me you saw nothing."

Amina brushed her daughter off with a wave of her hand and took a heavy sip of tea. Leaning forward, she said, "Fatwa. A wife doesn't need to see. Especially after all these years. A wife knows. And when her husband says he has seen a strange woman cavorting in his garden and is going to run after her... Well, what else am I supposed to believe?"

Amina broke into another tempest of tears. She had been a saint all her life, she cried, had sacrificed everything for her Choudry and his children, had given up her family for him, her friends. Had come all the way to America. All for him. And this was the thanks she got?

"No, Fatwa," she said at last, loudly slurping her tea and banging the glass down onto the saucer, "I will not even ask about him anymore. I will not even try to find him. He must come back to me and beg my forgiveness. He must swear to me that he'll give up all this nonsense. Seeing God! Hmmph! Saving the president! Huh! Am I to believe such nonsense? Does he think I am that stupid? Oh, what a foolish husband I have!"

She stared off bitterly into nowhere, tried to imagine the woman who had lured her Choudry away. She must be young, she thought. Young and cheap. With long hair. And lots of makeup. Yes, she was sure there was too much makeup. Henna all over. And bright red lipstick and thick eye shadow. What else do men look for? Then she bent forward, placed her tea glass on the wobbly coffee table, folded her arms and said: "I am going to stay put here until he returns. I swear to God! I'll not move once from this couch until he gives up all these foolish ideas of his and comes back home."

"But, Mama," Fatwa responded with a note of apprehension.

Amina cut her off before she could continue.

"There is nothing more to say," she said, leaning back. "I have sworn to God. I cannot go back on my word."

And Amina folded her arms and sat rock-still, so still that she began to blend in with the faux-French couch on which she was firmly perched.

Meanwhile, Choudry blissfully pursued the woman who had mysteriously appeared to him in his garden. Clutching his prayer beads between his fingers, he prayed fiercely for guidance and wondered where this luminous creature who hovered gracefully in the air would lead him.

Like a pilgrim embarking on a religious journey, he followed behind, followed blindly, without questioning either her intent or the probability of her existence. Trailing luminously ahead of him, she floated like a temptress, alluring and hypnotic. And after the passage of what seemed like a short eternity, Choudry concluded that she could not possibly lead him into harm for she emanated nothing but serenity and warmth.

This beatific vision, this saintly radiance floating in the air before him like a gentle star must certainly be a creature of God, he thought, a divine emissary sent to intercede on his behalf as he carried out his mission, and recalling his Christian friends and their very strange, their very mythical beliefs, he concluded that she was very much like the Madonna. A black Madonna sent by God to—

Choudry abruptly stopped himself. Cupping his hands in the air, he begged for God's forgiveness. He was verging on apostasy, on rejecting all he had been taught to believe in. Here he was, a Muslim—yes, a Muslim, *alhamdulillah*, although not a good one—and he was following this glowing apparition, this spritely vision who beckoned him like a seductive imp, but he did believe in the Virgin Mary and the miraculous birth of the Prophet Jesus and—

Pearl halted in midair and turned her glowing face toward him with a benign, reassuring smile.

"Trust me," she said.

Her voice was soft and soothing, and Choudry stopped his silent blabbering, for he did not want to offend this charming creature—this gentle genie, he thought with a bashful smile—and, instead, he put his trust in God and in the mesmerizing vision suspended delightfully before him, and followed her as she took off into the air again with the speed of a bird.

Soaring through the ether, Choudry was transported as if in a dream. Soon, everything around him was covered in a fine mist, as if he were encapsulated in a bubble of air, transparent yet opaque, as if he were watching the world pass by through a thin layer of plastic film.

Below him, a strange topography unwound like a coil of gauze. There were wisps of clouds and odd patches of flimsy trees. Choudry stared in wonder as a jagged geometry of green fields and silvery rivers passed below him. Everywhere he looked, he could see undulating mountains and gorges that dropped precipitously into the depths of the earth. Then, without warning, there was darkness, and then the silent presence of strange looking animals whose eyes glowed eerily at him through the shadowy night.

Choudry clutched his prayer beads to his chest as lightning streaked through the thick, brooding sky and, invoking God's ninety-nine names, he closed his eyes and waited for death. When he opened them, he saw that they were now three, soaring through the air like a trio of birds lost in a violent whirlwind.

Feverishly fingering his beads, Choudry begged for forgiveness, prayed that God would absolve him of all the sins he had committed during his long, tedious life, and pleaded for a safe and speedy return from this wondrous, fearsome hallucination.

At last, the world came to a stop. The blurry haze slowly lifted, and Choudry was greeted by a deep, frightening silence, a silence so acute that he thought he had reached the gates of heaven. Through the stillness, he could hear the soft sound of a gentle breeze and the sweet cooing of birds in the distance, and he closed his eyes and swooned.

The first thing Choudry saw when he awoke was a small thatched hut, a coil of white smoke rising from its crude chimney. Beside it, in the middle of an open field, sheep grazed lazily in a vast sloping valley. Ducks quacked and waddled in a nearby pond, and cows stood idly, swishing their tails in the bright, misty sunlight. On the opposite side of the hut, a water buffalo, tethered to an oddly twisted tree, gazed off into the distance. And beyond, where the valley came to an abrupt end, stood the snow-capped mountains he remembered from his childhood, looming grandly in all their majesty.

Choudry's face beamed with emotion. He kissed the ground and praised God with a grateful tear in his eye. But then, standing up, it struck him that all of this was impossible. How, he thought, could he be back in his ancestral home? What strange powers did this extraordinary being possess, this ungodly spirit from whom goodness and tranquility seemed to emanate? Surely, he must be dreaming. Surely, none of this could possibly be real.

He turned to Pearl for an explanation, but instead of the sublime vision that had mesmerized him during his journey, he saw a strange man standing before him—a man who seemed vaguely familiar, a man whose face was oddly deformed, whose image seemed a silhouette against the bright sunlight, whose skin flickered, like a nervous light bulb between shades of black and white.

"*Allahu akbar*," he shouted in surprise.

Leaning forward, he could see that the man had no mouth and appeared dimwitted and pathetic as he stared blankly back at him.

"Who are you?" Choudry asked, though the man obviously did not have the means to answer.

"I will leave you now."

Pearl hovered over the thatched dwelling, her image as wispy as the thin line of smoke floating up from the chimney.

"I have done God's work," she said.

"But... but..."

The voice that arose was deep and scratchy, more like a groan, and Choudry jumped back, now convinced that this malformed individual, whose appearance bore a resemblance to what might be called human, was nothing more than an evil demon ready to snatch his very soul.

"Please do not leave me with this horrible devil!" Choudry cried.

"I am the president of the United States."

The words arose from nowhere, had no origin and no distinct reality. Choudry only knew that they were there, coming, it seemed, from the clouds, and he stared in disbelief and remembered the voice at the Tidal Basin and wondered what sins he had committed to deserve this punishment. He remembered Amina, remembered her astonishment when he had returned from his walk among the cherry blossoms, and he longed for her reassuring touch, for her knack at bringing him back to reality. He yearned for his troublesome children, for his narrow-minded son-in-law, and he recalled those lazy Friday afternoons, when he would sit quietly, waiting for his family to gather for their weekly dinner after Kazi's return from prayer, and all he could think about now was waking up and finding that this had all been a dream, an awful dream that belonged to someone else, and that beside him lay his loving wife, eyes open, ready to nag him for yet another blissful day.

But Choudry knew he was not asleep. He knew that Pearl was as real as the silver wedding ring on his trembling hand, that the man who stood before him was more than a figment of a dream, a dream he was sure could not possibly be his, for whatever abilities he might boast, he did not have the capacity for such imagination. And since he could not flee this tenacious nightmare by waking up, he looked for another means of escape and, spotting the door to the thatched dwelling that seemed to beckon him, he quickly ran inside, secured the latch and searched for a safe place to hide.

Late at night, curled up in front of the fire that hissed and snapped like a sinister snake, Akram would pretend to be asleep, would lie and wait. Sharir would be wrapped up in his ancient tomes, carefully perusing the brown, brittle pages, mumbling irritably to himself as he searched for new ways to extend his scourge, when the heavy volume would fall out of his hands with a loud thud as it struck the massive wooden table where he conducted his work. Slumping back helplessly into his chair, he would descend into a deep irrepressible sleep, his breathing irregular, his eyes as leaden and still as if he had been overcome by some deadly disease or as if he were under a powerful spell from which even he could not escape. Imprisoned in this stubborn stupor, he would not wake until late the next morning when he would loudly demand his breakfast and a tub of scalding water to make his ablutions as if nothing unusual had happened the night before.

As soon as Sharir was safely trapped in the bowels of slumber, Akram would jump up and sneak off quietly, making his way down the massive jagged steps that led down to the caves. Standing before a solid stone wall, he would mumble the words that Sharir had made him swear never to reveal, and the wall would grind open to a dark, torch-lit chamber where Sharir stored his secret treasure: tarnished coins of gold and silver, strings of tangled, precious jewels, glittering diamonds, blood-red rubies and other gems sparkling under the flaring light, all piled high like a pirate's booty.

Once, Akram hid in a small tunnel and spied as Sharir dug through the deep treasure, searching furiously as if something had been lost or stolen.

"Goro!" he bellowed. "What have you done with it? Goro! Have you found it? Have you made off with it?"

Then, retrieving a mysterious wooden box which he clutched tightly to his chest, he quickly calmed down and began chanting quietly as he greedily rubbed the smooth surface before plunging it back into the coffer and covering it up to once again hide it.

"You shall never find it!" he shouted. "Never!"

Balancing precariously on the narrow ledge that day, Akram watched curiously when his foot suddenly slipped, causing a loud avalanche of stones to crash into the bottomless precipice. Sharir froze. His eyes blazed with anger, and he raked the area with a look so evil that Akram was sure he would be found and severely punished.

"Goro! Where are you?" he hollered, and his voice echoed violently through the bottomless caves.

On that day, Akram understood the importance of that secret box, and he vowed to one day discover its significance.

But first he needed to perfect his magic, to strengthen his knowledge and learn whatever he could so he would one day be able to destroy his master and free himself and his village from his malevolence.

And so tonight, having waited patiently for Sharir to succumb to his mysterious sleep, he hastily made his way through the cavernous tunnels, following a path he had discovered over the long, endless months of his captivity that led to the outside world.

Out in the open, he cautiously made his way through the thick, ghostly forest. Trees jumped out at him in the stillness as if they were animate, and the night sky was so hidden by the thick foliage that whatever shadow Akram possessed was quickly swallowed. The hooting of owls punctuated the silence, and the occasional cry of a whimpering wolf pierced the heartless night. As he struggled through the thick thorny brush which swooped out and snapped at him, he felt as if his soul was slowly being sucked from his body.

In the middle of the thicket was a small clearing, unhampered by trees that shone brightly under the moonlight as if it were day. Here, behind a bush laden with dark red berries, Akram kept his secret stash—a small pot with herbs he would reserve in his pockets while gathering ingredients for Sharir's potions, a notebook where he would write down the spells and incantations he had learned from his master, and the small prayer book his mother had tearfully sewn into the inside of his shirt the day his father delivered him to Sharir.

Each night he would rest briefly from the harrowing journey, stilling his fears of the dark forest, bowing down in prayer and asking for God's guidance and protection. Then, satisfied that the spirits had been stayed, he would take out his notebook and carefully record what he had learned that day. Spreading out his herbs, which he had tied up into little packets, and lighting a fire where he would place his cauldron, he would practice the magic he was slowly mastering—mixing powders, concocting potions, reciting incantations—all in preparation for one day triumphing over Sharir. He paid special attention to the properties of each element—what effects each had: how certain combinations could cause illness or make one's opponent fall immediately into a hundred-year trance, how to create antidotes, how, especially, to create mixtures that would shield one from harm.

On this night, Akram experimented with bezoars, the magic stones that could combat most any wizard's brew. Combined with the right incantation, his master had told him, they could defeat most magic. So Akram began to mix up a potion, throwing herbs into the cauldron as he stirred and chanted:

Let the impure be gone
Let evil be overcome
Moonstone, dragon horn, lionfish spine

Akram had carefully ground the bezoars according to Sharir's instructions. As he added them to the mixture, the cauldron sparked and flashed, the moon darkened and the forest lit up like a conflagration.

Akram shuddered as a roaring wind tore through the haunted woods, nearly lifting him off his feet, and he feared he had released some force he was unable to control. As the earth thundered and shook and a fierce downpour of rain drenched the forest, leaving him soaked and shaking with cold and fear, he wondered how to stop it.

Akram reached for his stash and pulled out his prayer book. He recited a verse and implored God's help. Then, as if nothing had happened, a sudden calm fell: the rain stopped and quickly dried up, the moon once again shone bright and peaceful as it had before, and the deep impenetrable darkness reclaimed its eerie sovereignty over the forest.

Akram looked nervously about. He wanted to make sure he had not conjured some spirit that now lurked in the darkness waiting to attack. Satisfied, he hastily gathered up his belongings, hid them behind the berry bush and hurried back to Sharir's mountainous citadel, where he jumped into bed, shivering with excitement.

Chapter 6

THE WHITE HOUSE, to use the words of Candice Brice, who was always as precise as possible—later, when she related the events that were quickly reshaping the nation to her official biographer—was in a tizzy.

She was sitting in a mahogany chair in the Oval Office, facing the vice president, who had now fully assumed the role of commander-in-chief.

"There's no use…," she began, turning to address President Thorne's cabinet members who, after Larry White's disturbing appearance on the evening news, had nervously gathered for yet another emergency meeting (an historic meeting, she later emphasized, a significant summit of political players which had categorically changed the course of the nation) "There's no use," she repeated, "in panicking. No need to get ourselves into a dither."

She scanned the room with her sharp eyes, settling back into the hard, chair with icy calm and ease, with a sense of composure that defied the circumstances and with a smile that seemed as if had been chiseled from stone.

"What," the vice president started (his tone was just shy of annoyed, she would later say, his face as expressionless as that of a department store mannequin). And then he paused, flustered, eyed her mechanically, struggled with his feelings of disdain for this upstart of a woman, and then continued in his trademark monotone voice, "Just what do you propose, Miss Brice?"

He was perched imperiously behind the president's desk, the flag flagrantly furled behind him, the thick, gold window drapes framing him as if he were a figure in a portrait. His lack of patience, now that he was in full command, was clearly evident from the blank look on his face, and he gazed at Brice as a man, his stomach betraying his hunger, would impatiently regard the acquaintances he had gathered to dine with as they slowly and methodically readied themselves for a leisurely lunch.

Not to be outdone (for she considered him the root of most of the problems the administration had experienced since its inauguration, regarded him as arrogant, implacable, single-minded, and thoroughly self-absorbed), Brice glued her glassy stare right onto the vice president's lifeless eyes and calmly proceeded.

"Mr. *Vice* President," she began, emphasizing the first part of his title. She tried to hide her contempt, but her perfectly white, evenly-spaced teeth bared themselves as she spoke. "The man we saw on TV was obviously an imposter. I mean…"

And to make her point, she pointed to her own, rich chocolate skin, then to the vice president's pasty epidermis, and gestured with her hands and face as if to indicate how obvious the evidence was.

The head of Homeland Security cleared his throat and edged his way in to ward off a confrontation. He was a man of diminutive appearance, which in no way reflected his role in the administration, though his personality could at times be just as miniscule. Yet, he wasn't one to run from a fight, for conflict, after all, was the very nature of his business.

"While what you say is true," he said, looking at Brice, "you cannot deny that the voice we heard was the president's. Surely you don't believe that what we heard was simulated."

"We are looking into that right now," Drove said, breaking in.

Up to that moment, he had remained quiet, patiently hoping that they might fully comprehend the gravity of the situation, hoping, yet not fully confident, that they would put aside their differences in the interest of unity. Now, convinced this would not happen soon enough, he felt it his duty to the president and to the country to step in.

"Given the current technology," he continued, "we believe that might be a possibility."

"Then what do you propose?" the vice president asked.

His biography (unlike Brice's, which would come much later) was currently in the works, commissioned just weeks before the advent of these events, and he wanted to make sure that this moment in history, when the country was in dire crisis and he had been propelled into a role he had never sought (for that's exactly how he would have it portrayed), would demonstrate his rigor and decisiveness.

"Surely you don't expect us to wait around for some lab report while the president's life is in danger. We need to be resolute. We are not mice, Mr. Drove."

Mark Drove bit his cuticles and spat them out subconsciously at the floor. It was a habit he had developed when he first entered politics, when he needed to think, or when he was in the presence of individuals he did not consider his equal. His opinion of the vice president, which he constantly hid under a stalwart, stone-like façade, was less than charitable, but he now required his cooperation—needed him to come to a decision that would meet his expectations—and, while striving to hide his disdain, he searched for a way to convince him to act in a reasonable way.

"No, Mr. Vice President," he said. "We are not mice. And we should not behave as mice. Nor should we behave—"

"I'm glad you see it that way."

The vice president smiled. A flat, dry smile, that is, for the vice president did not have time for emotions, even when he was about to get his way (and he did not want his biographer to get even a hint that he was enjoying this moment of glory). He looked around the room, taking his time, fixing his small, round eyes on each of them as if to hypnotize them so they would better accept what he was about to say.

"Because what I'd like to propose is that we call in the National Guard and deploy them in Southeast."

The room went silent, shifted from panic to shock. Not since the riots of the 1960s had the National Guard been deployed in the nation's Capital, and they all knew the implications of such a move.

"We'll need an urban combat unit, just in case," he continued.

The vice president went on to lay out his plan, emphasizing the need for heightened security, the necessity—the absolute need—in this day and age, when urban warfare was quickly becoming a reality, to control the masses, minimize dissent, manage the media—all legal, he emphasized, all, he insisted, within the bounds of the Constitution.

"Nothing too drastic," he stressed.

But as he laid out his plans, and as the president's cabinet members politely listened, they could not help notice a gradual change in the vice -president's appearance. His pale white skin took on a soft, furry look, and his deep, resonant voice slowly diminished, becoming small and squeaky. Then, in an instant, as they watched and listened, the figure sitting behind the president's desk simply disappeared.

"Vanished! Into thin air," Brice would later explain with a smug smile (much later, when the world had become a totally different place) to her trusted biographer.

A moment went by as what had just happened registered in their tedious minds, for they were a somber group, and not much used to reacting to sudden surprises, at least not when they happened right in their very presence. Then, Candice Brice once again took control. Speaking in a calm, collected voice, she called out:

"Mr. Vice President. Mr. Vice President."

When there was no response, she turned calmly to Drove. Getting up from his chair, he stepped behind the desk. And though not a word came from his mouth, they all understood from the look on his face that something terrible, something incomprehensible had just occurred.

The members of the president's cabinet, prepped for disaster and no longer immune to extraordinary circumstances, all stood up and gathered behind the president's desk. And as their faces slowly dropped, one by one, they stared in silence and disbelief as they found, sitting on the chair, a small white mouse, which studied them cautiously with its beady eyes, then stood up on its hind legs and fingered its mouth with the tips of its tiny paws.

Instinctively, Brice picked the mouse up by its long, spirally tail and examined it as if she were in Biology class. It was a gesture meant to demonstrate her strong, analytical nature, an image for posterity showing her lack of fear, even when faced with the presence of a nasty, mangy rodent. For spineless people, she believed, did not make good leaders, nor did their tales make for good biographies, which, after all, were meant to sell and make money. And when she finally spoke, just after enough time had gone by to create the proper impression, it was with such fortitude and decisiveness that she was sure history (and her faithful biographer) would portray her in a most positive light.

"I don't believe I have ever witnessed events such as those we have seen over the last few days," she said dryly, holding the mouse high up in the palm of her hand. "If I didn't know any better, I would say that this was an act of war."

The room went silent again, for despite their collective experience, despite what they knew about terrorists and espionage and nuclear armaments, they had absolutely no knowledge of how to deal with what they were now witnessing.

"Do you know what this means?" Drove said, at last, his voice breaking the silence.

Bracing for the worst, they all turned toward him and waited for him to continue.

"It means," he said (and he bit his words, for he did not want to say what he knew he could no longer avoid), "it means that the Speaker of the House will now assume the duties of the presidency."

These words dealt a further blow to everyone in the room, for not only could they no longer hold back from Congress the astonishing events that had occurred over the past few days, but the opposition—an opposition eager to assert its identity—would now be fully in charge.

President Thorne recited the Lord's Prayer once again and shrank back beside the fireplace in the cold, musty cottage. The crackling fire set his nerves a-jitter, and he gathered up a sheepskin covering, a crudely made rug he found lying beside the stone hearth, and wrapped it tightly around his body.

He had rushed inside to escape the chilly morning, forcing the latch loose, then shutting the door against a world that seemed strange and alien to him. Now, between amens and Our Fathers, he sat in the dimly lit room, his spindly head half-hidden in the sheepskin wrap he clasped tightly with his hands, and wondered what would become of him.

He was not a coward, he insisted to himself. He was simply afraid. Or at least that's what he tried to convince himself it was. It was a natural instinct, he thought, his body trembling, and thinking back to his childhood, he remembered how he had been bullied as a child, how he had run off when the kids in the playground who had seemed twice his size, intimidated him, tormented him with their cruel boyish games. But despite these incidents, or maybe because of them, he had learned to face life's challenges with his courage screwed up tightly like a wound up spring.

So now, trembling with cold (it was the cold, he insisted, that was making him shake so uncontrollably), he sat beside the hissing fire, relentlessly reciting the Our Father, and peered guardedly through the shadows at the strange man hunched over on the floor at the other end of the room.

For the first time in his adult life, he was on his own—no advisors to assist him, no wife to comfort him in his moment of need, no servants to tend to his wishes. He had no way to call for help—no phone, no pager, no emergency button to press. And, what was worse, he had to think for himself, make decisions on his own, figure out how to survive in a hostile, foreign land, a place, it seemed, with no appliances, no running water, not even a working toilet, until his certain rescue.

For surely they were out looking for him at this very moment. Surely the Marines were on the way. After all, he *was* the president of the United States and he *had* been kidnapped. Abducted by a strange woman in the middle of the night. A seductress. A double agent, no doubt. A sly woman whom the enemy had employed to trick him into following into captivity. And the man who was now holding him hostage was most assuredly a terrorist. A wanted criminal. He had seen them on TV and he knew perfectly well what they looked like— swarthy, oily-skinned men with greasy hair and big noses and fat, unseemly bellies covered with wrinkled, faded clothing. Just like the man now moving about erratically on the floor across the room.

President Thorne watched as Choudry bowed and knelt, as he stood up and raised his hands, now silent, now whispering, moving in odd ways he had never before seen. He was obviously agitated, he thought, or perhaps it was a secret code, a way of communicating with his cohorts, letting them know that he had succeeded in capturing their target, devising ways to torture him and then finish him off. He knew their ways. He had heard about them at his morning briefings.

And so he watched and prayed, feared and trembled and waited for his fate to be decided.

Turning his head from right to left, Choudry finished up his prayers and petitioned God for guidance. After the extraordinary ordeal he had been through, he felt an urgent need for religion, and he wiped his face piously with his huge hands as he strained his eyes, attempting to discern through the shadowy light the man draped in a locally-made carpet at the opposite end of the room, a man who claimed to be the president of the United States

How, he thought to himself, had he gotten into this situation?

Trapped with this odd-looking, freakish man in an isolated village in a far-off part of the world. *His* village. *His* part of the world. The place where he had grown up. The place he had spent his childhood before leaving for the city, before marrying Amina, before packing up his life and emmigrating to America. Except it now seemed as alien to him as an exotic island, as strange and inhospitable as an empty desert, and he could not imagine, for the life of him, how he had ever lived here.

He wanted to go home. He wanted to be in his bed, wake up next to his wife, who would get up as she always did and make him his breakfast while he got ready to go to the shop. Where were the days when things were simple? When a man could get up in the morning, take a nice, peaceful walk down by the Tidal Basin, enjoy the quiet of the morning, inhale the gentle fragrance of the cherry blossoms and revel in their serene beauty. After all, he was a hard-working man, a good husband, an attentive father. Didn't he deserve some respite from life's toils and troubles?

With a loud sigh, Choudry leaned down on his hands and heaved himself up off the floor.

At the other end of the room, President Thorne flinched at Choudry's sudden movement. Sensing that things were about to change, he gathered the sheepskin even tighter around his body and prepared for the worst.

"If you touch me," he said nervously, "I'll mark you as a man."

The sound of his voice echoed through the bare cottage like the moaning of a cow, like strange music falling on tone-deaf ears. "There'll be a mark on you, and sooner or later they'll find you."

President Thorne listened for his words to resonate, and when they didn't, he touched his face with his fingers and decided that he must be in a drug-induced state, for what other explanation could there possibly be?

Choudry watched President Thorne fumble in the darkness like a madman and wondered if this could really be the president of the United States. For while he bore a strange resemblance to the man he had seen on the daily news, he could not help but think that the leader of the most powerful country on earth would surely be able to communicate more intelligibly. Certainly, he thought, his appearance would be more comely, more statesman-like. Nothing like the individual cowering on the floor, his hair disheveled, his face contorted, his clothing as plain and simple as a shepherd's. No, the president of the United States, of *his* United States, of the country he had proudly emmigrated to, would not have the countenance of one who seemed perpetually in doubt.

"You cannot speak?" he said at last, his voice shattering the hollow silence like the snap of a frozen tree.

Choudry stepped barefooted across the room and peered into President Thorne's startled face.

"I'm warning you," President Thorne said. He pulled the sheepskin closer against his body and dislodged the IV stand which came crashing down against the earthen floor. But the words did not come out. Instead, his attempt to speak amounted to nothing more than a mumbled groan.

"You are sick?" Choudry asked, gently setting the IV upright.

President Thorne looked suspiciously at Choudry's large nose and his rough features—his puffy, black eyes, his thick swollen cheeks, his chin doubled over in layers of fat—and he knew this show of kindness was a trick that would soon turn into unrestrained violence. Wasn't that how they normally did it? Befriend the victim, then break him down slowly?

"Do you want me to fetch a doctor?"

"You understand," President Thorne said, "that the United States Army is now out looking for me in full regalia. No building will be left untouched. No stone unturned. The valleys will be swarming."

Choudry gazed in pity as President Thorne struggled to speak, as he jerked his head about and emitted a deep, pathetic moaning. And he understood that the man sitting before him on the floor like a poor villager—this pathetic mute who had called himself the president—could not communicate, much as he tried his best to articulate.

"Here," he said. He reached into his pocket and pulled out a pencil and a tattered pad splattered with blood from his butchering block. "Sorry," Choudry said, apologizing for the smudged bloodstains on the paper. "They're from my shop. I'm a butcher," he quickly added. "Go on. Take it."

But President Thorne, having now heard the word butcher and seeing the spots of blood spattered across the page, could no longer control himself, and he tottered wildly like a buoy in a violent storm, expecting any minute for the interrogation to begin, for the man who stood before him, feigning kindness, to turn on him suddenly and begin his torture. Babbling like a madman, he said in no uncertain terms that if he were to lay one hand on him, he would be marked for life, his family would be detained, locked up and held as collateral, and his country would be invaded and destroyed. The United States would not stand for its leader to be kidnapped, and not one American would rest until he had been released.

Choudry watched President Thorne struggling helplessly on the floor, listened to the mutterings emanating from deep inside his throat, trying to make their way out of his hapless face, and wondered nervously what to do. He remembered the voice at the Tidal Basin, recalled the command he had been given. Could it be, he thought, that this man was afflicted with some strange disease? Or had he suddenly gone mad? But what could he do? He was just a poor butcher. A humble immigrant who wanted nothing more than to return to his shop, skin a chicken, quarter a lamb, grind beef for his customers. And what help could he possibly get for him, here in this tiny village, far removed from civilization?

"My name is Choudry," he said uneasily after President Thorne had finally collapsed on the floor exhausted. "Fuzzaluddin Choudry. My friends call me Fuzzy," he added with a laugh. "I am an American citizen. You are the presi—" Choudry hesitated. He was stunned, confused. What, in Allah's name, was he thinking? Then, looking straight at President Thorne, he said, "Is this true?"

President Thorne sadly nodded his head.

"*Allahu akbar!*" Choudry shouted, as the reality suddenly struck him.

Choudry stood up on his bare feet. His body began to shake and his voice became loud and agitated.

"I am sorry," he said, his voice trembling. "Allah has ordered me to do this. *Allahu akba*r. How," he cried, "can I execute His orders? Look at me, Look! I am a plain man. Can't you see that? And you! The most powerful man in the world. But I will not let that stop me. I must do what I've been told. *Allahu akbar! Allahu akbar!*"

President Thorne's eyes bulged as Choudry worked himself into frenzy. This, he thought, was it. This was when things would turn ugly, when he would be stripped naked, would be beaten until he no longer remained conscious. Others would come. They would rip out his fingernails, hang him from his feet, burn his skin with acid. He knew their ways. Had he not discussed these techniques with his intelligence agents? Had he not authorized similar treatment to protect his country? He closed his eyes and cursed the day he had decided to run for office. He now understood how horrible it all was, how utterly heartless power and politics could be, and he began to loath every decision he had ever made since his rushed inauguration. Better to be on his ranch. Better to be working in an office, making millions, far away from the horrors he was now facing, horrors he himself had sanctioned in the name of national security.

"Lord, forgive me for what I've done," he cried in a desperate prayer.

"*Allahu akbar.*" Choudry shouted, as he suddenly realized that, were they found, he would be accused of kidnapping the president of the United States, of holding him hostage. And no matter how much he explained, no matter what he said, no one would ever believe him.

"*Allahu akbar,*" Choudry cried. And he lifted his hands in the air and gazed at President Thorne with the look of a man who had just committed the most horrible crime.

"The Lord is my Savior," President Thorne shouted, tears streaming down his face. "The Lord is my Savior."

Inside The Blazing Path of Light Ebenezer Baptist Church, LLC, in Reverend CJ Willis' cluttered office, Larry cowered like an unreformed sinner. He was in a quandary. He was trapped, and he didn't like being trapped. If he left, he would be assailed by the press, who were camped outside the church, waiting to get a glimpse of the man they had dubbed "Doublemouth." There would be no escape. But if he stayed, he would remain at the mercy of the unscrupulous Reverend Willis, who held the threat of the even more unscrupulous media over his head as a means of keeping him from running away.

"They'll stir-fry you the moment you leave these premises," he said to Larry shortly after he had bolted the church door shut. "They'll snatch you up with their long, heartless claws, swallow you up, and spit you out piece by piece."

Then, softening his face into a smile and modulating his voice into a gentle song, he said: "Here there is sanctuary. They can't touch you. You're under God's protection. *My* protection."

Hunched over himself in the worn chair beside the reverend's cluttered desk, Larry sulked like a child and listened unwillingly to his words.

Meanwhile, Reverend Willis began to use his cramped quarters— the room where he had penned his modest weekly sermons—as a base to disseminate word of the miracle that taken place at his humble sanctuary. Working feverishly, he faxed press releases, made phone calls, and did telephone interviews with the local media. God, he pronounced, had seen fit to send a sign to mankind, using his unassuming church as the medium. The time had come, he maintained, for men to mend their ways (women, it seemed, did not have much mending to do, save for pants and shirts and other shabby garments, for they did not merit mention), for the world to come to its senses and return to God's straight and narrow path, for politicians to end their grip on corruption and serve the people as God had meant them to: with love and kindness and no regard for personal gain. Peace was imminent, he announced, and world destruction a palpable possibility should people refuse to obey God's will. This, he insisted, could be the only possible explanation for the appearance of a creature whose unnatural form masked a glowing goodness that shone radiantly from deep within. For despite his wretched-looking countenance and the cacophony of voices that seemed to arise as if from the very depths of hell, he had sought God's forgiveness and had been saved through the goodness of His grace. Surely, this was a sign to all of God's creatures. Surely, this was a lesson for all, if only they would heed it, amen.

And, he would add, at the end of each interview, as a casual aside, just in case it had not been made subtly clear, forgiveness would surely be granted to any who joined his humble mission.

Larry half listened, half ignored the Reverend's words, his mind wandering back and forth between bouts of self-pity and the pesky preacher's prophetic proclamations. Sometimes, he almost believed his words, sometimes dismissed them as hogwash. On the one hand, he could not deny the inexplicable transformation of his face, the strange voices, the words that seemed to rise up from nowhere, and since there was no other plausible explanation, the one that Reverend Willis offered seemed to make sense. On the other hand, he knew, somehow, that Reverend Willis, whose show of kindness masked his true motivations—motivations Larry could not yet comprehend—was not to be fully trusted. And then he concluded that, either way, it made no difference, for none of it would restore his appearance, change him back to the way he used to be. And he sensed that he was forever doomed to a life of torment, would remain an oddity, a freak sought out by curiosity seekers, until the end of his days.

And then he remembered his deeply-held convictions, long formulated since the days of his adolescence, his belief that ministers and priests and others of that class of men who dealt in the business of hopes and dreams, were simply out for their own benefit. Profiting from the misfortunes of others. Offering them promises and then demanding donations in return. Was Reverend Willis any different? Was he not a charlatan in priest's clothes preying on the trust that his followers willingly gave him?

"A bunch of bull," he said out loud from one mouth, as Reverend Willis concluded his final interview and hung up the phone. "*Our Father,*" he recited from the other.

Upon hearing these utterances, Reverend Willis made a quick note for his upcoming sermon and decided, serendipitously, to focus on the theme of doubt—the class of spiritual doubt that this poor creature was experiencing at this very moment, an uncertainty similar to that which

Jesus Christ Himself had suffered in the Garden of Gethsemane the night before his crucifixion. It would be his Easter Sunday homily and would fit the season as well as the current circumstances surrounding his storefront mission.

"It will be my best," he announced, eyeing Larry with a self-satisfied smile. "But there will be hundreds, thousands of worshippers. Where will we put them all?"

"No building will be left untouched, Larry's uttered. *"No stone unturned."* "Damn," he shouted. And then, in a prophetic voice: *"the valleys will be swarming."*

With a puzzled look on his face, Reverend Willis echoed Larry's words and tried to comprehend the meaning of what he had just heard. Was this a prophecy? An enigmatic prediction? Was this strange creature, who now seemed to him as beautiful as he was horrible, capable of foreseeing the future? If only he could remember his lesson on divination.

Reverend Willis jumped up from his chair and rushed over to his overstuffed bookcase, repeating Larry's mysterious message to himself as he searched for the textbook he had found so arcane during his studies that he had eventually abandoned it for something much more practical.

"The valleys will be swarming," he said out loud. "But there are no valleys here," he declared, turning to Larry in consternation. "Just streets and buildings where people live and work. And then there's the White House, the Capital building, the national monuments. No hills, no fields. Just wood and concrete. Granite and steel."

And then, as if the entire landscape had lit itself up for his benefit, he shouted with a sudden glow of understanding that emanated from his face like a burning bush: "The national monuments! Right there in the National Mall. 'The valleys will be swarming.'"

Reverend Willis contemplated this phrase more deeply.

"Yes," he shouted jubilantly. "The valleys will be swarming with worshippers. There, my friend, we shall hold our Easter service. On the grounds of the National Mall. In the valley of granite and steel. There we will move our humble church for all to come see. For all to worship."

And Reverend Willis, his mind racing at lightning speed, began to plan for the coming Sunday's Easter celebration. Rain was predicted, he said, so they would need to provide shelter. And then there was the sermon he needed to prepare—and a wonderful sermon it would be—inspiring, filled with hope: the hope that this creature, like the Lord Himself, symbolized from his miserable position in life. And there would be donations—lots of them, he predicted—and he would need to hire ushers—volunteers, naturally—to collect them. And, of course, there was the publicity. How else would he attract the masses? How else would he draw world leaders to his humble Easter service?

"We must alert the media," he said to Larry.

Reverend CJ Willis, who until now had ridiculed the cadre of reporters that had gathered outside the entrance to his church as nothing more than a bunch of useless chatterers, who, having found renewed purpose like a down-and-out man who finds a lucky coin abandoned in the gutter, rose from his chair, his face beaming with joy, and marched out of his office, straight to the front door of his modest house of worship. Larry followed like a lost puppy and stood beside him as he unlatched the lock and flung it open, causing them both to squint as the blinding light flooded into the darkened room.

Several seconds later, after their eyes had fully adjusted, after the dull drone of voices that greeted them had diminished to utter silence, they gazed in awe at the throng of people who had had gathered outside the church and were patiently waiting to catch a glimpse of the man who some were beginning to call a savior. Their eyes swollen and tearing, their noses dripping, and their mouths covered as they sniffled and hacked, they numbered in the hundreds and stared in wonder at Larry and Reverend Willis, as silence settled like a comforting blanket and they got their first glimpse of the man they had come from all walks of life to see.

"*The Lord is my Savior!*"

Larry's voice echoed through the hushed stillness as the press aimed their cameras and captured his image like trained hunters adeptly capturing their prey.

"The Lord is my Savior," the crowd repeated, weakly. Then quickly, spontaneously, they began to echo the phrase louder and louder in strong waves of fervent prayer, zealously and in unison, until no other sound in the run-down neighborhood could be heard.

Reverend Willis beamed with joy. Lifting his hands high up in the air, he recited a prayer of thanks and knew at last that his time had finally come.

The moment Amina solidified on the faux-French couch, the Choudry residence was transformed into a hub of scientific curiosity. Rigid as an exotic statue, her hands frozen in eternal despair, her head turned to the side and facing upward, toward the Koranic verse pinned haphazardly on the wall, Amina sat like a giant stone and neither moved nor breathed nor showed any sign of what might be called life.

As soon as Fatwa witnessed her mother assume this dubious position, she quickly called the doctor, and word soon spread through the medical community of the human petrifaction that had taken place at an ordinary house in a residential neighborhood in Arlington, Virginia—a petrifaction that seemed to penetrate the entire body, yet allowed it to somehow remain alive. It was a modern day miracle, a phenomenon that no one had witnessed before, for while Amina showed no signs of physical activity, the fact that she was not dead was evident from the warm glow of her tawny skin and the perpetual sparkle in her deep brown eyes, which remained wide open, blinking every so often, and pursued anyone who entered the room.

What was even more curious, however, was the fact that she would occasionally move, spontaneously and for no particular reason, wrenching her stone-hard body out of its statue-like position with a loud, rumbling reverberation. Looking around as if nothing extraordinary had happened, she would speak to the doctors and scientists who were studying the cause of her curious condition and admonish them for their uncalled-for attention.

"I shall not move from this place," she would stubbornly announce as if to say how much they were wasting their time. And turning her head toward the particular expert of the moment, she would add: "I have sworn to God."

Then, just as suddenly, she would settle back quietly into her fossilized state on the faux-French couch, like a figure that had been meticulously chiseled on an ancient frieze, and nothing, not even the steaming temptation of a freshly cooked lamb biryani, placed on the table before her like a tantalizing offering, could make her budge.

The experts were baffled. Here was a woman who, from all appearances, seemed as solid as rock, who showed no signs of life, except for her occasional rumblings, who did not eat or drink or even breathe, and yet she remained alive. And what was even more perplexing was the fact that she had apparently not been affected by the flu epidemic that had afflicted the rest of the population, for she showed no symptoms whatsoever.

"It's amazing," said one doctor, as he placed his medical instruments back in his case. "She has no heartbeat. Yet, she is most definitely alive."

He scratched his chin and contemplated the mystery, which, he insisted, held the key to health and longevity, and faded into a haze of contemplation.

"You are foolish," Amina said, pivoting toward him and startling him out of his scientific ruminations. "Just like all men. There is nothing of interest here. Nothing to understand."

And then she resumed her rock-like position, as solid and motionless as a statue of an Indian goddess, not flinching even when the medical researcher waved his hands before her eyes or touched her calcified skin, much to Kazi's vociferous chagrin, to test her responses.

As word spread by word of mouth and via the ever-vigilant media, the house soon became a Mecca for those seeking to be cured (a comparison that disturbed Kazi to no end), for it quickly became apparent that anyone who entered the Choudry residence was immediately healed, and so the designation stuck like flypaper.

Soon, long lines of people queued up outside the house of miracles as everyone waited to touch the hand of the saint with the curative powers. Ailing and desperate, they entered through the front door—

ordinary people, people who had never before believed, who had never before been to church, priests, politicians, Hollywood celebrities—bearing gifts and carrying offerings of food and incense, donating money and livestock and other sacrificial trinkets, which they humbly placed before the woman in the dark orange sari with the matching scarf covering her head.

Bowing before her and mumbling entreaties, they reverently stroked her hand and snaked through the living room into the kitchen and out the back door. It was a system that Kazi had devised when he realized there was no way he could stop this idolatry, and, with the assistance of his children, the traffic flowed as smoothly as could possibly be expected, given the large crowds of ailing individuals, which grew by the hour.

Soon, the lines of sick and crippled individuals wound around the house and stretched out onto the street, where it uncoiled itself like a snake's long and weary tail, and Kazi was forced to quit his part-time job and join his wife, who had moved in permanently with her mother in order to accommodate the twenty-four/seven vigil that had developed.

"Allah has forbidden you to be alone in a room of strange men," he said in explanation, fingering his long, stringy beard and staring sternly at his wife. But Fatwa, observing the women and children who were patiently waiting to get a glimpse of her mother and who clearly outnumbered the men, knew perfectly well her husband's real intention, for he did not need much of an excuse to get out of going to work.

Meanwhile, Amir soon realized the profit potential of his mother's newfound position in life, and quickly put his recently acquired MBA skills to work. Here in his mother was a woman with the ability to cure the common cold, and she was suddenly the focus of world attention. And so, to maximize that potential and to protect her against commercial infringement, he decided to incorporate her as a religious entity, and he hired a team of lawyers (she needed legal protection, he insisted, or she would be taken advantage of) and an able architect of Asian origin to build a shrine so they would be able to collect tax-free donations.

"We'll do like they do in the East," he said.

"*Astaghfirullah*," Kazi protested. "May God forgive you. This is nothing but idolatry. Are we becoming Shiites?"

"America needs a shrine where pilgrims can flock to and pray," Amir insisted. "Besides," he added, appealing to his brother-in-law's overzealous convictions, "maybe they'll decide to become Muslims."

Then, one day, a pair of suspicious-looking men arrived at the door. Dressed in long, black trench coats and carrying mysterious briefcases in their leather-gloved hands, they announced that they were from the American Pharmaceutical Association, a subdivision of APE, and said that they had come to look into the disturbance at the Choudry residence, a disturbance that was creating shockwaves throughout the industry. They needed to investigate why none of the original inhabitants of the Choudry household had been infected with the flu bug when everyone else had succumbed, as expected. And why, they added with much consternation, anyone who stepped into their house was instantly cured.

"We are baffled," the first one said, scratching his bald head with the overly-bitten nail of his index finger.

"Flabbergasted," the second one echoed. Short and shout, and with a pudgy little belly, he had a round, weary face and a gray moustache that hugged his mouth and made him resemble a walrus. He folded his arms over his paunch and stared indignantly at Amir.

"When we issue a flu alert," he continued, "we never fail."

"And when we release a flu vaccine," said the first one, "we are always on the mark."

"Except for this year."

"Except, somehow, for this year."

"We need to investigate."

"We need to look into this thoroughly."

They took a breath and looked at each other as if to confirm that they were on cue.

"We need to understand the exact nature of what's going on," the first one continued.

"We need to understand," said the second, "so that another incident like this never happens again."

And so these two competent representatives, who had been duly dispatched by the esteemed pharmaceutical industry, went on in remarkable synchronization, speaking of the urgency for cooperation, implying, ever so subtly, that Amina's mysterious therapy amounted to nothing more than an unfair business practice—an invasion of their specialized territory—and insisting that, once they came to an agreement, everyone would benefit.

"*Everyone*," the first one emphasized, glancing around the room from beneath the frame of his dark glasses and resting his heavy eyes on Amir.

"I will need to consult my lawyers," Amir responded when they were finished.

"Amir!" Fatwa protested.

"Hold your tongue, woman," Kazi scolded.

But Kazi's castigation of his wife was immediately interrupted by a loud, rumbling that caused the floor to shake violently. Sounds of panic were soon replaced by a hushed silence as everyone in the room turned their eyes toward Amina and watched her twist herself angrily out of her petrified state and point irately at the two men.

"You are talking nonsense," she said to them, unwinding her stiff body and glaring at them with an evil eye. "Just like my husband. Just like all men. May Allah put a pox on you!"

And the two men immediately broke out into a painful rash and began coughing and sneezing uncontrollably. Amina smiled naughtily and settled back comfortably into position on the faux-French couch. Astonished, they looked from Amina to Amir, then back to Amina.

"We will be back," the tall one said.

"We will certainly be back," the short one echoed.

And the two men rushed out of the room, holding their noses and covering their mouths in a desperate attempt to suppress their symptoms.

Sharir clenched his fists until the veins popped out against the baggy sleeves of his black robe, then sent his hands crashing down on the table, sending an angry thump through the eerie silence that filled the room. He paced about the chamber nervously, furiously cursing in his deep, hollow voice. Reaching up as far as he could, he stretched his hands out of the loose-fitting sleeves, his bony fingers extended to their limit, and bellowed from the depths of his hoary soul.

After all these years (hundreds of years, months and decades and centuries of casting spells, extracting elixirs, delving into tomes of enchantments he had inherited from his forefathers to rediscover forgotten incantations), he felt as if maybe he was beginning to lose his touch. He knew that magic had its limits, that spells could wear off or, even worse, miss their mark, go terribly awry. He understood that even the most carefully executed hex could eventually be thwarted. Yet, after all the havoc he had wreaked, in an effort to avenge the ills committed against his family, something—or someone—was beginning to interfere with his schemes. Someone, it seemed, who was potentially more powerful than he.

"Goro!" he hollered.

The sound of his voice swelled through the empty chambers, ricocheting against the solid rock that encased his cavernous hideaway, dying away slowly into a faint murmur.

Sharir hurried toward his work table with long, spindly steps, and stared feverishly into his crystal ball. He marveled as Amina effortlessly undid the evil he had so carefully planned. She was good, he thought, with a slight curl of his thick lips. This woman, who had suddenly been imbued with magical powers, was wielding them with such ease and effect that, for a moment, he looked on with a strange sense of pride.

But good was not what he wanted!

He picked up the crystal ball and hurled it across the table. It crashed against the hard, wooden surface and rolled back and forth in a narrow arc, swaying like a restless pendulum until it came to a stop, resting its hard, clear surface against the cold stone wall. Sharir peered silently at it, his eyes piercing and fiery, then spun around, his loose robes fanning out in a whirl of fury. "Counter spells, counter spells."

He repeated the words as he stared into the blazing fireplace and tapped his bony finger against his gray, sunken cheek.

"Akram!" he bellowed.

Rubbing the sleep from his eyes, Akram came scurrying into the room and stopped before his master with his head bowed toward the hard, stone floor.

"Yes, Master."

"Look," Sharir said, pointing to the crystal ball. His voice was less vehement now, filled with uncertainty, the tone of an apprentice whose experiment had suddenly gone wrong and who looks to his tutor for guidance. "Look," he said again, this time more forcefully, "at what that woman is doing."

Akram began to tremble. He peered timidly into the crystal ball, which lay horizontally on its side, and watched as Amina cast her spell over the two men who had come to investigate her mysterious ability to cure. Silently satisfied, he gazed as they broke out into a painful red rash and watched the long lines of people parading slowly through Amina's house, each pilgrim stopping briefly to kneel humbly before her, grasping the sleeve of her orange sari or kissing her ossified hand in hopes of making their afflictions disappear.

"Someone is interfering with my plans."

Sharir's voice was desperate, frightening. Akram didn't answer. No telling what his master might do when he was in this state. His fury was sudden, and he could turn like quicksilver. He shifted his eyes away from the crystal ball, stared blankly at the floor and waited apprehensively for Sharir's anger to burst like an overinflated balloon.

"We've got to stop this," Sharir said softly

He put his hands on Akram's shoulders, lifted his head up gently, like a father about to speak affectionately to his child.

"I've watched you," he continued. "Your powers are growing. Your spells are getting better. Together, we can stop this woman. Together," he said, raising his voice and squeezing his eyes into two balls of black fury, "we can put an end to Goro's doings."

Akram looked timidly at his master. He felt strangely relieved. For once, he was not being blamed. Instead, he was being praised by the great, fearsome Sharir. Then he turned his eyes downward and stared silently at the floor. He knew not to contradict him. He knew that, even though he was being commended, the wrong word—the wrong reaction—could send his master into an uncontrollable rage. Sharir needed to be appeased, and Akram understood that, despite his words of approval, he would never accept for his apprentice to become more skilled than he.

"You have taught me everything I know, Master," he said at last. "But my skills are nothing compared to yours."

Akram waited for Sharir to speak, to holler, to curse. Instead, he heard nothing but silence. He glanced up and noticed a sudden change in his master's appearance. Where once there was arrogance, he now saw only fear. And where once the deep lines that etched his ancient face seemed frightening and intimidating, he saw an old man whose once powerful position in the world was now in question.

Akram wondered if the time had come for him to put his plan into action. Were his powers indeed strong enough to defeat the mightiest wizard in the world?

"Akram," Sharir said softly, his voice now as weak as his face seemed frail. "I have been good to you, haven't I? Did I not shelter and clothe you? Did I not share my knowledge with you?"

Sharir's face was almost sad, his voice nearly pleading.

"Will you not help me just this once? Otherwise, my time will be up. I will be defeated. Destroyed. And Goro will win."

As he pronounced these last words, Sharir's face turned suddenly wicked. He pushed Akram away violently, stood up and bellowed:

"Goro. I will not allow it!"

Sharir set his fiery eyes on Akram and rushed toward him like a madman.

"You," he said, lifting Akram up in the air with one hand. "It's been you all along. Right under my nose. I should have known. Disguised as a shepherd boy."

"No, Master," Akram pleaded.

Sharir flung Akram across the room as if he were just a pebble. Akram fell to the floor and watched as Sharir cautiously approached him, cursing him as vehemently as he could.

"Goro," he said. "Face-to-face at last."

Sharir lifted his hands up in the air and turned his face upwards.

His voice rose as he chanted an ancient spell that Akram had never before heard.

The ground began to rumble. The room flashed with lightning, and a swift wind rushed through the chamber.

Sharir turned toward Akram with a madman's smile. Fearful for his life, Akram put his hands in his pocket, squeezed the magic stone he kept there and recited the incantation he had used in the forest.

As suddenly as the wind had swept through the room, it reversed itself, becoming loud and violent and sucking every object in its path with the force of a vacuum. Sharir held on to his blue turban as his hair and clothes trembled from the wind's force. Akram gripped the leg of the table and prayed for a miracle.

Then, at once, the wind stopped. Everything in the air crashed to the ground. A deafening silence settled eerily on the empty room. The bright light brought on by the maelstrom disappeared, leaving only the dull glow of the torches, their flames having mysteriously survived the windstorm.

On the stone floor, still and unconscious, lay Akram and Sharir as a last bit of breeze calmly exited the caves.

Chapter 7

THE SPEAKER OF THE HOUSE was a gracious lady who hailed from a prominent California political family and had become well acquainted with the inner workings of politics at a very early age.

"I know politics," she would say, smiling bittersweetly with wide eyes open, her finger tracing the side of her patrician nose, "like I know Ghirardelli Square. And believe me," she would add, with a slight twinkle and a quick chuckle as if to tantalize the person she was speaking to, "I know Ghirardelli Square."

A strong member of what had recently been the opposition, and an even stronger opponent of the president, she had led her party to victory in the recent elections and had been overwhelmingly chosen to lead the new majority in the House of Representatives.

Bella Stromberg, or Bell as she was better known, was an impatient woman, though her public demeanor displayed nothing but tolerance and calm. Her smile was radiant, though one could tell immediately that she was not a pushover. And her perfectly coifed, subtly tinted hair, which complimented her handsome face, revealed a woman possessed with both classic beauty as well as the iron fist of one who wielded power effortlessly and, some would say, ruthlessly.

So, on this hectic morning, as she was at once putting on her makeup (a tiresome task which she felt compelled to do) and preparing to lead the House in a contentious vote which the minority was vehemently opposed to, she looked away from her handheld mirror as the door opened, and flashed a look of annoyance at the maid as she entered the room to announce that Mark Drove was on the phone insisting to speak with her.

"He was very persistent," the diminutive woman said in her own defense in her heavy Spanish accent. Then, as if to apologize for the intrusion and to get her employer's attention, she added, *sotto voce*: "he said it was urgent. A matter to be taken up only with you."

Bella Stromberg smiled. She understood the ways of her opponents as well as she understood that her own political career depended solely on their behaving in the very way they did. She knew that the president, whose strange public absence she attributed to a lack of leadership ("He's inept," she would insist whenever she got a chance, "unable to coordinate even a knife and a fork," a remark that always produced a smile at cocktail parties or with her colleagues in passing in the halls of Congress). She knew that he was adamantly and stubbornly opposed to the legislation she was currently promoting, legislation that would benefit ordinary working people and that the corporations were fighting tooth and nail. And she assumed that Mark Drove, who was as dull as the name he bore, had been enlisted to lobby her, to cajole her into reconsidering legislation that they would be unable to defeat. This was a president who was opposed to being opposed, she reminded herself, pleased with this odd turn of phrase, and the entire administration, especially the vice president, who was now somehow in charge, was having a difficult time dealing with the new political reality that had taken over Washington.

"Tell Mr. Drove," she said to her maid, "that I'm unavailable at the moment. Tell him we can meet in my office later this morning."

"But, ma'am," the poor woman insisted, "he sounded very serious. Almost... agitated."

These last words caught Bella's attention, for whatever else could be said about Mark Drove, he had never been known to become even slightly excited, no matter the situation.

"Very well," she said in such a way that her maid knew she was being dismissed.

Bella Stromberg, whose very name epitomized courteousness, mumbled under her breath as soon as her maid left the room, patted her hair in place, folded her lips in to smooth the lipstick she had jus applied, jerked her head to the side, gathered her thoughts as if she were gathering a cluster of marbles, and mustered up her usual smile as she picked up the phone on her desk and held it to her delicate ear.

"Mr. Drove," she said, pleasantly. "How nice to hear from you so early in the morning."

It was a typical, double-edged statement for Bell Stromberg, one which embodied both civility and her underlying distaste for a man she had nothing but contempt for.

She listened patiently to Drove's droning voice, maintaining her persistent smile as if it had been plastered on to her face and could not be removed. She batted her eyes, glanced at the floor, crossed her legs, and took careful note of each word that was being said to her. When Drove was finished, she said simply, "Yes. I'll be there immediately," and hung up the phone.

Bella Stromberg sat silently at her desk and contemplated the information she had just been given. Her smile, implacable as it seemed, turned upwards a degree, then, several seconds later, returned to its former position. She stood up, patted her hair and called to her maid to have the chauffeur ready the car for an immediate trip to 1600 Pennsylvania Avenue.

When she arrived at the White House, Bella Stromberg was escorted immediately to the Oval office, where she found the president's coterie sitting silently. As she entered the room, she understood from the glum expressions that greeted her that the situation was much more serious than Drove had conveyed on the phone. She gazed at each individual, mentally noting who was there and who was not, then turned to Drove and said, matter-of-factly, "Where's the vice president?"

Drove didn't answer. Instead, he threw an anxious look to Candice Brice, then asked Bella to take a seat.

"Ms Stromberg," he began, steady as always. "Our nation is facing a serious crisis. A crisis unparalleled to anything we have ever faced in our history."

"Mr. Drove," Bella broke in. "I am very well aware of how much this administration is opposed to the legislation I'm promoting—"

"Ms. Stromberg," Drove interrupted, stopping her in her tracks. He stared at her as if he were staring down a spider, at once wary of being stung yet ready to make the first strike if necessary.

"We are not here to discuss legislation," he continued. "We are here to discuss the threats that are being posed to our nation as we speak. Threats which are hard to explain—even harder to believe—but which we in this room have witnessed with our own eyes."

Drove paused, letting the silence speak to the gravity of the situation. For the moment, he was in charge, and he waited to see if she would challenge him. Then, when she remained silent, he went on to reveal the events that had taken place over the past several days. He described, as best he could (for he was not a remarkable storyteller), the tragedy that had befallen the president—how he had awakened one morning to find his mouth missing, his voice taken from him, his face deformed. How they had struggled to come up with a solution, "keeping the interests of the country always in mind." And how the president had suddenly disappeared, leaving no indication of his whereabouts.

"Of course, we assume he's been kidnapped," he stated, calmly, emotionlessly, as if he were relating the events of a tiresome movie.

He reviewed the steps they had so far taken, and how, no matter how they tried, they could not keep up with the ever-changing situation. When he finished, he folded his hands in his lap and took a deep breath, as if to indicate that what he was about to say could no longer be held back.

"Ms. Stromberg. The survival of the nation now depends on you."

Bella crossed her legs, nervously straightened her dress, and scrutinized each face in the room.

"And you have kept this from the American people?" she said at last.

"Really, Ms. Stromberg, this is no time for politics."

"This is not politics, Mr. Drove. This administration has constantly kept pertinent information from the public. And it's high time it stopped."

Drove looked to the president's cabinet members for a response. Finally, the head of Homeland Security spoke up.

"Ms. Stromberg. You do understand. Circumstances like these are difficult. We don't want to create panic in the streets."

"The American people have a right to know," Bella persisted.

"Ms. Stromberg," Drove broke in, hoping to fend off a political squabble. "Whether we have done right or wrong will be left for history to decide. And, if you, as commander-in-chief, decide to reveal what has occurred, that will be your decision."

Bella carefully weighed the words she had just heard. Her placid smile quickly pursed itself and her expression began to mirror those in the room.

"Mr. Drove," she said at last. "I demand to know what's become of the vice president."

"Ms. Stromberg."

It was the voice of Candice Brice, a woman, who like Bella, bright and determined, had made it up to the top. Brice stood up, solemnly approached her, reached into her pocket, and then held out her open hand, upon which sat the mousified vice president. Bella Stromberg, always calm and cool, immediately lost her veneer. She shuddered at the sight of the mangy-looking rodent, and then smiled angrily.

"Is this some kind of a joke?" she said, standing up and taking a step back.

"This is no joke, Ms Stromberg," Brice responded. "Early this morning, while we were all in this room discussing how to deal with the president's disappearance, we all witnessed this... this sudden metamorphosis of the vice president."

The mouse spun aimlessly around in Brice's hand, then sat up on its hind legs, set its beady eyes on Bella, and hissed.

Bella Stromberg jumped back and looked at them in disbelief. As was always the case when dealing with this administration, she could not quite determine what was true and what was not, what was being kept hidden from her and the American people and what was being revealed as if through a tiny crevice that no one could fully peer through. She looked around the room again, took note of the severity of their looks, and tried to determine if she was once again being tricked. Set up in some political ploy that would test her mettle against theirs.

"Mr. Drove," she said, "if what you say is true, I am ready to assume my constitutional duties. If, however, this is some kind of political trick, which, I'm sorry to say, your party is famous for, I will make sure that it backfires in a way you will never forget."

"This is no trick, Ms. Stromberg," Drove said. "I assure you of that. Like it or not, we need your help. And the Constitution warrants that you, as Speaker of the House, are next in line to assume the presidency. We, Ms. Stromberg, have no control over that."

Drove's face was sad, defeated. His political career had been brilliant. He had fashioned victory for the party where victory seemed impossible. But now, circumstance had intervened and there wasn't anything he could do but give in.

"Very well," Bella said, a look of triumph passing briefly over her face. "But I must warn you that I will be forced to discuss this with my party. We must have buy-in from all stakeholders."

"I understand, Ms. Stromberg," Drove responded. "I understand."

"We will be here to advise you," the attorney general said, speaking up for the first time. "If you so choose, that is."

"I'm sure you will be," Bella answered curtly.

And with that, Bella Stromberg stood up, took a parting glance at the miniscule vice president, who wiggled his nose nervously in the air, and walked curtly out of the room.

Amidst President Thorne's mum pleas for extrication from captivity ("The Lord is my saver," he kept saying, "Our Father," he kept praying) and Choudry's exhortations for guidance in carrying out his most dubious mission ("*Allahu akbar*," he repeated over and over), a violent storm broke out. Torrents of rain drenched the valley. Fists of lightning punched the sky as the earth rumbled mercilessly like an angry god.

Faced with a power greater than either of them could defeat, they looked to each other for solace, the one an unlikely model of refinement and grace, the other a perfect specimen of hard, manual work and the Darwinian laws of survival. Forgetting their differences, forgetting the possibility of torture and death, on the one hand, the uncertainty of how to proceed with a mission that was nebulous at best and that involved the most powerful man on earth, on the other, they embraced each other like long lost brothers and sat in trembling comfort as the earth shook and the sky opened.

The storm raged on for hours, and the rain poured down as if the oceans had been unleashed. Fighting his fears, Choudry stood up and opened the door to witness nature's ire. The eye of the storm was centered high up in the mountains, and while the wind gusted furiously and the rain poured down relentlessly in the valley, the eerie webs of lightning remained high above with their unnatural glow.

Choudry closed the door to the hut, and the cacophonous downpour muffled into a steady, deafening roar. Stepping lightly across the room, he approached his improbable companion and sat down quietly beside him.

President Thorne watched him from the corner of his eye, sullen and quiet, like a frightened child.

"You should relax, Uncle," Choudry said.

It was said with kindness and with a gentle look that took President Thorne by surprise. He gazed suspiciously at Choudry and attempted a smile from behind his shapeless face as the earth shook from a new roll of thunder.

"The storm is centered in the mountains," Choudry said. "We will wait for it to pass. Then we'll make our way out of here."

The rain drummed loudly against the roof of the hut. President

Thorne eyed his captor tenuously and wondered what he should do. He was trapped, and he had no choice but to make the best of things, to rely on himself and his own God-given instincts.

"They say an evil wizard lives up there," Choudry continued. "When I was a little boy, I used to hear the stories. 'We must be very careful,' the elders would tell us, 'else he will destroy our village and eat our children.' I never believed them. I always thought it was just another old wives' tale."

Choudry began to relax as he remembered his childhood, and the trembling in his body started to ease. Though now, as an adult, he detested their superstitions, their willingness to believe in even the most ridiculous of claims, he looked back fondly on their simple ways and their uncomplicated outlook on life. An outlook, he now thought, somewhat amused, that no American—not even his own children, whose roots, after all, led back to here—could possibly understand.

"One day," he went on, "a violent storm approached the village. Just like this one. Only the rain never fell. For days, the lightning flashed and the wind gusted and the earth shook with thunder. All eyes looked up there to that mountain. Everyone prayed. They asked for Allah's forgiveness. They begged to be forgiven whatever sins they had committed. The storm went on and on until it seemed the mountains would be consumed by the lightning. Until it seemed the hills would explode and come crashing down, destroying the village in their path. Until, they all thought, the earth would open up and swallow everyone. Then it stopped. Just as suddenly as it had begun. There was silence. Dead silence. Gradually, the village returned to normal. People tended their sheep again. They made bread. They milked their cows and gathered honey. They tried to forget the storm. But, no matter how hard they tried, they could not. And the more they tried to forget, the more they believed in that evil wizard."

Choudry turned to his companion and smiled. And for the first time, President Thorne felt safe. Here, he thought, was a simple man. An honest man. And for some reason, he no longer felt threatened. For some inexplicable reason, he knew in his heart that the person sitting before him could not be capable of causing harm.

Looking directly into Chourdry's eyes, he extended his hand. A warm smile filled Choudry's face. He took President Thorne's hand in both of his and, as if he had just met his father after a long absence, kissed it and gently touched it to his forehead.

"Friends?"

President Thorne tapped Choudry's hand in acknowledgement. Then he reached for the blood-speckled pad and began to write.

"My name is Gerald Thorne." he wrote. "President Gerald Wellington Thorne."

He held out the piece of paper. Choudry read it, and his eyes opened wide and his lips began to tremble.

Then, on another sheet of paper, President Thorne wrote: "I have no mouth, as you can see. It just disappeared one morning."

And, on another: "I don't know how I got here. I just did somehow."

Choudry read this last note and set it on the ground with a sigh of relief, for he knew that at last there was someone who could understand the ordeal he had been through over the last couple of days. Taking a deep breath, he began to relate the strange events that had happened to him, about the vision he had witnessed at the Tidal Basin and how he had been commanded to save the president of the United States.

"To save *you*," he said, looking directly at President Thorne with a look of confusion on his face. Then, with a smile, after a long silence, he said: "Maybe, we need to seek out that evil wizard."

He laughed at himself for saying this, laughed because now, after all these years—after all the events that had taken place during the past few days—he was beginning to believe that some magical force had entered his life.

"Maybe," he said, "the elders were right. Maybe, whatever is up there has some strange power over us."

Choudry had not finished saying these words when the storm suddenly broke. A deep, heavy silence fell over the valley and a ray of sunlight edged its way through the crack in the doorway.

Instinctively, they stood up and walked to the door, opened it and stepped out into the bright, clean sunshine. The valley glistened under the pure, gleaming light and the sweet sound of birds rose up in place of the clamorous storm as the fresh smell of the newly washed valley filled their lungs.

A clamor of thunder rumbled in the distance, and Choudry pointed toward the mountaintop where a dark cloud and bursts of lightning continued to ignite the sky.

"That, Uncle, is where the villagers claimed the old wizard lived."

He pointed to the dark cloud.

"That," he said, "is where we must go."

Choudry looked to President Thorne as if he were a child looking to his father for assurance.

"What do you think?' he asked.

President Thorne took Choudry's hand in his. He tapped it gently and nodded and allowed the sparkling sunlight to smile for him.

The Blazing Path of Light Ebenezer Baptist Church, LLC was witnessing a frenzy of activity like it had never before seen as the church was packed up and readied by the day laborers the Reverend CJ Willis had hired in front of the neighborhood 7-Eleven after numerous promises of salvation, food and spare change, and the guarantee of sanctuary ("The feds cannot touch you," he promised them, "as long as you are in my church," even though he was not quite sure they had understood a word he said).

The simple wooden altar was placed near the entrance to the church. The wobbly folding chairs, which filled the hallowed chamber during services, were stacked neatly in rows beside it. And the two rickety bookshelves, purchased at a local used furniture shop, each holding a Bible, a pile of ragged, recycled religious pamphlets that Reverend Willis had accumulated over the years, and an assortment of frayed collection baskets, were emptied and placed near the back door. The cross was carefully removed from the wall, as were the plastic-framed posters of Jesus and the Virgin Mary, and the portable lectern, a long, rectangular corrugated pegboard box fortified on the sides with metal strips, was moved off to the side of the hall, where it would stay until it was ready to be loaded onto the U-Haul truck. As for the faded vinyl stained-glass decals, which had been originally promoted as reusable, they were carefully peeled off the windows, placed in protective sleeves (plastic bags from the grocery store down the street) and stored in boxes that had been donated by the self-storage facility around the corner.

After spending the night meditating on how best to organize Easter services on the National Mall—how to attract the right people, how to exert the most influence on the world's rich and powerful, and how to accommodate the masses he was expecting—Reverend Willis spent the entire day calling around town, making preparations, and arranging to spread the word. And to allow for the maximum number of people and to emulate the resurrection of Jesus and His ascension into Heaven, he had ordered, after much thumbing through the yellow pages, the perfect, most flexible structure ever to be erected on the lawn of the National Mall.

"It will rise as Jesus rose," he proclaimed to Larry, who was deep in lamentation, hunched in misery on the broken-down couch. "It will mirror the miracle of the resurrection," he insisted, hoping to jolt Larry out of his melancholy.

When Larry refused to respond, Reverend Willis stood up from his chair and marched to the church entrance. Unbolting the doors, he stood before the gathering crowds and announced in a loud, resounding voice: "Church services will be held this Sunday—Easter Sunday—in the valley of granite and steel—in the world's largest, most portable church. The erection—marking the resurrection—will take place promptly at sunrise."

And, he added, almost as an aside so as not to take attention away from the magnitude of the occasion, to emphasize the relationship between the physical and the spiritual, he was hereby renaming his mission.

"From now on," he proclaimed, "it will be known as The *Portable Inflatable* Blazing Path of Light Ebenezer Baptist Church, LLC."

For, he declared, he would now be able to travel across the country with his church in tow.

The crowds cheered loudly at this momentous announcement, and the Reverend CJ Willis, proud and elated, looked on like a king observing his loyal subjects. Easter services would be magnificent, he thought to himself, marking one of the most glorious occasions in the history of mankind. And his name would be forever associated with it. All that was left for him to do was to write his sermon, a simple homily that would capture the inspiring beauty of Easter, and then lead the procession from this humble spot to the National Mall—the valley of granite and steel—a passage, he thought to himself, equivalent to that of Moses leading his people through the desert, or of Jesus Himself on the road to Calvary. As for the legalities of erecting a structure on public grounds without a permit, he concluded that God's laws would take precedence over man's, and that God's rule would ultimately prevail. Surely no one would stop them from holding Easter services. They would stake their rights, set up their church and occupy it, and no amount of intimidation would stop them.

Larry, meanwhile, languished in his misery, in an atmosphere he had not been exposed to since his childhood, being, as he was, more acquainted with the neighborhood bar than with the local church. He pined for Pearl, who had not yet returned from her mysterious flight into the ether, and bemoaned his physical deformation and his senseless captivity (for Reverend Willis would not allow him to leave, insisting his life would be in danger). Having succumbed to this irreconcilable situation—a man with two mouths, a man possessing two voices, a man with a personality that seemed to be split in two—he concluded that there was nothing left to do except wait and see how things would turn out.

He had given up hope that he would ever return to normal or that those around him (he glanced angrily at Reverend Willis, who had returned from his proclamations and was now busy writing his sermon) had any interest in helping him, other than for their own personal gain. At the same time, he relished in his newfound fame, for the press corps scrambled for his attention at his brief appearances at the entrance to the church, and his name and his now legendary face appeared in newspapers and on televisions alike.

It was an astonishing accomplishment for someone who had not finished high school, for Larry White was suddenly being recognized as a kind of sage—his words were quoted and his opinion sought after. And his two mouths, which moved in unsynchronized fashion, spouted off expressions so enigmatic that they were pronounced both brilliant and sublime.

"*This house is haunted with the histrionics of our nation,*" he would say, from one mouth, as the crowd eagerly awaited his council.

"And damn anyone who enters it," he would shout from the other.

"*No building will be left untouched. No stone unturned. The valleys will be swarming.*"

"Tell me it's not true. Tell me I'm in the middle of a bad dream."

And his esoteric words and a sublime rush of emotion would move the crowds to tears.

But Larry was miserable. He missed his job and he missed his buddies at work. He missed the Saturday nights when he would go out carousing with his friends. And he missed his apartment, and the soft, lumpy bed where he would sleep off the previous night's bout of drinking and nurse his lingering hangovers in the mornings. But, most of all, he missed his Pearl.

"Pearl, baby," he would shout, prayer-like, sitting in the empty church chamber and looking upwards toward the heavens. "Where you at? Come back to me, baby. I know I've not always been good to you. But I'll change. You'll see."

But Larry's prayers went unanswered, with the hushed, echoing silence of the empty hall his only reply, and no matter how much he begged, no matter how hard he prayed (suppressing that word deep under his breath as he did so), Pearl did not return. She was lost, he concluded. Forever. Had floated away, far, far away into never-neverland, never to be seen again.

"Mr. Willis," he said at last, as the good reverend worked frantically on his Easter homily. "Reverend. Father. Whatever. You got to help me. Please, sir."

"Not now, Larry," Reverend Willis answered, "I'm in the middle of Sunday's sermon. It will be great, Larry. Inspiring. And the crowds will be there to see you. The word will spread. The donations will pour

THE WIZARD AND THE WHITE HOUSE

in like manna from heaven. We'll be famous Larry. Rich and famous."

"But all I want is my Pearl back," Larry cried.

"Pearl is in the Lord's hands now," Reverend Willis responded somberly, looking up now from his notebook. "We must never question Him or His intentions."

"But Mr. Willis—"

"No buts now, Larry. We are all God's instruments. God's receptors. And we must prepare ourselves for His great day. Ah," he sang as if in a dream, "and what an erection it shall be!"

Reverend Willis, pious as ever, drifted off into reverie, as Larry relented, torn and hopeless, slumping back into his chair, and cursed the day he had ever touched liquor to his poor lips.

"The Devil's milk," he said to himself, remembering his wife's words. "A potion for the poor."

Surely something was not right with the world, he thought. For if God had wanted him to have two mouths, he would have been born that way. And if God had wanted Reverend Willis to lead the nation into salvation, then surely this could have been done without his help.

Then, Larry had an idea. He would bring his plight to the press. To that news program where they helped people solve their problems. He would tell them everything: how he had woken up one day to find himself transformed into a horrible looking creature, how Pearl had brought him to Reverend Willis' church to help him return to normal, and how she had disappeared into thin air, floating away before his very eyes. Surely, they would be able to help him. Or at least get the word out to someone who could.

Larry rose from his chair like Lazarus resurrected and strode out of the office, leaving Reverend Willis lost in his ruminations. He felt stronger now, and he marched resolutely to the front of the church and unlatched the door. Opening it, he scrunched his eyes, swollen from worry and lack of sleep, as the bright light filled him with blindness. A sudden hush fell over the crowds that had been waiting anxiously for him to appear as he towered above them like a prophet ready to speak to his anxious disciples.

Larry looked out at them silently. His two mouths trembled with fright. Then the words began to flow as if both mouths had become one.

"Our Father, I've come here to save you, hallowed be Thy name, my name is Gerald Thorne, what a bunch of bunk, hogwash! I just wanna save myself, from the Devil's milk, the Devil's milk, Thy kingdom come, a potion for the poor, don't touch that shit to your lips, that shit's nasty, Thy will be done, look what it's done to me, all I wanna do is go home, go home and be with my Pearl, on earth as it is in heaven, the pearly gates of heaven, I'm lost, lost in this valley, give us this day, cows and sheep, and oh, my God, my lips, my mouth, our daily bread, my Pearl, she just flew away, and forgive us our trespasses, she done flew away like a ghost, up there in those mountains, in this valley, I ain't done nothing wrong, as we forgive those who trespass against us, the rain will wash us away, and lead us not into temptation, the Lord is my Saver, Lord Jesus save me, Lord Jesus save me, but deliver us from evil, save me from this nightmare, get these damn lips off, offa my face! The Lord is my Saver, I am the president of the United States. Amen."

The crowd was mesmerized, and the press corps recorded his every word, but this last utterance was lost on the crowds as they went wild and burst into chants of, "the Lord is my Savior."

For a moment, both of Larry's mouths broke into a smile. Then, as the crowds swayed back and forth, chanting and waving their hands in the air, the church door opened and Larry felt himself being yanked by the collar as Reverend Willis, whose peaceful reverie was rudely interrupted by the raucous commotion outside his church, came rushing out in a panic. Always ready to save his flock and ever mindful that Larry could run off at any minute, he pulled him back into the safekeeping of his church and bolted the door shut.

Amina, solid as a bronze bust and radiating the serenity of an ancient goddess, began to weep. Frozen in time on the faux-French couch with her face lifted upwards in a gesture of eternal piety, her tears dripped slowly onto the floor before her sandaled feet and accumulated into dark, damp stains that slowly widened and consumed the hand-woven oriental carpet. And though she cried silently, an occasional whimper could be heard echoing through the hushed silence of the little shrine that the house had become, and though she did not weep in steady streams, the tears were abundant enough that they soon began to gather into tiny puddles.

Fatwa placed a green plastic basin she had purchased from the local dollar store before her mother to catch the tears and prevent the carpet from becoming saturated and mildewed, but soon the green basin began to overflow, and it was replaced by a larger bucket, and eventually by an even bigger clay urn which had been hand-fashioned back in Amina's village just after her marriage to Choudry.

The long lines of pilgrims that snaked daily through the house gradually grew larger. Word of Amina's miraculous cures spread, and people traveled from near and far to pay homage to the saint in the orange sari, as she came to be known, and to dip their fingers into her holy tears. Rich and poor, they came seeking a cure for their untreatable ailments or to bathe their wounds in Amina's wondrous lachrymation. Cripples arrived on crutches and wheelchairs; lepers, draped in cloth, entered the makeshift shrine barefoot and limping, and cancer victims, with no hope for survival, journeyed, seeking a last desperate chance at life and the prospect of dipping their fingers into the sacred liquid that trickled from Amina's stony eyes.

Recognizing the value of his mother's tears, Amir began handing out little glass vials so that visitors could gather the precious drops to take home. Standing beside her petrified, statue-like body, he would gently click the tiny containers in his hand to draw their attention, and though he did not charge for them, a sign above his fossilized mother stated that donations would be welcomed—donations, he explained whenever asked, that would help support the Amina Foundation, an explanation that was enough to elicit generous offerings.

Kazi, meanwhile, his clothes disheveled, his beard even more unkempt from the long hours he was keeping, remained conflicted about the goings-on in his mother-in-law's house. On the one hand, he bemoaned Amir's idolatry and continually begged him to cease his heathen ways. On the other, he welcomed the opportunity to proselytize to the desperate individuals who filed non-stop through the crowded house.

"Allah will not like this," he would say to Amir in those rare moments when there was a lull in visitors. "You are associating another with Him."

But Amir would not listen, and he continued to collect money and hand out commemorative artifacts and devise new ways to profit from his mother's fortuitous condition.

Eager to save his soul from eternal damnation, Kazi decided to set up a prayer area in the next room—a spot facing Mecca where he placed a small rug, a verse from the Koran, which he stapled fastidiously to the wall, and an electronic clock, set for the Washington, DC area, that played the *azan* at the five appointed times.

Standing at the entrance to his makeshift chapel, he would invite visitors to enter, asking them kindly to remove their shoes, and lecture them on the benefits of Islam, enjoining them to reject the paganism his brother-in-law was promoting in the next room (as well as whatever faith they had been so misfortunate to be born into) and to join him on the one true path to God.

"God is very great," he would proclaim. "He has given us guidance for this life and the next. God is very, very great."

And though his attempts to bring them into the fold were treated with the utmost respect, his pleas fell on deaf ears, for their chronic ailments had already been cured by Amina's miraculous tears, and they went off with their little vials and their commemorative trinkets and ignored Kazi's fervent appeals for conversion.

Disappointed, Kazi implored Allah's mercy, begged, on his knees, for forgiveness, invoked God's wrath on those who would not obey His commands and performed his prayers at each appointed time, remaining steadfast in his mission to call the misguided and the misinformed to the true path of Allah.

But the Choudry family was not all business and faith, for despite the show of reverence and the appearance of relative tranquility, a pall of fear had fallen on each of them. Ever since the unannounced visit by the two pharmaceutical representatives ("Since when do members of the American medical profession make house calls?" Kazi asked skeptically one night over a meal of rice and lamb), they had become the target of sundry and repeated warnings. Anonymous phone callers threatened to turn them over to the Department of Homeland Security as suspected terrorists if they did not cease their unauthorized activities. Unsigned letters were left in their mailbox demanding that they close up shop and forget any nonsense about sainthood and miraculous cures. And mysterious packages started showing up on their doorstep, causing the bomb squad to set up a permanent base in front of their house.

Then, one day, a man, claiming to be a religious scholar, arrived at their front door. Refusing to join the line of idolaters waiting to get inside, he rang the doorbell instead and waited patiently for a member of the household to answer. When news of the man's presence reached inside, Amir abandoned his post and went to greet the stranger, who promptly reprimanded him for his blatant apostasy and threatened to take the sword to his neck.

"Your family members will be sacrificed," the tall, lanky man said in perfect English, his face hidden behind a black scarf. "Your house will be torched. There will be nothing left."

Amir brushed him off nonchalantly and threatened to report him to the police should he show up again, but back inside, he stood nervously beside his mother's altar and began to feel as apprehensive as the rest of his family.

"Shallow threats," he said nonchalantly to Fatwa, after telling her what had transpired. But his warm, charismatic smile had now vanished, and his face became a mere expressionless façade.

Even more disturbing was how the news media, which had originally treated the story of Amina and her mysterious miracles with interest and enthusiasm, suddenly turned on the Choudry family, referring to them now as charlatans and insinuating that they were part of an insidious plot hiding behind what they termed "religious charades," and warning people of the legal consequences of association, should anything be proven against the family.

Channel 7, in an investigative piece aired on the evening news, claimed that the stone-like saint was "nothing more than an illusion created by dim light and the power of suggestion," and that the urn of tears simply contained filtered ocean water, dripping from a little tube hidden behind Amina's head.

"This so-called saint," the news reporter concluded as the camera zoomed in on Amina's calcified image, "is nothing more than a cynical imposter, bent on fooling people into handing over their money, money which could possibly fall into the hands of those who wish to do America harm."

The media's coverage was so slanted and so negative that even Kazi, who continued to rail against the idolatry his family was perpetrating, said out loud, in between supplications for God's mercy, "This is nonsense. We are not charlatans. We are not terrorists. They are just against us Muslims." And then he immediately implored God for forgiveness for defending his family under such circumstances, though he insisted to himself that it was the right thing to do.

"Amir," Fatwa said to her brother late one night when the lines of visitors, succumbing to the fear-mongering, had trickled down to just a few brave souls, "I'm afraid. The children are being taunted at school. Our lives are in danger."

Fatwa gazed at her mother, solid as stone, silent except for the slow drip of tears, and began to sob. She was physically exhausted from the activity of the past few days, drained and confused from all that had taken place since her father's vision at the Tidal Basin and his sudden departure. She missed her mother—missed sitting with her, sipping tea and talking, gossiping about the neighbors and the latest trend in saris. She missed her father who had run off with a strange woman (though she still refused to believe her mother's claims) and was nowhere to be found. And she missed her husband who was so busy trying to convert the masses and fending off attacks on their religion that he no longer had time to taunt her.

"Fatwa," Amir responded, "it's all right. People are just angry. We're safe here. Mama will protect us."

He turned tentatively toward his slate of a mother, seeking reassurance, then looked back at Fatwa and forced a smile.

"*Astaghfirullah*," Kazi shouted. "May God forgive you for all that you've done. Can't you see that you are doing exactly what the Koran has forbidden us to do? Associating another with Allah?"

"Kazi," Fatwa protested, wiping her tears and raising her voice, "enough is enough. Don't make things worse. We're all wrong."

A humbling silence fell over the room at Fatwa's words. It was unusual for her to speak up, especially to her husband, and her uncontrolled outburst revealed to them just how grave the situation had become.

"Well," she said, looking from Kazi to Amir and feeling suddenly emboldened, "what are we going to do?"

Just then, the room began to rumble, and Amina yanked herself out of her stiff, stony sleep.

"How many times have I told you how foolish you are?" she said angrily. "Just like your stubborn father."

She stretched out her arms and legs as if she had just awakened from a long, soothing slumber, yawned from side to side to get her jaws moving again and sat back comfortably on the couch.

"Fatwa," she demanded. "Get me some tea. Oh, how I miss my tea! And bring me some biscuits."

"Yes, Mama," Fatwa said obediently hurrying off to the kitchen.

"Amir," Amina ordered. "Get me my footstool. And Kazi," she said, turning an angry gaze toward her son-in-law. "Change those clothes. And go trim that beard. If there's one thing I can't stand, it's a man with an unkempt beard."

"But, Auntie," Kazi protested.

"Allah has not ordered us to be untidy. We are supposed to be neat and clean."

"But, Auntie," Kazi repeated.

"Now!"

"Yes, Auntie."

"And clear these good people out of the house and have them wait outside. We will show this world what we are made of."

"Yes, Auntie."

By the time Fatwa came back with a steaming pot of tea, the room had been emptied of all remaining visitors. Kazi returned in a clean set of clothes and with his beard neatly trimmed, though still long, and

Amir gently set the footstool down before his mother after having moved the urn of tears off to the side. The lights were on, the candles extinguished, and, except for the signs and crowd control posts, the trinkets and flowers strewn throughout the parlor, and two stray sheep and a lowing calf that had been left behind, the room had returned to normal.

Fatwa poured the tea into the little glass cups she had set on the tray, and Amina rested her legs on the footstool and took a long, indulgent sip, letting the warm, soothing liquid linger in her mouth.

"Ah," she sighed. "Tea. God's gift to mankind. Don't you agree?"

She took another deep, noisy sip, then set her tea glass on the table and looked at her family.

"Now," she said. "We must gather everyone together. Outside. In front of the house. At dawn, we will march. To the valley of granite and steel. There we will all find the answers we need."

Bewildered, they stared at Amina, then looked at each other silently. If she had been an enigma while she sat petrified on her faux-French couch, she had become even more so now that she had returned to normal. She had never before given orders to anyone, especially not in such a curt fashion, and she had never been known to speak in riddles as she seemed to be doing now.

"Auntie," Kazi ventured, filling his mother-in-law's glass to appease any anger that might arise from his question, "where is this valley? And what answers do we need? Do we not have all the answers we need in the holy Koran?"

"Silence!" Amina shouted.

She lifted the glass to her mouth and indulged herself again in the precious liquid.

"You cannot understand," she said, "because you refuse to understand. Because you are blind. Yes, *alhamdulillah*, we have the holy Koran, and yes, *alhamdulillah*, it contains all that we need to know. But in order to understand it, you must be able to see. '*Deaf, dumb, and blind, they will not return.*' Does not the Koran say that?"

"But, Mama," Fatwa began.

"There are no buts, my daughter," Amina said. "Allah has put each of us here on this earth for a reason. It is our duty to find that purpose and act on it. Now, you will all make way at dawn—you and all the good people who have come to this house—and you will see."

"And how do we get to this valley, Mama," Amir asked.

"Now you ask me such questions, my son? Yet, when you want to build shrines and swindle people you do not ask?"

She gave Amir a stern stare, an uncanny, enigmatic look that would remain with him until the end of his days.

"Just follow your instincts," she said at last, "and you will know."

And with that, the house began to rumble and Amina settled back into her petrified position on the faux-French couch.

"Mama, wait!" Fatwa cried. "Don't go!"

"Just follow your instincts. I will be there to guide you."

And Amina quickly hardened, firm and resolute, the steaming tea glass dangling from the crook of her right index finger like a priceless jewel.

Akram slowly opened his weary eyes and tried to remember where he was. A strange, oppressive weight made his head seem as heavy as lead. He felt as if he had been in a deep, relentless sleep—a restless sleep that had caused him to have dreams he could no longer remember, but that seemed, as he waded through the veils of his nebulous memory, to have been filled with fear and horror.

As his vision slowly came into focus, the fog began to lift from his memory. He was a prisoner. Or a servant. A slave. Sold, as far as he could remember, as a sacrifice—an appeasement—to an evil wizard to protect his family and their humble village. Had it all been just a dream, he wondered? Was he now in his house, his mother and father nearby, his brothers and sisters sleeping peacefully beside him?

Akram scanned the dark room and tried to make out where he was. Then he heard a sound—a weak groan—a moaning that reminded him of how the village elders had described death as it approaches with its deliberate, heavy feet.

Jumping up like a frightened animal, he peered through the darkness. Lying on the floor, illuminated by the dim, waning fire in the hearth, he could make out a figure. Slowly, the haze lifted from him like a black chador. Slowly, he began to recall what had happened, and he understood then that it had all been real. Quickly he felt inside his pocket and breathed a sigh of relief when he found his magic stone.

Sharir stirred in the darkness. Akram scampered off like a mouse trying to escape from the claws of a vicious cat before it awakes, and quietly made his way down the stone steps he had scaled countless times when setting off to gather magic herbs for his master.

Deep down in the depths of the caverns, he came to the solid wall of rock he had seen Sharir mysteriously enter. Trembling, he grasped the magic stone in his pocket and chanted the words he had heard his master recite, and watched as the stone wall slowly ground open with a loud roar.

His heart thumping, he walked through the newly forged entrance. His eyes agape, he marveled at the treasure he now saw up close for the first time, scattered in heaps and piled up high in large wooden chests throughout the vast torch-lit chamber. Huge coffers overflowed with coins of gold and silver, strings of cool, white pearls were strewn across the floor, and jewels of many colors, shapes, and sizes sparkled under the light of the torches that burned brightly in their sconces on the cold stone walls.

Never before had Akram seen such beauty. As he looked around the room, he imagined his family and the people in his village. With such riches, they could all prosper. No one would go hungry. No one would have to toil from dawn to dusk.

Then, Akram remembered the wooden box he had seen Sharir greedily clutching. Hastily, he began to search. He rummaged through the treasure, pushing aside crystal baubles and golden scepters until he found the wooden box that he knew was more precious to Sharir than all the treasure in the room. As he carefully retrieved it from its hiding place, he heard a loud cry, and he turned around and saw Sharir standing at the entrance to the chamber, leaning against the stone wall, weak yet defiant.

"Goro," he cried, weakly. "Give me that box."

Akram stared at Sharir. His heart was filled with terror at the sight of his master, yet the yearning to be free burned even more painfully than his fear. His first instinct was to obey, but he knew that his chance at liberating himself and his village from the clutches of Sharir would be lost. He would surely be killed and the village and everyone in it destroyed.

Looking Sharir straight in the eye, he took a deep breath and said, "I am not Goro. I am Akram."

Akram felt emboldened by his own words, and he took a step closer to Sharir.

"The boy you took from his village and have kept here a prisoner."

"Akram," Sharir said, cowering as Akram came closer. "Give me that box and I shall give you all the treasure you desire."

Akram smiled as he felt himself become transformed. With each word he said, with each step closer he took toward Sharir, he became bolder, stronger, less fearful and unsure. No longer would he be treated as a slave. No longer would he be ordered around. As he watched Sharir cowering on his knees, a man defeated, he knew he now had the upper hand. Towering over Sharir, he felt he was no longer a boy, that, as night becomes day, he had now waxed into a man.

"For years, you have tormented our village," Akram said. "Kidnapping children. Holding them for ransom. Intimidating their fathers. Threatening to destroy our homes and our livelihood. Now it is time for us to be free."

Akram held out the wooden box and fumbled for the latch.

"Don't open that box!" Sharir shouted. Then, looking pitifully at his one-time apprentice, he pleaded. "Akram. Haven't I been good to you? Haven't I taught you everything you know?"

"I don't need a box to defeat you. *Master.*"

Akram felt the latch with his index finger. Ignoring Sharir's pleas for mercy, he recited a prayer, disengaged the tiny lock and slowly opened the mysterious wooden container.

Chapter 8

Easter morning arose in the nation's capitol like no other: warm and glowing, the heavens brushed with a scattering of stars, and a bright, stippled sliver of golden moon. Despite predictions for rain, the skies were crystal clear, and the only clouds that appeared were light, fluffy puffs kindled by the fierce backwash of moonlight.

Despite this dazzling celestial exhibit, most residents of the greater metropolitan region slept peacefully, blindly hiding their heads in their pillows and ignoring the calls for rebirth and renewal that had been stapled on street posts and splashed across billboards throughout the area. There were, however, those who kept avid vigil, who had spent the night in silent observance, who solemnly awaited the dawn with its bright promise of enlightenment and hope.

Outside The Portable Inflatable Blazing Path of Light Ebenezer Baptist Church, LLC, the faithful prayed quietly. Holding candles in their upheld hands, their heads bowed reverently, they waited for their self-appointed preacher and their newly-anointed prophet to appear, ready to begin their rapturous march.

Inside, Reverend CJ Willis sat in silent contemplation, his eyes heavy from lack of sleep, his fingers numb from writing, and prepared for what he hoped would be the most celebrated, the most prodigious day of his career. Focusing on the Bible cradled in his hand and trying to quell his anxious mind, he meditated on the trials of Jesus Christ in the Garden of Gethsemane, and pondered the elusive promise of spiritual riches, brushing aside the earthly ones that kept prying their way into his devout deliberations (*the church coffers will overflow*, a soft voice whispered in his ear, *baskets will multiply like loaves of bread*).

Having put the final touches on his Easter Sunday sermon, he now prepared himself for the most challenging day of his life. The multitudes would converge on the National Mall—the valley of granite and steel. The rich, the famous, the most powerful would be in attendance, and his name would be forever engraved in the permanent annals of history. His moment had come, and success would soon be his.

Sitting beside the good reverend, Larry dozed off and awoke in constant fits of restlessness that brought back the days of drunken stupor, when sleep and consciousness would often merge into one. And in those rare moments when he managed to rest quietly, his eyes tightly shut, one or both of his mouths would spout such aphorisms as to make Reverend Willis both smile with anticipation and cringe in utter fear.

"*God has sent me an angel*," he shouted in one fitful moment. "And damn the souls of anyone who gets in my way!"

"Fight the demons, Larry," Reverend Willis shouted in desperation.

"But Mr. Willis, Reverend, sir," Larry said, startled awake. "I want to sleep. And the demons just won't let me be."

"Sleep is the Devil's lure, Larry. A temptation to cloud the mind. Fight it, Larry. Fight Satan's lair. Let God's grace flow through you. We must pray. We must show the people who gather today what we are made of."

"*May the Lord protect me*," Larry said despondently.

"That's the spirit," Reverend Willis said, pleased.

"And damn the rest to hell!"

Ever hopeful, Reverend CJ Willis ignored this last egregious outburst and wandered back into his own musings, filled with worshippers flocking to his portable church, which towered majestically over the monuments on the National Mall—worshippers bearing witness, dropping down on their knees to confess their sins, passionately lifting their tongues into a cacophonous chorus of beseechment while digging their feverish fingers into their purses and pockets and filling his baskets with coins and bills.

"Yes," he shouted, much to Larry's dismay. "The time has come at last! Rise up Larry. Rise up and let us begin our glorious journey."

Back in Arlington, the Choudry residence was no less fraught with preparation and apprehension, though the Easter holiday was not their particular dish of rice.

"God forgive them," Kazi lamented. "Worshipping rabbits and eating chocolate. What kind of religion is that? If only they were Muslim!" he exclaimed.

Having spent the night reciting verses from the Koran and seeking forgiveness for participating in his in-laws' blasphemous activities ("How," he kept thinking, "could they have strayed so far? How could they associate a woman with God?"), he now reluctantly assisted Amir in cobbling together a last-minute dais on which to carry Amina's petrified body.

As the two men labored, Fatwa sat before the computer and frantically searched the Internet. Baffled by her mother's cryptic entreaty, she Googled and queried and meandered through cyberspace, attempting to locate the enigmatic valley of granite and steel.

"There's no such place," she said at last, wearily setting aside her mouse. She looked to her stone of a mother in desperation and strained to hold back her tears. She had always heeded her entreaties, had never once disobeyed, but this time she was stuck, unable to comprehend or abide.

"She said to follow our instincts," Amir shouted as he bound the last planks of wood together with rope.

"Follow our instincts?" Kazi said. "Our instincts are to follow the true path of Allah. Not to participate in paganism and idolatry."

"Kazi!" Fatwa protested.

She glared angrily at her husband. She was adamant, determined to obey her mother's wishes no matter what, just as she had been on the night of her wedding, and giving him a look she had learned from her mother, she curtly said, "We will do as Mama says."

Kazi blinked nervously, mumbled an inaudible reply, and firmly tightened the length of rope around his mother-in-law's make-shift platform with a humbled grimace on his face.

"And may Allah guide us and keep us safe," she added, just to be sure he had understood.

"*Insha'llah*," Kazi responded, lifting his hands in supplication and mumbling a prayer. "May Allah guide us and protect us on this unholiest of days. *Insha'llah*," he insisted. "God willing!"

"Amen," Amir answered, and he curled his mouth into a smile as he inspected their handiwork with pride.

"*Amin!*" Kazi shouted back at him. "It's *Amin!*"

And, on this early Easter morning, while the Choudry family busily prepared to carry out Amina's cryptic wishes, while Reverend CJ Willis sat in his church engulfed in solipsistic visions of grandeur, while Larry furiously fought his demons and prayed blindly for a return to normalcy in his own modest, peculiar way, the White House, no less busy, was fraught with solemn deliberations and reactive planning.

Bella Stromberg, having been secretly sworn in as president ("No need to alarm the public," Mark Drove insisted as the chief justice of the Supreme Court administered the oath of office, and then, surreptitiously, under his breath, he whispered to one of President Thorne's closest confidants, "I'm still searching for a way out of this,") President Bella Stromberg, now officially, though not publicly, having been issued the oath of office—the first woman to hold her hand to the Bible in this most distinguished of ceremonies (she had worn a very special, expensive French perfume for the occasion, over the protest of President Thorne's coterie who insisted she put on a fragrance of American origin), sat down with her cabinet (which was actually President Thorne's, for she had not had the time to prepare, to appoint, to even think about who she might want to advise her) and wondered what course of action it would now be best to pursue. For having been suddenly propelled into this new and formidable role, she now had to deal with the various crises that she had inherited from her predecessor (*a total buffoon*, she thought, secretly, smiling to herself, *incapable of even coordinating a noun and a verb*).

Bella Stromberg, ever the diplomat, crossed her dainty legs, swished a length of hair out of her vision, batted her radiant eyes, and said at last, "Our first order of business must be to locate the former president," (and she subconsciously, unwillingly put a stress on the word *former* as she secretly hoped that he would never be found), "and to locate those responsible for these incredible events that have been taking place."

"Ms. Strom—Madam President," Drove said, tackling this last word as if he had just bitten into a piece of steak which was both tough and overcooked.

"Yes, Mr. Drove," Bella answered, tapping he finger impatiently on the table.

Drove observed her curiously. She had not been president for more than ten minutes and she already looked old and weary. Her hair seemed suddenly duller and the wrinkles on her face more pronounced. His first instinct was to let her suffer just a little, to refuse to offer any advice at all, to refrain from filling her in on what had already been done, but his sense of patriotism overcame him and he reluctantly continued:

"We have already dispatched Special Forces to search for the Pres—the *former* president," he said. "And we have top scientists looking into the strange transformation of the vice president, as well as into President Thorne's facial situation."

"I see," Bella responded. "And?"

Drove hesitated. Then he said: "There are forces gathering—domestic forces—which we see as a threat to our nation's security."

"And what exactly are these forces?"

"A certain minister, right here in Washington. A Reverend—?"

"CJ Willis." Candice Brice, sensing Drove's hesitancy, completed Drove's sentence like a schoolgirl who, having waited patiently to impress the teacher with the correct answer, finally seizes the opportunity to speak up.

"Yes," Drove continued. "Reverend CJ Willis. A wily fellow, it seems, and his strange accomplice, a certain Larry White. They have been preaching an odd mixture of politics and religion."

"Larry White," the Secretary of Homeland Security interjected, "has a facial deformity. He speaks in riddles and seems to mesmerize the masses."

"And then there is the Choudry family," Brice added, with a smug smile on her face, for though she was not particularly fond of Stromberg, she was, after all, a fellow woman, a brethren sister who had made it through the ranks, and she felt a sense of pride in being in the same room at this historic moment and detected a window of opportunity for herself.

"The Choudry family," Drove continued. "Pakistani immigrants. The husband is a local butcher and recently tried to break into the White House. He, too, has disappeared. The wife claims to have special powers and has been attracting all sorts of people to her house, which has been made into some sort of shrine. It's been all over the news."

"Yes," Stromberg said, "I see." And though she had read about all of this in the papers, she did not really see what the relationship was to everything else that had occurred.

"We feel there is a connection between all these events," Brice explained, sensing Bella's confusion.

"And has anything been done? Analyses, surveillance?"

"All of the above," Drove answered.

"And?"

"Both of these groups are planning to converge on the National Mall. The one to hold Easter services. The other—well, we're not quite sure, but we do suspect something… shall we say, not kosher."

"And the *former* president?"

"Well we can't say for sure," Drove responded. "But you can put two and two together. A Pakistani immigrant—an Islamist, I might add, though I don't like to point fingers, but given the current climate in the world—this individual disappears at the same time as the president."

"I see," Bella answered.

Bella Stromberg became somber. The elation of becoming president—the historic precedent she had set—suddenly disappeared. Feeling the weight of circumstances she could neither change nor control, she listened to everything the members of President Thorne's cabinet had to say and digested it slowly and carefully, as one digests a big meal that sits heavily and unbearably on the stomach. After considering all the angles—the facts she had been given, the political climate she had inherited, the personalities sitting across from her in the room who were known for their utmost contempt for her and her brand of politics—she said, "Very well. Then I think we should show up at this reverend's Easter services."

"But—"

"There are no 'buts,' Mr. Drove," Bella responded.

She planted her eyes firmly on his, then slowly scanned the room to establish her authority.

"I have always been a hands-on person," she said. "And while the office of the president may curtail that somewhat by its very nature, in this case I want to see exactly what's going on. With my own eyes. With all of our eyes. And Easter services will provide the best way for us to do that."

"Very well, Mr.—Ms. President," Drove said, reluctantly. "I will arrange then for Secret Service protection."

"Yes, Mr. Drove. Please do that."

"Beggin' your pardon, Madam President," the Secretary of Homeland Security said, clearing his throat. "If I may point out—I'm Jewish."

"Well, Mr. Secretary," Bella responded, in as culturally sensitive a way as she could possibly muster under the circumstances, "then you will only have to bear the cross for just one day."

She slowly surveyed the room again to see if there were any disagreements, any challenges to her carefully formulated decision.

"Put on your Sunday best," she said at last. 'We are going to attend Easter services."

On this same Easter morning, deep in the Hindu Kush Mountains, where a mysterious electrical storm was lingering over a particular patch of rocky terrain, President Thorne, who, unaware of the goings-on back in Washington and who believed he was still the president of the United States, was busy clambering up a steep, winding path with his trusty companion, Choudry, who steadfastly led the way forward. It was a path that wound, beneath the dark clouds, through the rocky hills to the hidden entrance of an infamous cave where the evil wizard was said to live. Or at least, as Choudry continually repeated, each time he stopped and put his hand on his distended belly to catch his breath and ask for God's forgiveness, it was what he seemed to remember from his murky childhood, at least what he was led to believe, and he could not quite say for sure whether or not he had ever put much stock in it or whether or not he believed in it even now.

"The elders always told us not to wander off in this direction," he said as he gasped for air. " 'The evil wizard will snatch you up and roast you like kabob,' they told us. Superstitions," he said, leaning against an outcrop of rock. "Wives' tales meant to keep little children in their place. Don't you think, Uncle?"

President Thorne smiled and nodded, though his smile was

invisible, and his nod was more a reaction than a consent.

Yet Choudry persisted in his precipitous pursuit, determined to find the cave, whether to prove that the wizard really existed or to finally put to rest this childhood myth he could not say, and President Thorne grunted in acknowledgement, though whether he agreed with Choudry or not was not quite clear, either.

Trailing alongside him, President Thorne huffed and puffed from the strenuous climb and towed his dwindling IV supply behind him like a child tugging his toy wagon, wishing for this arduous journey to come to a quick end, thinking only of the comforts of his ranch: his gregarious wife sitting quietly beside him, the fireplace crackling, soothing and warm, an idyllic life he now yearned for more than ever. He was weary, longed to rest in his own comfortable bed, to sleep a deep, deep sleep, then open his eyes and find himself lying under the gentle rays of the morning sun, the birds chirping innocently in the trees, his horse, Dolphin, neighing cheerfully in the open field nearby. And throughout this reverie, he failed to give one thought to the White House or to his responsibilities to the nation, except to admit, ever so secretly, as if some surreptitious spy could read his thoughts, that he was ready to give up politics, to escape the Nation's Capital, once and for all, to leave the Beltway madness and all its machinations behind him, and go back to living a normal, more simple life.

"This is my maiden voyage," he said to himself. "A maiden, made-in-America voyage exported to... Where am I, anyway?"

And President Thorne looked at Choudry and it no longer mattered. He could be anywhere, he thought. And yet he wasn't. He was here. Wherever here was. And he was with this fellow, a fellow human being, whoever he might be. And all he needed now was to get back home, safe and sound. And, somehow, instinctively, he knew he would. If he had survived his days in the White House—dealing with the opposition, reacting to international crises of one sort or another, keeping his eyes in front, behind, and to the sides of himself to make sure no one was attempting to usurp his authority, to undermine him, to trick him, confuse him, subtly steer him into making decisions he might not otherwise make—then he certainly could survive this mysterious, difficult journey in a strange and ancient land, a journey that had begun to open his eyes.

He had put his trust in Choudry, having had no choice, really, but to do so. Still, after having spent all this time with him, and with a mind that was clear and uncluttered, now that he was on his own and far away from his advisors, he had found in Choudry someone who accepted him for what he was, someone who had no expectations of him, someone who wanted to help him, not for some reward or political recognition, or to achieve some unspoken goal, but for the sake of helping another human being in need. And it was this honesty, this rare, chivalrous attitude, that endeared Choudry to him, that was now helping him get through these most trying of times.

"God has sent me an angel," he said to himself.

He observed Choudry from the side of his eye as they continued their strenuous climb. His unshaven, blubbery face, which had not long before frightened him, now brought him comfort. His slovenly and rather common appearance, which had caused him to search for cover and to tremble in his shoes, now made him feel relaxed and safe. With this once sinister-seeming individual at his side, who at this very moment was carefully carrying his IV as they climbed up the jagged path, he knew his life was in good hands.

"God has sent me an angel," he repeated, out loud, as loud as he could say it though he knew no one could hear him.

And if they ever got back alive, he would recommend Choudry for a presidential award. Before the entire nation, he would honor him as a national hero, and the world would come to know what pride Americans took in their country, even those who had just recently arrived.

The air was dry, and lightning lit up the eerie, blue-gray sky. As they continued their climb up the steep mountainside, the earth rumbled with the angry sound of thunder, and the clouds, having already given up all they had to surrender, hovered ominously above, moving slowly along with them as if steering them forward.

"Over there," Choudry shouted.

He pointed to the mouth of a nearby cave.

"I will go in, Uncle," he said, as they caught their breath. "You can wait for me here."

President Thorne shook his head. He pointed to himself and to Choudry and then to the cave, indicating they would go in together.

Slowly, carefully, they entered the dark, dank cave and made their way deep into its cavernous belly. In the darkness, they could hear bats squealing and the sound of rodents scuttling off at their approach. A bright light glowed in the distance and moved as they approached, retreating as if guiding them forward. Choudry peered at President Thorne through the darkness and slowly followed the tiny light deeper into the cave's endless belly.

At last, they came to what looked like a flight of steps—huge rocks that led up to a landing where the light now shone, beckoning to them like a lure. As they climbed, they could hear voices, low muffled mutterings that gradually became louder. When they reached the top, they came to an opening.

Following the beam of light, they entered a huge chamber lit by torches that lined the walls. As their eyes adjusted, they could see huge chests of treasures—gold and silver coffers of bright, sparkling jewels— and then they saw a boy and, cowering on the floor, a man whose appearance was both frail and frightened.

"I don't need a box to defeat you. *Master*," the boy was saying. "In the end, it will be you who defeats yourself."

"No, Goro," the man shouted. "Please."

The boy held a small wooden box in his hand which he slowly drew open. As the old man begged for mercy, a bright glow emanated from its aperture, and the figure of a woman, bathed in radiant light, emerged like a genie from a magic lantern.

"It's her," President Thorne shouted, looking to Choudry. "She's come to take us home."

Like a child, he clapped, jumped up and down, knocking the IV down. Then, suddenly, he realized that he had just spoken, as the words echoed through the huge cavern, and he looked at Choudry and repeated, loudly and clearly: "It's her."

As the glowing figure hovered gently above them, smiling down at them in a shower of light, Choudry recognized the woman he had seen in his garden, the one he had followed without quite knowing why, who had transported him back to his childhood village.

"*Allahu akbar*," Choudry shouted joyfully.

Pearl smiled down kindly at them. Then, she turned to Sharir, cowering on the ground and staring up at her in fear. Silently, she waved her hand and Sharir shriveled up into a dry, brittle ball, and, in an instant, he disappeared.

Akram stared in wonder. Realizing he was now free, he smiled for the first time since his captivity, and shouted for joy.

"Go," Pearl said to him with a gentle smile. "Go to your people. Tell them the days of darkness are now over."

Akram ran off, rushed from the caves he had come to know so well, hurried back toward his village, which, in his childish mind, would still be the same as the day he had left.

"Now," Pearl said, turning to Choudry and President Thorne. "It's time to go. Are you ready to return?"

"Yes," Choudry said.

"Yes," President Thorne shouted. And tears fell from his eyes—tears of joy, tears that fell from knowing, as he lifted his hands to his face, felt each nook and cranny, that he had, at last, returned to normal.

"Yes," he said. "I'm ready."

Chapter 9

Back in Washington, the sun began its slow ascent into a cloudless blue sky still sparkling with stars and a fine sliver of moon. Rays of sunlight peeked shyly over the horizon, blushing into a deep crimson and reflecting on the calm waters along the banks of the Potomac.

As the birds stirred into wondrous song, warmly inviting the city to awaken to the uncertainty of a brand new day, as the city's residents gradually rubbed the night's dreams and delusions from their weary eyes, as the newspaper carriers loaded their delivery trucks like drones, as the priests and politicians, the white collar professionals, the lobbyists, the government clerks, the salesmen and women of the great consumer machine, the transit workers, the street peddlers, the day laborers, native and immigrant alike, as the newly and secretly sworn-in president made up her face in one of the most historical rooms in the White House (for she, herself, having made her bed in the Lincoln Bedroom, was now making history), as the citizens of this great metropolis stirred into consciousness, Reverend CJ Willis, his arms uplifted like a shepherd standing on a hillside, ready to lead his flocks to lush pastures, stood in front of the entrance of his modest Southeast mission, where the fading decal of a broken cross clung relentlessly to its grimy storefront surface.

Like Moses looking down at his tribe, he surveyed the crowds waiting breathlessly in the street for their prophet to appear. Smiling broadly, he took a deep breath of cool morning air and began:

"My dear friends and followers," he called out to the hushed silence. "God has sent me an angel."

Reverend CJ Willis, his oratorical skills honed to perfection, his voice smooth and polished, was ready now to rouse the throngs, ready to march, to lead his followers forward and claim victory. Looking down at the eager crowd, he paused to garner their anticipation, then pointed to Larry who stood beside him, like a lost child who had put his hope in the one adult who had recognized his plight and now waited anxiously to be rejoined to his loved ones.

"An angel," he continued, "disguised as a savage beast."

Weary from lack of sleep, discouraged from his futile quest for an end to his miserable condition, Larry gazed sadly at Reverend Willis, angry on the one hand at having to endure his manipulative broadsides, too drained, on the other, to do anything about it. Then he turned his heavy eyes to the crowd with a look so pitiful that their curious faces turned to sadness.

"When I first set eyes on him, my heart trembled in fear. I thought to myself that, surely, Satan himself had appeared. But then, praise the Lord, praise the Lord, I realized that God was testing me. That He was showing me that good things don't always come in beautifully wrapped packages. And hallelujah! Hallelujah! I saw the goodness that this creature had to offer me and mankind."

"Praise the Lord," the crowd shouted.

"My brothers and sisters in Jesus, the time has come for us to follow the Lord's path. To let this wretched creature—this man you now gaze upon with pity—show us the way to God's mercy. Today, God willing, on this glorious Easter Sunday, and with this good angel's assistance, we shall bask in God's grace and share in His blessings. Amen."

"Amen."

"May the Lord have mercy on us."

"Amen."

"May the Lord guide us in His grace."

"Amen."

"May the Lord see fit for us to follow on this journey."

"Amen."

"May the Lord see fit that you, my friends, bestow upon us your trust and generosity as we seek the riches only He can bestow on us."

"Amen."

"Let us now rise and go forward. To the valley of granite and steel. There, we shall all be equal in the Lord's eyes. There, we shall worship and become one. There, the Lord's grace shall shine down upon us like a bright light and, God willing, we shall enter His kingdom and bask in His goodness. May the Lord bless us with His bounty."

"Amen."

As Reverend CJ Willis concluded his homily, as Larry gazed, dazed and confused, at the crowd that now beheld him as if he were their king, as the gathering of worshippers solemnly and reverently amened to the good reverend's entreaties and raised their voices in fitful shouts of hallelujahs, a bright light appeared in the sky, a light small yet vivid. All eyes looked up, all mouths hung in silent wonder as it hovered gently above them and shone down on them like a soothing beacon. As if on cue, Reverend Willis pronounced, "The Lord has given us a light to guide us."

And with that, Reverend CJ Willis, until recently the pastor of a small neighborhood congregation, strode down into the street, his Easter surplice fluttering on the gentle morning breeze. With a reluctant, stupefied Larry at his side, he made his way to the front of the crowd and led his super-sized, instantaneous congregation toward the grounds of the National Mall.

And the bright star guided them, like a signal at sea. And it lit their way as they marched solemnly through the broken streets toward the shining, promised valley of granite and steel.

Meanwhile, over in Arlington, on the opposite side of the Roosevelt Bridge, another crowd waited eagerly: a throng of well-wishers and cure-seekers who had gathered on the front lawn of the Choudry residence to pay homage to the woman they all believed possessed the secret to health and longevity. Faithful devotees, they stood in front of the modest house, silent and reverent, anxiously anticipating the momentous emergence of Amina's stone-like body from the dilapidated wood-framed structure.

As the sun's rays twinkled over the horizon, the door to the house swung open, and the wooden dais, which Amir and Kazi had hastily put together overnight while Amina's followers were faithfully keeping vigil, emerged into the cool morning on the shoulders of six men who had been chosen to bear her.

Like the Hindu goddess Kali, she stood, perched majestically on the flat, wooden platform, crouched, as if still sitting on the faux-French couch, balanced precariously on one leg, the other folded gracefully over her knee. Her head was poised heavenward, and her glass, full of steaming tea, dangled gently from the crook of her index finger and glistened in the rays of the rising sun.

Behind Amina's petrified body, Amir appeared, dressed in a black suit and tie. Next came Kazi, proudly clad in his finest *sherwani*, made of premium, worsted wool, accompanied by Fatwa, who was wearing a colorfully patterned *jamawar lehenga*, a matching headscarf wrapped loosely around her hair, and their four children, quiet and sleepy-eyed, all in their mosque-going best.

Ever vigilant against the idolatry his brother-in-law was promoting and always ready to spread the true word of Allah, Kazi stood tall and proud, like an imam ready to lead prayer, his long beard, now trimmed but still stringy, resting gently against his chest. With his arms folded in front of him, he commanded the crowd's attention and began to speak, solemnly and ceremoniously.

"*Allahu akbar, Allahu akbar. Allahu akbar, Allahu akbar,*" he chanted, his deep voice ringing through the quiet morning. "My dear brothers and sisters in Allah," he began, and then, remembering that the individuals gathered before him were not yet Muslim, he backtracked. "My dearest brothers and sisters. We are here this morning, *insha'llah*, not to pray to an image. Not to worship rabbits and eat chocolate. Not, *alhamdulillah*, to pay our respects to this mere spectacle of a woman."

As Kazi spoke, the ground began to rumble, increasing in intensity with each word he pronounced, and Amir shot him an angry glance. Fearing his mother was about to aim her wrath at his fanatical brother-in-law, he turned to the congregation and smiled calmly.

Kazi glanced over his shoulder at his mother-in-law, perched like a stuffed bird on a makeshift stand, and nervously fingered his beard. Satisfied that she was still firmly trapped inside her ossified shell, he cleared his throat and turned back to the crowds.

"God is very great. God is very great," he began again, tentatively this time, as the rumbling decreased and he felt more assured. "God is very great. God is very great. Brothers and sisters. My dear mother-in-law, this woman you see here as a mere statue, is a wonderful, kind woman. She came to this hostile land—to this country where we Muslims are not welcome—and did her best to live a good life and raise her family. But she got lost in this... in this jungle, and has been trying ever since to find her way. Her husband has run away from her on false pretenses. And she, with all her strength, with all her faith in almighty Allah, has demonstrated her lament by the appearance you are witnessing here now."

Kazi stopped and turned to his wife for reassurance, resting his warm, brown eyes gently on hers as he had not done since their wedding night. Fatwa smiled back at him, proud of his newfound moderation and leadership, and nervously adjusted the scarf on her head.

"But," he continued, turning back to the crowd, "my mother-in-law is not a goddess. God forbid. She is not to be worshipped or set before Allah as a partner. We must not be making an idol of her, bowing down before her and paying homage with prayers and money."

Amir began to fidget. His eyes opened wide and he moved his

hands about as if he were trying to prevent himself from drowning. All his dreams of success and money—everything he had worked hard for over the past few days—were about to be destroyed by the fanatical words of his obsessive brother-in-law, an extremist who, he suddenly decided, had no right to be speaking to this crowd. Lifting his head high, he stepped forward.

"What my brother-in-law means, ladies and gentlemen," he said, struggling to reinterpret Kazi's words, "is that my dear mother has come to show us a new way. And so, as you come here to be cured of your ailments and donate generously so we can build shrines around the world and help others just like you, you should respect her for what she is: a woman with special powers that are meant to help all of mankind, regardless of religion or creed."

The ground shook more forcefully now, and all eyes turned toward Amina whose body, frozen in time, slowly moved as she wrested herself out of her solidity and stared angrily at everyone.

"Shame on you!" she scolded. "Shame on all of you!"

She gazed in disbelief, scowled at the crowds, who were bowing and prostrating themselves before her, then turned crossly to her family.

"You have made a mockery of me," she said. "You have made a mockery of Allah and all He has taught us. May Allah forgive you all you have done!"

The crowds stared fearfully at Amina. She smiled back timidly at them, then frowned, then grimaced. Then, noticing the tea glass dangling from her index finger, she curled her arm up to her lips and nervously took a loud sip of the soothing libation.

"We are not here to make fools of ourselves," she continued, "nor to make a fool of Allah. We are here to serve His will and to help those around us."

She paused to take another sip of her tea as she formulated her thoughts.

"We are nothing but sheep," she continued. "Sheep in a den of wild wolves. And God is our shepherd. Our guide and our protector."

Kazi, who had never heard his mother-in-law speak so eloquently before, fell suddenly to his knees. With the deepest fervor, he said:

"Auntie. Those are the most beautiful words I've ever heard you say."

"Silence," she shouted.

She stared angrily at her son-in-law until he turned his eyes silently and humbly to the ground. Then, inhaling the scent from her tea cup, she took another long, loud sip.

"Several days ago," she said, "my foolish—my *husband*—had a vision. And because I did not have faith in him, he ran away. But Allah has shown me my mistakes. Faith is what is lacking in today's world. Faith in ourselves. Faith in those around us. Faith in God. But, *alhamdulillah*, Allah has shown me that we are here to help one another. And if we don't understand each other's difficulties, if we don't know how to help each other through this life, we must at least try. Or else we will lose each other. And, if we lose each other, we will lose ourselves."

Murmurs of approval rose from the crowd. Amina adjusted the scarf around her head and took another long sip of her tea.

"Now," she said, "we will go. *Insha'llah*. To the valley of granite and steel. There, I believe, I will find my husband. There, I believe, we will all find what we are looking for."

A long silence followed. Amir waited to see if his mother was finished. Satisfied, he looked to the crowd and quickly said: "Amen!"

"Amen!" the crowd responded.

"*Amin!*" Kazi shouted, rising up from the ground. "It's *Amin*."

Standing atop her dais, Amina morphed back to the same calcified position she had assumed since the day her husband had disappeared. A ray of sunshine cast its light on her shiny tea glass, forming a shaft of light that extended down to the sidewalk and pointed forward like a beam from a lighthouse.

"Look!"

Fatwa pointed to the light and understood. Gathering her children around her, she turned toward Amir and Kazi, and with a firm look of conviction, led the marchers forward.

The goings-on at the White House, though less lofty in nature, were nonetheless filled with pomp and purpose. As agreed, Bella's cabinet members (not hers, she kept insisting, for she would never have chosen such an insipid group of individuals, would dismiss them as soon as she had a chance, she promised herself, crossing her legs like a proper lady and waiting for the last of President Thorne's tedious counselors to appear), these secretaries and bureau chiefs gathered ceremoniously in the Oval Office just before dawn as planned, dressed in their church-going best, ready to descend on the National Mall to observe what they could, as they were bid to do by their newly sworn-in leader. And though ready to execute her orders, their demeanor and the vapid look on their heavy-eyed faces indicated their lack of faith in what they considered to be a fruitless and uncalled for diversion.

Sitting at the presidential desk with a presidential smile smeared across her weary face (for she had not slept the whole night, had quickly discovered that the Lincoln bedroom was not all that it was cracked up to be, had sat up instead, practicing her presidential gestures and perfecting her presidential walk), she nervously drummed her dark red fingernails against the hard, wooden surface, gathered her thoughts in a mind that was less than clear, and put on a guise of calm and patience to mask her annoyance with the Secretary of Homeland Security, who had not yet arrived.

"Madam President," Drove said, letting out a sigh that betrayed his disdain for the current situation (*how,* he thought to himself, *could he wake up one day and find that the opposition had taken over, just like that?*) and his uncertainty as to how to address the first female president ("madam" seemed too lofty, too French, and then, smiling to himself as he recognized the tawdry innuendo, he decided that, yes, it was indeed the perfect salutation). "*Madam* President," he repeated resolutely, a huge smile eating up his smallish face, "if you will excuse my ignorance," he said, "I fail to fully understand the exact purpose of this expedition."

"Really, Mr. Drove," Bella responded. "I'm quite surprised."

She scratched the edge of her mouth with her manicured fingernail (a French manicure, no less, Drove noted, with a deep coat of polish to contrast with the pastel suit she was wearing).

"I would think," she continued, "that you would have more interest in finding the former president."

She smiled, with just a slight air of triumph. Drove looked at her as if he were looking through a glass of water; her face was clear, yet unfathomable, and he could not be certain whether she really believed they would find the president (for to him, he was still the president) right under their noses, or whether this was a ruse meant to buy time while she and her allies consolidated power.

"Ms. Stromb—" he started. "Madam President. We have every appropriate agency working on this. Surely you don't doubt their abilities. Surely you don't mean to put all of us in a compromising position. I mean, we could all be taken out in one fell swoop."

"Mr. Drove," Bella responded, coolly. "You and your agencies have had a week to resolve this crisis. A week in which the American people—in which Congress itself has been kept in the dark."

She stopped a moment to let this last remark sink in. Drove observed her closely, as if he were looking through a jeweler's eye, as if she were an abstract painting, for despite her appearance of polish and composure, none of the parts added up.

"I am a woman, Mr. Drove," Bella continued, "in case you hadn't noticed. And women have intuition. And I truly believe that by attending this Easter service that the reverend you mentioned is holding today, we are going to discover something that none of your agencies so far have learned."

Candice Brice, who until now had been sitting quietly with her hands oddly placed in her lap, began to twitch in her seat. Not one to remain silent, she was trying to decide whether to speak up; not one to mince words, she suddenly found herself, after at last having made her decision, shredding and chopping her phrases and sentences as she wrestled with her natural affinity toward a woman who, like herself, had struggled to make it, and her dislike for this particular individual and the political philosophy she espoused.

"Madam President," she said. "I am a woman, as well. I, too, have intuition. But..." And here she lost her train of thought, was left hanging as if the ladder she had spent her career climbing had suddenly been pulled out from under her.

"Ms. Brice," Bella said impatiently.

"The point is," she said. And again, she could not gather her thoughts, was left speechless and helpless and utterly disconcerted.

Bella watched with a slight curl in her smile as Brice wiggled and waggled in her chair like a self-conscious schoolgirl. Then her eyes fell on Brice's lap where the vice president, a mere mouse, sat resting comfortably. Detecting the silence and embarrassment in his self-appointed caretaker, he raised his head, wiggled his mouth, and scurried about in Brice's lap, stopping to observe each and every one in the room. Setting his beady eyes on Bella, he stood up on his hind legs, licked his front paws, and began to hiss rabidly.

"Ms. Brice," Bella said, suppressing a chill that scaled her spine. "Please keep that *thing* out of sight."

"That *'thing,'*" Brice responded with a look of annoyance, "happens to be the vice president."

"*I* will decide who the vice president is."

Bella's tone was icy and her eyes pierced the room.

"Times have changed, Ms. Brice. This is a new day for America, a new—"

But before Bella could continue, the vice president let out a loud rabid hiss and lunged. Leaping into the air and spitting through his teeth, he landed directly in Bella's perfectly coifed hairdo and dug his claws deep into her scalp.

Bella jumped up and yelped as the members of her cabinet (not hers, she pleaded, please not hers) rushed to her aid. Taking a deep breath to calm herself, she closed her eyes, then opened them and looked angrily at Brice.

"Kindly remove the vice president from my hair, Ms. Brice," she said.

Brice reached for the vice president, but the mangy little mouse hissed vehemently at her and she quickly withdrew her hand and retreated.

"I'm afraid he has no intention of leaving," she said, and she grinned a grin that bared her perfectly straight and brilliantly white teeth.

Bella took another slow, deep breath and attempted to focus. She would not let these insidious individuals ruin her plans, and she would certainly not let a scurrilous little rodent stand in her way.

"Very well," she said. "If that's the way you want it. If that's the way *he* wants it, then so be it."

And with that, Bella quickly reached for the corner of her desk, swiftly retrieved her Easter bonnet, a newly purchased straw hat with a wide brim and a spray of silk springtime flowers, and clapped it down over her head, trapping the vice president inside.

At that moment, as President Bella Stromberg assumed a calm, innocent smile, as her finest Easter bonnet jiggled and joggled on top of her head, as the secretaries and bureau chiefs watched in wonder at the spectacle that was taking place before their eyes, the door to the Oval Office opened and the Secretary of Homeland Security entered, wearing a black yarmulke and a prayer shawl around his shoulders and holding a well-used prayer book in his hand.

"Just in time," Bella said in a clear, steady voice.

She batted her eyes and smiled. Calmly adjusting her bonnet, she retrieved a straight pin from the depths of her purse and jabbed it through to secure it firmly, poking the whimpering mouse of a vice president in the process. Glancing around the room, she smiled, with just a touch of self-satisfaction, and said to the good Jewish secretary, "We were just about to leave for Mass."

Chapter 10

FATWA FOLLOWED THE NARROW BEAM OF LIGHT glowing from Amina's tea glass and led her mother's star-struck followers— the sick, the needy, the lost and crippled, the homeless and the indigent, all of whom had come to be saved and cured, coddled and cared for—down the neat and tidy Arlington streets, down through the luminous morning that had burst across the greater metropolitan area. Amir marched by her side, tall and proud, while their drowsy children tagged along, sleepy-eyed and yawning, yearning to be back in their warm, comfortable beds. Bursting with piety, Kazi reluctantly followed beside them, clutching his prayer beads in his right hand and mumbling stringent supplications of praise and forgiveness.

With Amina perched high in the air like a contorted ballerina, teeter-tottering on her wobbly wooden dais, they crossed the Potomac River, marched resolutely across the Roosevelt Bridge, wielding candles and incense burners whose trails of smoke reached up to the heavens, towing and tugging a small, stubborn herd of bleating sheep and lowing cows, and made their way down along Constitution

Avenue, pursuing the glowing light that guided them steadily toward the enigmatic valley of granite and steel.

Amina's rigid body bobbed in rhythm to the footsteps of the six ushers who reverently transported her, while her fervent devotees followed behind, clutching vials of her sacred teardrops close to their hearts, beating their breasts in solemn contrition, and repeating the chants that Amir shouted from his strident bullhorn.

"All praise to Amina!"

"All praise to Amina!"

"Welcome, O Queen!"

"Welcome, O Queen!"

"O healer! O giver of life!"

"O healer! O giver of life!"

"May the Divine One grant you peace and well-being!"

"May the Divine One grant you peace and well-being!"

Kazi countered these blasphemous outcries with desperate exclamations of *Allahu akbar* and attempted to transform their unholy mantras into proper praises of God, but his voice grew scratchy and hoarse, and he was soon drowned out by Amina's spellbound disciples and by the competing prayers and supplications of the countless assemblies converging simultaneously on Constitution Avenue and marching in droves through the jam-packed streets.

Kazi watched in amazement as the crowds teemed and swelled, choking the streets like swarms of ants. He hadn't seen such multitudes since his pilgrimage to Mecca some years before, and he fingered his prayer beads and marveled at how similar these throngs of unbelievers seemed to the faithful pilgrims who converged on the holy city each year. But instead of arriving at the most sacred place on the earth, they were gathering instead at the very heart of western decadence—the center of capitalism and consumerism and secular tyranny.

"If only they were Muslims!" he shouted into the deafening din.

Exasperated, he raised his hands and shook them furiously in the air and begged for Allah's forgiveness. No, he corrected himself, they were not at all like pilgrims. They were more like animals, like flocks of birds, lost in the midst of their migration, coming together, disoriented and confused, and wondering how to reach their final destination. Yes, that was much better, he said to himself, relieved, childlike, satisfied. And his face beamed with piety, with self-righteousness, and he marched and chanted praises to Allah, fingered his prayer beads feverishly, and wondered how he had gotten himself into this irreverent situation, he, a devout Muslim, who had spent his entire life in the praise and worship of almighty Allah.

When they arrived at last at the National Mall, every inch of the vast lawn was crammed with worshippers and spectators, oohing and ahhing and staring in wonder at the newest monument to have risen at the center of American culture: a huge, fully-inflated plastic cathedral, towering high before them like a giant Moon Bounce. Kazi gazed, his mouth wide open, his beard flittering on the morning breeze, as the improbable structure quivered in the rising sun from the rush of air that kept it afloat. Majestic and imposing, its bright colors glowed hypnotically in the brightening sunrise, a remarkable, spectacular monument with soaring walls of neon orange and towering steeples of vibrant yellow.

"Allah," Kazi murmured, overcome by its magnificence and fascinated by its marvelous design.

The crowds converged on the fluttering church like bees drawn to a mysterious hive, and solemnly entered, climbing up through its swollen portals, mesmerized, immune to the possibility that, should the air pumps suddenly stop, they would all quickly perish inside.

Overcome with emotion, Kazi lapsed into irreverence and once again remembered the *Hajj. Were these people not moved by the same feelings?* he wondered. *Did they not have the same depth of fervor? The same profound faith?* Then he stopped himself, raised his hands in supplication, and chastised himself like a child for his sinful thoughts. Turning to Fatwa, he shouted over the clamor. "We must leave this place at once."

Fatwa looked away and proceeded as if he had not spoken. Maintaining her steady pace and ignoring his stubborn demand, she raised her head high and forged ahead, a fearless commander—a veritable Joan of Arc—leading her troops to glory.

Amina's petrified body floated gracefully as they made their way through the crowds, an implausible statue, a sublime symbol of hope and transcendence that attracted more and more faith seekers over to their side.

"I demand that we leave at once!" Kazi shouted adamantly to his wife. His face was a shriveled ball of anger, and he aimed his angry eyes straight at her and pointed a bony finger.

Amir lowered his bullhorn and glanced apprehensively at his sister, then hollered over the deafening din. "This must be it," he shouted. "The valley of granite and steel."

"But where do we go?" Fatwa asked.

"Straight ahead," Amir answered, pointing to the orange and yellow cathedral.

"To a church?" Kazi shouted. "We are going to a church?"

"Kazi," Fatwa shouted angrily.

"Are we not Muslims?" Kazi protested again. "Do we not have our own place of worship? Allah forgive us! We cannot enter a church! I refuse."

But as he protested, the earth trembled, and the more he objected, the stronger the rumbling became, until a loud voice broke through the noise and commanded, "March on!"

And so they did. They marched toward the colossal, colorful cathedral, marched as the crowd behind them grew larger and larger, chanting *All Praise to Amina*, clutching their precious vials, beating their remorseful breasts, and staring blindly at the enormous, hypnotic Moon Bounce of a church.

And the multitudes trailed behind, followed Amina dressed in her bright orange sari, as she stared blankly toward the sky with her cup full of steaming tea dangling from her index finger, through which glowed a narrow beam of intense light. And though Kazi continued to protest, though he railed against the idolaters around him and extolled the teachings of the one true religion, he did so in much more muted tones so as not to further invoke the wrath of his errant mother-in-law.

Making their way among the thick, teeming crowds, they headed toward the main entrance to The Portable Inflatable Blazing Path of Light Ebenezer Baptist Church, LLC, a garish neon sign blatantly announcing its presence above the doorway.

Holding out his hands in supplication and begging forgiveness with multiple *Astaghfirullahs*, Kazi respectfully removed his shoes and climbed through the huge quivering portal.

Inside, he watched as the crowds streamed in through the arched entrances of the plastic structure. Catching themselves as the ground below them bounced from the force of the air pumps, they carefully navigated the shifting floor, swayed like boats on the open sea in hopes of being transported to a new level of spiritual awakening. Like children at a spectacle, they gawked at the brightly colored chandeliers that dangled from the vaulted ceiling, marveled at the replicated gothic columns that embellished the precarious structure and helped support its weight and gazed at the stained cellophane windows through which the morning sun filtered, casting multi-colored shadows on its already vibrant walls and on the members of this swiftly gathering congregation.

Then, the sudden vibrato of an organ filled the church, its hollow strands of music producing sounds that would never have been heard in a mosque. And, out of nowhere, a choir burst into jubilant song:

I stood on the river of Jordan
To see that ship come sailing by
Stood on the river of Jordan
O, see that ship sail by

"Worse than rabbits and chocolate!" Kazi shouted in disgust.

Unable to control himself any longer and hoping to bring reason to this assembly of bewildered souls, he shouted as loudly as he could: "Can't you see the error of your ways? Reject this idolatry and come to the true path of Allah!"

But his desperate cries were lost to the sound of the choir, the steady drone of the air pumps and the gasps of wonder and shouts of joy, as the crowd admired their new house of worship and anxiously anticipated the glorious service they had come to attend. With clapping hands and stomping feet, they joined in the singing, swaying to the rhythm of the air pumps, as new arrivals continually flocked into the already crowded church, kneeling and bowing on the bouncing elastic floor, lifting their arms and shouting cries of hallelujah.

"And they call this religion!" Kazi lamented.

Meanwhile, outside on Independence Avenue, a fanfare of sirens crescendoed as Bella Stromberg's official motorcade arrived.

"President Bella Stromberg, if you please" she chimed with a radiant smile as she disembarked from the presidential limousine and posed for reporters. "And this," she added with a slight curl of her hand, "is my entourage."

Surrounded by Secret Service and closely followed by President Thorne's coterie ("Not mine," she insisted to the press with a sigh. "The sooner I can replace them, the better."), she paraded like a model, marched across the great lawn in her high-heeled shoes and strode awkwardly into the bouncing cathedral, her head held high, her patrician smile firmly in place, a woman who had made it, fortuitously, to the top, a woman who drew every eye upon her as she climbed inside the fluttering structure.

Dressed in a mauve skirt with a fresh corsage fastened to her twill suit jacket, she batted her eyes incessantly and waved presidentially at the crowds as they turned to get a glimpse of the remarkable looking woman who had suddenly appeared, who proceeded carefully down the winding aisle like a tightrope performer navigating a thin length of rope, who struggled to balance herself on the pointy stilettos she had chosen to match her impeccably pressed suit.

"Remember," she whispered to Mark Drove as she grabbed on to his pinstriped suit to steady herself, "follow your instincts. For once," she added, and shot him a glance that caught him off guard, "try to think like a woman."

Drove staggered down the aisle like an unwilling groom, his arm curled tightly around hers, his legs wobbly from the moving floor. Warily navigating the wavy passageway, he turned his face toward hers and grinned as her Easter bonnet, fastened with multiple straight pins to restrain the agitated vice president ("the *former* vice president," Bella reminded herself smugly as he hissed under her floral hat and dug his claws further into her scalp), budged this way and that.

At the front of the church, in the very first pew on which was scotch-taped a makeshift sign marked "VIP's," Bella and her reluctant entourage took their seats as Reverend CJ Willis stepped out onto the altar clutching a golden scepter in his right hand (a secondhand walking stick he had picked up at a neighborhood thrift shop) and wearing the finest Easter surplice he could rent. "No need," he had confided to Larry, "to pay good money for something to be worn only once."

Like Jesus on the Mount, he looked out onto the congregation, his arms outstretched, his eyes gleaming in the rays of colored light that filtered down on him through the cellophane stained-glass.

Surveying the jam-packed cathedral, his face beamed like the morning sun. He was pleased with the turnout. He was pleased when his eyes lit upon the dazzling Bella Stromberg sitting royally with her stunning Easter bonnet teetering jubilantly back and forth. He was pleased when he observed her venerable-looking entourage balancing themselves on their seats in the front row, and at the man in the yarmulke, grasping his prayer shawl as he sat down as if he were fearful of losing it. He was pleased that the media had come with their cameras. And he was pleased when he beheld Amina's statue-like body, perched ethereally on its wooden platform, wending its way down the aisle and through the crowds as if floating in thin air, clutching her dangling tea glass through which shone a single ray of blazing light. And though he did not know who any of these individuals were, he understood that he had succeeded in attracting the most diverse group of people he could, given the short notice. and he raised his hand and thanked God for his skill and his training, and imagined the accolades that awaited him as a result of his tireless efforts.

Larry stood on the altar beside his self-appointed caretaker, dazed as a sojourner lost in the wilderness. Looking out into the crowded church, he stared incredulously and shouted, "Damn!"

As he tried to calm himself, as he tried to focus instead on his horrid condition, which he knew would take his mind off his fears, the congregation silenced into a hush and waited for their newly-proclaimed messiah—the one who had been touted in the fliers Reverend Willis had posted all around town—to speak. And they stared in wonder, and anxiously awaited his sublime words. But their wonder soon turned to disappointment, and their disappointment to disillusion, and they soon began to mumble and stir.

And then, angry voices arose from the crowd. For, unbeknownst to Larry, his face had returned to normal and, rather than the monstrous-looking creature they had come to witness, the sublime individual who embodied their hopes and dreams, who spoke in multiple voices and spouted riddles that dazzled and confused, they beheld instead an ordinary looking man, a normal human being they could have met anywhere on the streets or seen on the six o'clock news.

As the shouting increased, Larry hid his face fearfully in his hands and stood trembling before the angry worshippers. For the first time in his life, he was truly afraid, and he reached back into his memory for words of comfort from his childhood, tried to remember a prayer his Aunt had taught him, words that had never held much meaning but that he now muttered with the utmost sense of urgency.

Reverend Willis was so busy surveying the crowds and congratulating himself that he did not take notice of Larry's transformation back to normalcy, but as the crowds clamored, he recognized that something was terribly wrong and he rushed up to the pulpit, spread his arms out to gather their attention and quell their anger, and shouted in a voice that resonated above the cacophony.

"Brother and sisters. Welcome. Welcome to worship."

The church fell into silence as Reverend Willis' amplified voice echoed throughout the inflated structure.

"Jesus welcomes you," he said. "Jesus welcomes you to His church and to His celebration of renewal."

Kazi fingered his beard and listened curiously to Reverend Willis, watched with skepticism and with surprise, and noted the similarity between the reverend's words and the tone he was used to hearing during Friday prayer. But though the message may have been similar, the means to it was not, and he got a hold of himself, and begged God for forgiveness and shouted, in a loud voice that bounced off the plastic walls of the church, *"Allahu akbar."*

Hearing this utterance, Reverend Willis lowered his arms and scanned the congregation, his eyes resting on Amina's statue-like presence, her dangling cup of tea steaming like an incense burner.

"Jesus welcomes you, sister," he said to her. Then, looking around the congregation, he exclaimed: "Jesus welcomes each and every one of you to His house of worship. For Jesus is the Lord of the universe."

"*Allahu akbar*," Kazi shouted again. "Can't you see the error of your ways?"

This time, Reverend Willis spotted Kazi standing beside Amina's dais in his off-white *sherwani* and skull cap, tall and majestic and fingering his long, stringy white beard.

"My dear brother," he said to him, "we are all sinners in God's eyes. But Jesus is Lord. That's why we must worship Him. That's why we must accept Him as our Savior."

Kazi eyed Reverend Willis suspiciously. He wanted to launch into his own sermon on the teachings of God, wanted to lecture him on the temptation to worship false idols, of giving into erroneous beliefs and lapsing into heresy but, at that moment, a bright glow appeared at the top of the church and all eyes moved upwards toward the vaulted ceiling where the figure of a woman slowly emerged. Hovering peacefully in the air, her stomach slightly swollen, she smiled down warmly at the crowd of worshippers, her hands spread out in a gentle, comforting gesture.

"Allah," Kazi cried out. "Save me from this show of idolatry!"

The congregation, though, was appeased now, for they had come here to be moved, to be dazzled, to be delivered from their mundane lives and transported into a higher realm of existence. Hopeful now, their wishes on the brink of being fulfilled, they broke out into spontaneous praises and bellowed "Hallelujah!"

Larry, who was still covering his face in fear, slowly removed his hands and looked up.

"Pearl!" he shouted, holding back his tears. "Pearl, baby. You've come back to me."

Bathed in a bright light, Pearl slowly descended from the arched ceiling of the inflated cathedral, down toward the center of the altar where her husband waited blissfully. The crowds looked on in silence, and the only sound that could be heard was Kazi's quiet Astaghfirullahs as he peeked fearfully through his fingers and wondered how he had come to find himself in this place of witches and jinns.

As Pearl gently landed on the altar, the light she was bathed in gradually faded, and two figures emerged, one on each side of her: President Thorne, his face now whole, gazing apprehensively into the packed church, his fear of crowds now returning in full force, and Choudry, his big belly protruding through his wrinkled pajama shirt, looking around uncomprehendingly, like someone suddenly awakened from a sleepwalker's trance.

Except for the sound of the humming air pumps, the church was silent, and the worshippers stared in wonder at the three angels who had just descended from heaven. Then, a loud rumbling arose, and the fluttering church shook even more as Amina slowly stretched out her arms and emerged from her state of petrifaction. Looking around as if she had just arrived to a foreign land, she climbed off her dais and shuffled her way up to the altar like a pilgrim after a long and arduous journey.

"Choudry?" she said, as she approached her husband and blinked her eyes. "Is it you?"

"Amina," he shouted with a great big smile.

His eyes filled with tears, but he lowered them to the floor as Amina's recalcitrant look twisted into a scowl.

"Choudry," she scolded. "Where have you been?"

Choudry couldn't answer. He didn't know how to explain the miraculous journey he had been on. How, he thought, would she believe him when he himself did not believe the things that had happened? And so he stared at the ground in silence, gazed at his feet like a child incapable of assuaging his mother's anger.

"Just like I thought," Amina said at last. "Running around with a strange woman. Acting foolishly. Allah knows where you've been and what you've been up to!"

"Amina. Believe me. It's not what you think."

"Not what I think? You should be ashamed of yourself. Running off with this woman and abandoning your children. Choudry. Look at me. Have I been a bad wife?"

"Amina, please. Not in front of everyone."

"Not in front of everyone?" she said incredulously.

She turned around and looked at the crowded church. Unfazed, she turned to Pearl, took note of her swollen belly and said: "What have you been doing with my husband?"

Before Pearl could answer, President Thorne stepped forward. And though his legs were trembling with fear as he looked apprehensively at the large crowd, and though he felt as if his knees would buckle under him and fail, he placed his hand firmly on Choudry's shoulder and, looking straight at Amina, said in a loud, clear voice:

"This man, my dear woman—your husband—is a true blue American hero." And turning to Choudry, he said: "Heckuva job, my friend."

Amina scanned him from top to bottom as if he were a discarded dishcloth.

"And who in Allah's name are you?" she said.

At these words, the trembling in President Thorne's body miraculously ceased. Until now, he had assumed that everyone knew who he was, that, wherever he went, he would be immediately and unquestionably recognized. This woman, with her direct style and her simple statements, was now making him reassess that assumption. He put his hands to his face, felt each spot to make sure he was whole again, opened his mouth and moved his jaw from side to side. Then he looked sadly at Amina. Quietly and with the utmost humility, he said: "I am the president of the United States."

Quiet though they were, the words echoes through the inflated cathedral. The congregation gasped, and the anguished mutterings of Charlotte Wentforth Melloncourt Thorne ("This is most embarrassing, how inconvenient, how utterly thoughtless...") could be distinctly heard above the astonished din.

"Charlie?" President Thorne said, scanning the congregation for the First Lady's familiar face. But instead of his wife, his eyes fell immediately on Bella Stromberg, his longtime opponent, swaying in the front pew to the motion of the air pumps, her face frozen in shock, as if she had just found her husband with another woman. Her hat, showy and tasteless, just like her party, was moving around as if it were about to take off. Seated around her were his cabinet members, the ones who had sworn loyalty to him, looking at him as if they had abdicated their allegiance, their faces as blank and lifeless as storefront mannequins.

The Secret Service rushed up to the altar, but President Thorne put up his hand for them to stop, and the look of confusion on his small, narrow face turned into a sullen gaze of sadness.

"Allah," Amina said, breaking the silence. "And this is how you rule your country? Running off with foolish people and doing God-knows-what?"

"Amina," Choudry begged.

"Don't 'Amina' me," she scolded, turning to her husband. "All my life, I have listened to you. Obeyed your orders. Cooked and cleaned. Raised your children. And all without objection. Haven't I done that? Haven't I been faithful to you? Why, Choudry? Why? Why do you persist in acting so... selfishly?"

Amina adjusted the scarf on her head. Gesturing to the congregation with an outstretched hand, she looked at her husband and said in a calm, strong voice, "These people have come here to see better than this. Better than you. Better than this so-called president. Better than all the mockery you see here on display today."

Amina turned to the crowd and, with a look of consternation, said, "You cannot find happiness here. You cannot cure yourselves with all of this show. You must do it all from within. God wants it that way."

Choudry looked up at his wife as she spoke and his face beamed with pride. He had never heard her express herself so clearly, so eloquently before, and he understood that the simple woman he had been married to for so long—the one he had brought straight from the village - was not as simple as he had made himself believe.

"Amina," he said, when she was finished, when her words were answered by a quiet, unconvinced silence in the cathedral. "I want to go home. Uncle," he said, pointing to President Thorne, "wants to go home."

And for the first time in many years, Amina saw the sparkle in her husband's eyes. She noticed the kind smile on his chubby face, heard the gentle tone of his aging voice, a tone she had not heard in many a year. And she understood that the man she had married had now returned to her. She understood that she had been wrong to accuse him, and she knew that, no matter what, he would never do anything to hurt anyone, especially her. She had not, after all, been married to him all these years for nothing. A wife knows. And when a wife knows, she knows she is never wrong. But instead of smiling, she adjusted her orange headscarf and, taking notice of the tea glass on her finger, she took a silent sip of tea and said with just a slight look of annoyance,

"Home? You want to go home? All right. Then let's go home. But on the way, you must pass by the shop and get me some meat so I can cook your dinner."

"Yes, dear."

"I have not had a proper meal in days. And no dilly-dallying."

"Yes, dear."

"And don't forget the spices!"

"Yes, dear."

"He always forgets the spices!"

Then, turning to Pearl, she said, "If you have a husband, I suggest you get back to him. As quickly as possible. Husbands are like trees. You need to care for them or the fruit will become wormy."

Pearl turned to Larry and beamed like a schoolgirl. She had missed him during her flight into the ether, had feared she would never return to him again. Now, as he approached her with a look she had not seen in years and put his strong, gentle arms around her, she blushed and placed her hand on her swollen belly.

"Pearl, baby," Larry said. "Let's go home."

"Yes, Larry," she said. "Let's go home."

And Larry, who had not felt whole since the morning he woke up and found himself burdened with two mouths, kissed his wife in a way that made the entire congregation blush.

Just then, two of the most remarkable events occurred, events that would forever change the course of the nation's history.

Bella Stromberg, the remarkable, stylish woman who had fought her way to the top, who, until now, had sat silently through the spontaneous reunions that had taken place on the altar, let out a sudden and indisputably loud sigh of anguish, for she suddenly realized that she was no longer the president and, what was worse, that the most inept individual to ever lead the country (*an utter moron*, she thought to herself, in between hyperventilated gasps, *unable to even synchronize his left foot with his right*) was now back in charge.

Yelping like a mad dog as she tried to come to terms with this instantaneous reality, she stomped her high heel shoes against the plastic floor until the tip of her stiletto broke through the thick, shiny layers of the inflated church and created a loud, hollow pop that echoed through the chamber and was followed by a loud rush of air.

At the very same time, as the hissing increased, the vice president who, upon hearing President Thorne's voice, had become ever more agitated, finally managed to loosen the pins that Bella had used to secure her Easter bonnet and, lunging off her head, scurried down the aisle on his tiny feet toward the altar, creating an instant commotion among the already overtaxed and bewildered worshippers.

As the cathedral abruptly deflated, and as the cries of "Mouse!" filled the air, a panic ensued, and the crowds jostled and heaved and rushed toward the exits, as quickly as the shrinking, bouncing structure would allow.

"Come back!" Reverend Willis cried desperately. "The Easter service is about to begin!"

But Reverend Willis' pleas were ignored, and as the crowds dispersed, they punctured more and more holes into the sides of The Portable Inflatable Blazing Path of Light Ebenezer Baptist Church, LLC, which swiftly deflated and soon lay in the middle of the National Mall, a mere mass of plastic spread out like a giant melted, multicolored ice cube.

Epilogue

In a remote region of the Hindu Kush Mountains, in a tiny village called Kandamesh, a holiday had been declared, and the villagers were rushing about in preparation. *Tandoor* ovens spat out flames as bakers flipped steaming discs of bread inside their cavernous mouths. Freshly slaughtered lambs, stuffed with herbs and rice, their thick soft skin set aside for later use, roasted on open fires, emitting aromas that wafted throughout the mountainous village. And mounds of silken, steaming rice, gently laced with cardamom and saffron, were piled on large silver platters like beads of gleaming pallid pearls.

As if it were *Eid*, the feast following the month of sacrifice and fasting, strings of green and white lights had been twirled around the adobe mosque, the tallest structure in the village, and hung loosely along the sides of the slender minaret. And though it was only *asr*, the late afternoon when the day comes to its second life after the midday heat has subsided, their light radiated vibrantly despite the blazing sun that burned bright in the western sky.

Not since anyone could remember—not since the elders had been born, not since their parents had married, not since their grandparents had arranged for their blessed union—had the village known such joy or experienced such hope. Tongues wagged, extolling Akram's bravery; women praised his strength, men his accomplishments, and girls, not quite ripe for marriage, bantered as they helped their mothers with the preparations, wondering out loud who the lucky bride would someday be, each secretly eager she would be the one.

In the valley, on the outskirts of the village, where the villagers herded goats and tended crops each day, children ran freely, gathering flowers and stringing garlands. And in the thatched huts that dotted the valley like carelessly strewn pine cones, the village women, normally somber in appearance, put on their finest, embroidered dresses, donned vibrant, bejeweled headscarves, stained their eyes with thick strokes of dark-blue kohl, and tinted their hands with intricate patterns of amber henna.

In the center of the village, the men, wearing their finest white robes, patiently passed time at the local teashop. With white turbans swirled on top of their heads or black *karakul* hats pointing to the high heavens, they smoked hookah, drank minted tea, played backgammon, and waited for the festivities to begin.

And for the first time many could remember, they laughed—laughed like only free men can laugh—laughed openly and whole-heartedly. For with the death of Sharir, a dark pall had finally been lifted from their lives, and the villagers who, until recently, had known nothing but fear, now gathered up all the joy that had been suppressed decade upon decade, and put it on full display as if they were showing off their prized sheep.

At last, the sound of flutes and tambourines filled the village square, and a procession, led by the village elders seated atop donkeys festooned in multi-colored coverlets, slowly made its way through the center of the tiny town. Akram followed, donned in an intricately patterned *chapan*, riding, like a prince, on the finest camel, decked in hand-made, gold-trimmed covers. The village children danced and tossed flowers, and the women greeted him with jubilant ululations.

Akram felt like a hero and looked like a king. But tradition forced him to put away his pride, and he smiled modestly at the villagers and humbly accepted their show of thanks. Inside he was bursting with joy, and his handsome face shone as if it had just been buffed and polished. He was free at last, he kept thinking to himself, barely believing it, had defeated the evil one, had been rejoined with his family and was ready to resume the life he had been deprived of for several years. He waved at the villagers, lowering his eyes at the young maidens who gazed at him, peeking demurely from behind their silver-trimmed veils.

The festivities lasted for three days. Each day, lambs were slaughtered and roasted, goats and water buffalo were milked and rice was rinsed, laced with spices and cooked. Each day, the villagers donned a new set of clothes, clothes normally reserved for weddings, clothes which had been kept in storage for many a joyless year. Each afternoon, the lights on the mosque were lit, the singing and dancing resumed, and Akram was treated like a hero, paraded around town on the shoulders of his fellow villagers and praised for his strength and bravery.

When the celebrations were over, when the village returned at last to its normal way of life, the women removed their makeup and gold and went back to working the fields, and the men put on their everyday clothes and went about their daily business. The village baker baked his bread. The local imam called the faithful to prayer at the five appointed times. The older children returned to their flocks, and the younger ones to their play.

Life was peaceful. No longer did the people of Kandamesh fear the wrath of Sharir, no longer did they worry about their houses being destroyed or their children being snatched away from them. Eventually they forgot all about the evil wizard, and their fears were replaced with the daily concerns of life: who their daughters would marry, whether the rain would be sufficient that year, who would replace the village *omda* who had recently died from a sudden affliction.

Akram, meanwhile, settled back into his new life. Each day, he did the things he had done before his father had bargained him away to the evil one. Together with his brothers, he herded their flock of sheep and roamed the valleys and hills freely, as he had done before. He played his flute and sang wistful songs. And he dreamed of marriage and the family he would one day have.

But eventually, his thoughts began to drift, and memories of his days in Sharir's mountainous citadel overwhelmed him like drowsy dreams, enveloping him in their mysterious arms and taking him back to places that now seemed somehow appealing, that gradually lost all the odious associations he had once had while being kept captive there. He began to miss the caves he had explored while gathering herbs for Sharir's magic. He thought of the great fireplace where he would warm himself on cold nights, fall asleep after his chores were finished, or simply stare at as he dreamed of his freedom. And he felt a strange yearning to sit before its cavernous mouth and gaze into its furious flames.

And then he began to think of Sharir and, while his mind cringed as he remembered his severe, shriveled face, he began to recall the magic he had been slowly teaching him, the magic that, however steeped in evil it might have been, was tempting and intriguing. And every once in a while, he would put his hand in his pocket and clutch the magic stone he still kept with him at all times.

Soon, while he was herding his sheep, he began to slip away from his flocks and wander up to the mountains, making his way to his former place of captivity. There, he would delve into Sharir's books, lose himself in the evil one's notes and practice the magic he had come to love. At first, he would stay there for a day or two, going unnoticed by his friends and family. But soon the temptation seized him with the addiction of a drug, wrapped its long slender fingers around his mind, and his sojourns began to grow to a week, then a fortnight.

When he returned home, his parents would look at him without saying a word, then turn their eyes down in silent shame. And while they would never question him or reprimand him for abandoning his flock, they would stare at him strangely, quietly, for they knew somehow that something was terribly wrong, sensed that their son was slowly drifting away, becoming something they could neither understand nor control.

Akrams's father would finish his prayers and quietly beg God for forgiveness. He knew he was responsible for everything that had happened to his son, and he understood that he was slowly losing him. Akram's mother would sit by the light of the fire, mending clothes or tending to her daughters, crying quietly, wondering what would become of the child who had been kept prisoner for so long.

During this time, Akram befriended a boy named Wahid. He was a year or two younger than Akram, had bright green eyes that sparkled with alertness, and a kind, gentle smile that reminded Akram of the boy he had once been, long before he had been bargained away. Wahid would follow Akram to the fields, and everyday he would sit and listen attentively as Akram told him of his time in the evil wizard's citadel. His curiosity led to questions, and his questions to secret demonstrations of knowledge that all in the village would have frowned upon, had they known. And soon, Akram was teaching him simple acts of magic that sent thrills of joy and pride up and down his spine as he watched his apprentice grow in expertise.

"You have great potential," Akram said to him one day.

He smiled at Wahid. But it was not a normal smile. It was a smile that exhibited an aura of blankness, and behind that blankness was an enormous sense of greed, a feeling that he could possess Wahid if he wanted, bend him to his will and fashion him into whatever he wanted, like one would take a piece of wood and shape it into a cane or a bowl or a child's toy.

"This must be our secret," he said to Wahid one day, while they lay in the field. "You must never tell anyone."

"Yes, *Agha*," Wahid answered, addressing his friend with respect.

"One day," Akram continued, "I will teach you everything I know and, together, we will be the greatest magicians in the world."

He laughed innocently. It was just a game, he kept telling himself, as he wiped away the evil thoughts that kept creeping into his head. Just two boys dreaming up a fantasy that would dissipate into thin air just as sure as their youth someday would.

"Yes, *Agha*," Wahid answered waking Akram from his reverie.

Then Wahid rose, knelt, bowed his head, and kissed Akram's hand. Akram turned his head toward the mountains where the call of Sharir's caves echoed, summoning him.

Eventually, Akram and Wahid went to the citadel and never returned. Eventually, black clouds formed once again above the mountain that housed the underground caves, and occasional bouts of lightning and thunder shook the earth. Eventually, the people of Kandamesh came to understand what had happened, and soon a new pall of fear settled on them like a heavy blanket, and while they continued to go about their daily lives, tending to their business, their smiles disappeared like grass in the winter snow, their joy took flight, like birds leaving for an endless journey, and the villagers lived their lives like ghosts, like brown, empty husks whose presence harked back to a greener life.

Meanwhile, back in Akram's caves (for they were now fully his and he knew this as well as he knew his name), Wahid gathered herbs and did his master's bidding. Sometimes, he would doze off, as Arkam had, in his bed of straw, and sometimes he would wander the caves and dream of his life back in the village.

"Wahid!" Akram would cry, as he stared into his crystal ball or conjured up visions in the flames of the fireplace. "Bring me some asphodel!"

And Wahid would scurry about, gathering the herbs that Akram required while Akram stared into his crystal ball and planned his next spell.

Meanwhile, things at the Choudry residence began to assume a semblance of normalcy, at least as much normalcy as could be expected for a Pakistani immigrant family living in Arlington, Virginia, a family that had roused hope and suspicion in the nation with their manifestations of sainthood, their cunning requests for donations and other forms of nonstandard, non-American behavior.

Several weeks after Easter had come and gone (after the events that had fully erupted into the nation's consciousness before finally sinking back into the nether land of forgetfulness thanks to the adeptness of the ever-vigilant news media), the crowds had disappeared from the patchy suburban lawn, and Choudry's rusted, broken-down car now reoccupied its usual place in the cracked, weedy driveway beside the barren fig tree and the overgrown patch of mint that grew in front of their dilapidated garage.

Inside, the stanchions that had been used to control the mobs of devotees were finally removed, and the candles and other paraphernalia they had brought with them were packed and stored. The animals that had been brought to Amina as offerings were taken to Choudry's shop where they were slaughtered and, in the Islamic tradition, distributed among the poor. The faux-French couch, once a throne for Amina's calcified body, now sat humbly back in its place, across the room facing the *sura* which continued to hang crooked and unadorned on the living room wall.

In the days that followed, no mention was ever made of Choudry's disappearance and the journey he had been forced to embark on. Choudry kept tight-lipped about his extraordinary experiences, preferring to forget the visions he had seen and the quest he had been taken on, and Amina never brought it up, at least not directly; nor did she allude to the mysterious affliction that she had succumbed to. Her transformative powers were gone, and so was her ability to cure the sick. No longer could she shake the earth and sit stone-still at will, and no longer could she heal people of their maladies and afflictions. And if she had been asked how she had done it or even why, she would not have been able to answer except to say that it was God's will.

Now, whenever she sat on the faux-French couch, noisily stirring a sugar cube into her steaming tea, she did so as an ordinary woman, an everyday Pakistani immigrant lady wrapped in her trademark orange sari with a matching headscarf loosely wound around her neck, ready to deploy at the first sign of a male visitor. Whatever sainthood she might have assumed was totally gone. And though she often gave Choudry a stony stare, especially when he had done something to anger her, or chided her son-in-law, whenever he fell into one of his noisy bouts of intolerance, she also talked and laughed and played with her grandchildren. And, as she had done in the past, before she had been struck by her mysterious affliction, she spent hours in her kitchen, preparing meals that more than made up for whatever magic she had once been capable of.

"Choudry!" she would call out as she stood beside the kitchen window staring out into the garden and planning the day's meals. "I need meat! I need spices! Cloves. Cumin. Cinnamon."

"Yes, dear," he would answer from the living room, mumbling annoyances under his breath as the sound of pots and pans roused him from his afternoon nap. Then he would curl his lips into a slight smile as he heaved himself up from the sunken couch and made his way to the foyer to fetch his keys.

"And don't be late!" she would add. "You know what happened the last time."

And then, as if she had been magically transported, she would be hovering right in front of him, fixing his shirt collar so he would look presentable before he stepped out into the heartless world.

"It's a jungle out there," she would say to him, trying to smooth the wrinkles out of shirt. "People are just waiting to pounce. They'll talk about you. Say you look like you just came off the streets of Peshawar."

"Yes, dear," he would answer.

"Remember," she would add, now working on his hair which, no matter how she tried, still remained disheveled. "We are foreigners here. Foreigners who, unfortunately, are now well-known. And a foreigner is always a foreigner, no matter what."

"Yes, dear." And he would stare up blankly at the dusty chandelier where two burned-out light bulbs stood out more conspicuously than the ones that were lit, and wait for Amina to release him from captivity.

"You know, Choudry," she said to him one day. They were in the living room, drinking tea, waiting for Fatwa and her brood to arrive. Amina put her hands on her knees, leaned forward, and said in a voice that was almost a whisper, "I had a dream last night."

Choudry instinctively heaved a sigh.

"You and your dreams!" he said, waving her off and preparing himself for a long retelling of whatever strange visions she had seen in her sleep, complete with a thorough and convoluted explanation of what they portended.

"What's wrong with my dreams?" Amina said. "They are real. A woman knows her dreams. She knows what they are telling her. And I know that this dream forebodes something. Something not good."

And Amina began to recount the long dream she had had the night before, a night that had followed a wedding celebration they had attended, a celebration at which she had eaten slightly too much biryani and drunk just a little too much pomegranate juice. Choudry tapped his foot and fingered his fat belly through an opening in his shirt and prepared himself for the long-winded tale.

"There was a boy," she began, "living in a cave. And he was up to no good."

And though he feigned attention, Choudry immediately tuned her out, naturally, easily, as if he were listening to a soccer game that no longer held interest, drifted into thoughts of how he would one day retire, how, one day, he would finally find the peace and quiet he so deserved. He would sell the shop at last. He would take all the money and move back to Pakistan. There, he would have a big villa and a lot of land where he would grow tomatoes and raise sheep, and quietly watch the sun set at the end of the day. He would make new friends, and maybe find his old ones, the childhood buddies he had grown up with, and he would sit with them in the garden and drink tea and smoke hookah, while Amina, inside with the women folk, far enough away so he could not hear her but close enough so he could call her when he needed, could chatter away to her heart's content, talk of dreams and children and grandchildren, and even relate to them the strange days when she had been mistaken for a saint, when he had disappeared mysteriously with the president of the United States.

"It's not good, Choudry."

Amina's voice summoned him back to reality.

"Something evil is going to happen. I feel it in my bones."

Choudry sighed. Then he wiped his face in frustration with his two hands, held them in the air as if praying and stood up.

"Choudry! Are you listening to me! Choudry, I don't like it when you stop listening to me!"

"Yes, dear."

But that night, Choudry did listen to her, listened as he drifted off to sleep. He had no choice, really, for he was lying in bed, and she was sitting beside him, sitting up and chattering away, and though he did not pay attention to the words, he let his wife's voice filter into his consciousness, and eventually drifted off into the soft folds of sleep, and he smiled contentedly, for what better gift could there be in this world than to lie beside one's wife and pretend to listen as her voice chases you off into slumber.

Kazi, meanwhile, had reformulated his previous outlook on life. His attendance at The Portable Inflatable Blazing Path of Light Ebenezer Baptist Church, LLC (it was a long name, but it had kept flashing on the entrance to the structure and now stuck with him like chewing gum sticks to one's shoe), his visit that fateful Easter Sunday had been a revelation to him, had made him appreciate all he had been taught during his long and insulated life. And while he was convinced more than ever that the path he had been placed on at the moment he had been born was the one and only true way in life, he also now understood that there were others in this world who simply didn't understand God's ways. It was not their fault, he concluded, and he should not hold it against them.

And so he greeted everyone now as brothers, greeted them with a nod and a smile, ready to enlighten them whether they wanted or not, avoiding the sisters as much as possible, as had been instructed in the Koran, except, of course, for those in his immediate family who gladly accepted his new, modulated outlook on life. And while he still saw it as his mission to bring everyone over to the straight and narrow path, he did so with such humility that even Fatwa was surprised, and she praised God for finally tempering her husband's behavior.

"God is very great," he would say in a soft voice at any given moment and to no one in particular. It was as if he were talking to himself, as if he were trying to convince himself that he could make a difference with these simple words. "He has made this great world and all these great people for a very great reason."

He smiled to himself, grinned a smile of self-satisfaction, a smile that showed how very much at peace he now was with himself.

"*Alhamdulillah. Alhamdulillah. Alahu akbar.*"

All so gently. All so filled with his newfound convictions about life.

And he would pour his mother-in-law's tea, hand her the glass, humbly and respectfully, glancing up just so from beneath his brow and wondering to himself just what had happened to her that day when she had turned into a stone on the faux-French couch. And while he never asked her about her ability to transform herself into rock, while he never questioned the fleeting gift she had been given to cure people's illnesses, he would wonder to himself whether her powers had been a gift from God or whether she had been secretly delving into the evil art of witchcraft.

"*Astaghfirullah*," he would mumble whenever these thoughts entered his mind. "God forgive all of us."

And Fatwa would smile, not knowing what his utterances were about, and Amina would scowl, pointing a bony finger at him, reminding him with a not-so-gentle prod that, even though he had found a new mission in life, he still needed to find a job.

"It is God's will," she would tell him, bringing the tea glass to her lips. "Men should work. Women," she would add, after a long sip of her precious, golden liquid, "should remain in the house and sip tea."

And Kazi would turn his gaze down, avoiding his mother-in-law's stony eyes and silently ponder her words and the meaning of this very short, very great life.

And whenever Amir entered the room without the traditional salaam, ("Hey, guys," he now took to shouting as he opened the door), Kazi would simply stroke his long, stringy beard (which he now allowed Fatwa to trim on a daily basis), bow his head and silently say to himself, "*Wa alaikum salaam*." For that, he insisted to himself, was the proper way to enter a roomful of Muslims, though he no longer pushed the idea.

Amir, meanwhile, was forced to put on hold his dream of creating a worldwide network of shines in his mother's honor. After all, he insisted, he could no longer justify it since she had suddenly forsaken her life as a holy saint. ("How esoteric," he would ponder to himself, "giving up sainthood to lead a normal life.") Moreover, he could no longer afford it, for the donations had stopped coming in and his cash flow was now tilting toward the negative.

Still, he put his mind to work, as well as the skills he had developed from his MBA program, and at last settled on a business that found its inspiration in the strange events that had taken place while his saintly mother was assuming her rightful place in the world.

Mystic Tea by Amina was packaged in dark, mysterious-looking boxes with a picture on the front of a woman frozen in time, holding a steaming glass of tea to her lips. And on the bottom, just below the purple couch on which she was eternally perched, was printed the following inscription: *Tealeaves to Assuage Any Affliction*.

At first, Amina protested at the image on the box and the claim that was proffered.

"Amir," she said to him one day, "this is chicanery. You are fooling the people, and all in my name! God will not like it, my son."

But she soon stopped voicing her disapproval, for who was she to stand in his way. A son was a son, no matter what, and what more could a mother ask for than for her son's success. And besides, she now had something else to prattle about whenever she gathered with her circle of friends.

Mystic Tea by Amina soon became a hit, showing up in the trendiest of shops, and even making its way to the upscale markets around town. Amir could hardly keep up with the orders, and Choudry sat back, fingering his beads, and smiled as the money started rolling in as if they had started a charity for the latest natural disaster. At last, he thought, his son had made him proud, and he now began to advise him on how best to run his business.

"Don't fill the boxes so much," he would tell him as he watched him and Kazi toiling in their basement operation. And then, to Kazi's protests over his penchant for dishonesty, "Never give your customers too much of a good thing. Keep them coming back for more."

Amir would smile slyly in reply and then remove just a tablespoon of the tealeaves from the cellophane packaging before sealing it. Choudry would smile back in acknowledgement, while Kazi would frown, mumbling protests and begging for God's forgiveness.

But while Kazi looked down at the way Amir was cheating their customers, he was secretly pleased, for this left him just enough room to sneak a slip of paper with a short verse from the Koran into the boxes it was his job to seal.

And so the Choudry family went on living their lives, carefully navigating a course between the customs they had brought with them from the old country and the new ones they were trying to emulate, attempting, subconsciously, to define their version of the American dream.

And every once in a while—just occasionally—something strange would occur, something small yet inexplicable: A part of Amina's anatomy—a toe or a finger, or even an entire leg—would suddenly stiffen, then just as suddenly return to normal. Choudry would hear voices or see visions, suddenly and without warning, while sitting in his car or counting the money from his charity boxes. And at those times, while everyone pretended not to notice yet secretly feared the worse, Amina would look at Choudry knowingly and pronounce, "Did I not tell you? I'm never wrong about my dreams."

And then they'd go on, as if nothing out of the ordinary had happened, ignoring Amina and her dreams, hoping deep inside that nothing unusual would ever happen again, nothing like what had happened to them just before the advent of that year's Christian celebration of Easter.

Several months later—quite a few, in fact, for time does have a knack for flitting away when one is engrossed in life's daily conundrums—following the ordeal he had endured after an innocent shave and a not-so-innocent bout of excessive inebriation, Larry White was once again in the midst of shaving the heavy growth on his now intact face, when he let out a hair-raising howl and flung the red-tinged razor across the room.

Pearl, ever mindful of her husband's recent tendency toward edginess (for he had never been the same since that fateful day when he had inexplicably acquired two mouths), came rushing in, immediately and somewhat apprehensively (for despite the news media's adeptness at modulating the tenacity of current events, those directly involved do not easily forget the ordeals they have endured), and said in a muted voice, "Lord have mercy, Larry! Hush your voice! You'll wake the baby!"

Staring into the mirror, Larry wiped the crimson cut on his ashen face with a crumpled square of toilet paper.

"You trying to get outta going to church again?"

"But Pearl, baby," he said, pointing to the crack in the mirror which created a reflection he was not sure was real or not.

"No buts or ifs or ands now, Larry."

Her face was stern, and Larry gave her a look so mean for her lack of empathy (a word he had learned during his stay at Revered Willis' poor excuse for a church), that, for a moment, he thought she would burst into tears. Then, as if to compensate, he produced a great big smile as he remembered the child she has recently delivered, a plump little boy who had his father's features and his mother's temperament, and whom they had named ("they" being Pearl) Cornelius Jacob, in honor of the good reverend who had done so much to help them in their direst time of need.

"Now you hurry up and get ready for church," Pearl said. "And hush your whining. Ain't you got the spirit in you now? Ain't nothing gonna harm you once you got the spirit."

Pearl beamed proudly at her man. Her efforts had finally paid off, for having endured the worst indignity in life, he had returned whole and in full sight of salvation. And all through her efforts and the wise counsel of Reverend CJ Willis.

Pearl kissed Larry gently on the cheek and left the room, humming an old gospel tune as Larry grumbled, exasperated, under his breath and hastily finished up his shave with an uneasy eye on the reflection in the mirror.

The months following that fortuitous Easter Sunday when Larry's face had once again become whole—the remainder of the Spring, which bloomed and blossomed and added a striking patina to an otherwise drab section of town, and the summer that followed, which had begun mildly enough but then settled into its typical cycle of scorching days and tepid nights—those months had seen a gradual return to a life that was at once mundane and filled with delight for both Larry and Pearl.

Larry returned to his job at Union Station and was greeted, though hesitantly, by his buddies and coworkers as both a dubious celebrity and a fear-provoking freak. Though they admired him for his short-lived fame and envied him for the strange adventure he had been on, they avoided him like moonshine, were spooked by his very presence ("Got the Devil in him, he does," he overheard one of them whispering one morning as he was changing into his uniform in the basement locker room. "Man, the dude's bad news. Ain't no telling what he's bound to do. Best keep yo' distance!").

But eventually, when Larry's voice did not produce anything but standard sounds ("they say he speaks jus' like the Devil") and when his face remained singular and evenly-complexioned), the icy distance they kept began to thaw, and the old feelings of friendship and affection began to resurface, and soon they were laughing and joking with him just like old times and inviting him out to carouse with them on Saturday nights.

"Jus' like ol' times," they would say, teasing him.

But Larry would refuse. Had given up drink, he would tell them. "The Devil's milk," he would say, much to their surprise and chagrin.

And so Larry's friendships soon languished, went by the wayside, as often happens when one gets older and matures, though his former buddies pretended to be just as chummy with him as they had been before.

Pearl, meanwhile, no longer the beatific vision materializing in gardens and hovering above altars, returned to her Bible studies and her Sunday services and, once she had given birth (a miraculously painless delivery thanks to the mesmerizing marvels of modern medicine), soon settled comfortably into her new role as a mother. She doted on her newborn son, pampering him from dawn to dusk, making him smile and laugh and comforting him during his frequent bouts of uncontrollable colic.

Like all babies, Cornelius Jacob (or CJ Junior, as she took to calling him) kept his parents awake at night, howling just when they had gotten to sleep and raising hell until he was given his bottle, and, like all parents, Pearl and Larry managed to cope, getting up bleary-eyed in the morning and going about their daily business, half-asleep but fully blissful. And, like all babies who are given the proper nutrition, Cornelius quickly developed into a strong, healthy baby boy, though he soon acquired a strange twitch on the right side of his mouth which kept his parents on edge whenever it manifested itself.

"Pearl, baby," Larry would say sometimes, when no one else was around. "That child's got the Devil inside him."

Pearl would immediately scowl at her husband and look at him as if she were observing a stranger whose very demeanor suggested harm.

"Larry White," she would say, indignantly. "How can you talk about your own child like that!"

"Just look at him," Larry would respond. "I don't like it, Pearl. Don't like the way his mouth moves like he's trying to fight off something evil. Something he has no control of."

"He's just got a little itch," she would say playfully, ignoring her husband's comment, cuddling her precious baby boy and running her finger gently over his quivering mouth. "And if that's the way you feel about your own flesh and blood, Larry White," she would say crossly turning toward him and raising her voice, "then maybe he's just got a little bit of you inside of him. Maybe I ought to take him straight to Reverend Willis and get his opinion."

These conversations, like those between all married couples, would lead to quarrels that would stop just as suddenly as they had begun, only to be forgotten, though feelings of anger and resentment would fester somewhere deep down inside each of their hearts, though they'd continue to go about their lives as if nothing untoward had been said. Pearl would read her Bible, with one wary eye on Cornelius Jacob and the other on Larry, and would needle her husband into going to Sunday services to witness the Lord and ask for forgiveness. Larry would resist these overtures to the best of his abilities, insisting, out of ignorance, that salvation, once achieved, was once and for all.

"Forgiveness for what?" Larry would say. "What is it I've done now?"

But eventually he would half-heartedly oblige, whenever he could no longer ignore her entreaties or come up with a good enough excuse and, with his already elevated status at Reverend Willis' revived storefront church as a has-been prophet, he soon became a permanent pillar of that dubiously esteemed mission.

"The Lord has sent me a messenger," Reverend Willis would proclaim before his congregation in his mellifluous voice, as he launched into long, drawn-out, fiery sermons on the long succession of prophets and the singular message they had each brought to mankind. And he would rail against the ills of society ("Idleness is the child of insolence."), and how the Devil continuously manifested himself in new and unique ways ("His face is in every magazine, every newspaper, on every billboard you lay your eyes on."), implore his parishioners to give up their ways and follow the straight path ("The Lord's way or the doorway—the doorway to hell, that is."), and then elicit from them their reluctant generosity ("Give generously of your love as you give generously into the collection box.") as the service climaxed to a glorious close.

And because, on that fateful Easter Sunday, when his portable, inflatable church had regrettably burst into air and deflated rapidly with a rushing hiss that was greeted with apprehension by all in the immediate area (for in this age of terrorism, can one ever be too cautious or too sure?), trapping hundreds of worshippers in its heavy folds of gaudy plastic and creating a riot not seen in the Washington, DC area for decades, the good Reverend CJ Willis chose to settle back into his humble storefront mission and keep as low a profile as he possibly could so as to avoid any legal proceedings that might ensue. And as a result (though he would claim otherwise), he reincorporated his ever-evolving church, renaming it The True Almighty Church of the Lord's Ever-Lasting Revival and Mission, Inc., a long, convoluted name that demonstrated his special ability to adapt to the times.

"For just as the Lord transformed His life while on this earth, so, then, shall we transform ourselves, so, then, does His church transform itself throughout the ages."

Eventually, the grimy storefront window was wiped clean, the fading cross was replaced with a brand-new laminated replica, and the reusable cellophane stained glass window was peeled off for the very last time and, in its place, a real stained glass window, made of the finest plastic and imported all the way from China, was installed and glowed down warmly on the congregation when the sun was positioned just right in the sky.

"And God saw that it was good," the Revered Willis said, quoting from the Bible, to no one in particular.

And he settled into his role as pastor of a small but popular neighborhood church, slowly forgetting his dreams of grandeur, settled himself in his cozy chair in the overly cluttered office in the basement of his storefront mission, counting and recounting the proceeds of the week's collection money, with no worries to fret about in the world until, one day, Pearl, clutching Cornelius Jacob in her arms, peeped her head nervously through the door, and, hushing her child's rambunctious howling said, in a voice that was less than tranquil, "Uh, Reverend Willis?"

Looking up from his notes (for the good reverend was preparing the coming Sunday's sermon), he invited Pearl in. Then, startled out of his complacency, he glanced fearfully from her to the hellish looking child and let out a sigh that some would describe as desperate and others as unwilling acquiescence to God's incomprehensible will.

And so does the cycle of God's creation persist. So does our story of Larry and Pearl and their newborn child and their hastily trained pastor come to an end, though the ending, as one can plainly see, is just a continuation as all endings really are.

One day—and it was a most beautiful day, though one that portended something momentous and unusual—not long after his mouth had firmly and enduringly reattached itself to the place it had lovingly occupied on his forlorn and befuddled face, and soon after he had once again recovered the use of his ever-vexing and innocuous voice (a voice, he now admitted, that had gotten him into trouble more often than not, for not everyone was blessed with the gift of rhetoric and the ability to cogently string together a simple series of words), President Thorne was sitting in his den, reading the day's newspaper, comfortably settled in his favorite armchair, deep inside his quiet ranch in the back-country of the Texas wilderness, when a sudden, terrifying thought seized his mind, a thought that seemed to bring the very essence of his life to a perfect standstill. Anxiously, he lowered the paper and glanced, bewildered, around the room, reaffirmed that he was truly implanted in his own house, in the very setting he had escaped to after handing in his sudden and shocking resignation, and stared straight out the window where his horse, Dolphin, grazed tranquilly near a tall, shady oak tree under the warmth of the morning sun. Reassured, he let out a long sigh of relief.

"No," he thought. "I don't have to do that anymore."

And he lifted the paper back up to position, just close enough to block out the world yet far enough so he could decipher the enigmatic print on the page.

"Not today. Not tomorrow. Not ever again," he said quietly.

President Thorne smiled to himself—a big satisfied smile, a smile of utter relief, a smile, he was now capable of easily producing—and resumed his morning routine: scanning the daily comics, though, he secretly admitted, he often found it difficult to comprehend the cryptic form of humor they insisted on employing.

"Could it just be me," he thought, scratching his head, annoyed at the obtuseness that could sometimes make its way into publication. "Damn liberals, he mumbled. "Can never make their intentions clearly known."

Life had been good to President Thorne since his retirement—his abdication, some would say, his abandonment of a failed attempt at governing the nation. Ever since the ordeal of his mouth—and the odyssey he had unwillingly embarked on to rediscover it—and his inability to speak clearly (though that was a word most would not use to describe the utterances he had used during his tenure), he had begun to question the wisdom of the current, unworkable excuse for democracy, where the most vocal got their way, and the most vulnerable in society suffered as a result.

"I tried my best to do the right thing," he would repeat, even when no one was listening, "but all they did was whine."

Whine because they thought they were entitled to things they had no right to. Things that cost the nation. And all the while, the small minority of hard-working people suffered—the ones with ideas, with money to invest, the ones whose hard work created the wealth that everyone benefitted from. After all, hadn't he been taught to defend the rights of the minority? "Buy the people, for the people." Hadn't he read it over and over again in the history books? Hadn't the forefathers carefully framed the Constitution, structured the government so that no one faction trampled the other? Only they had never said who the people really were. So when he had decided, at last, all on his own (and with the coaxing of his trusted advisors), he was faced with wave after wave of resistance. No wonder nothing ever get done! No wonder the government was filled with stalemates, logjams and legislative congestion. Where were the days when leaders decided and everyone else just shut up and listened?

But now he was content. Now he could sit in his room, read the newspaper and not have to listen to one side or another. They had all complained, of course, his backers, the ones who had pumped money into his war chests, the ones who had risked their necks to make sure his presidency was seated after an unthinkable dispute at the ballots. But frankly, he couldn't give a damn—yes, he used the word freely now—for here he was, removed from the frantic pace of Washington, at peace at last, enjoying the frills of early retirement and not worried in the least about which judge to appoint, which senator chaired which committee (and there were many to fear in that arena) or whether to employ his veto power on some bill which some exasperating lobbyist did not favor, or simply put his John Hancock (he loved that expression, it gave the simple act of signing the authentic weight of history) on a document that, frankly, he had not read nor would have understood had he taken the time to do so.

Even his wife seemed pleased, though at first she had protested, had insisted it would make them pariahs in an already hostile society.

"What in the world will we tell our friends?" she had said to him, with her sleepy eyes and slow, Southern drawl when he had first announced his intentions. Then, just as quickly, as if something had suddenly changed, and with a tone of resignation and bitterness: "No matter. Your advisors will think of something. That dreadful Mark Drove will think of something. He always does."

And though she rarely spent much time with him nowadays (for she was always retreating to her bedroom or flying off to some exotic land where, she hoped, no one would recognize her), she had accepted his decision to leave the White House, suddenly and without explanation, and soon began referring to those days when he had lost his mouth ("How inconsiderate," she would confess to her closest confidants) and disappeared without even informing her ("How could you?" she said to him, one day, after he had returned, though he could not tell if she was referring to his disappearance or his reemergence), if she referred to them at all, as a social nightmare from which she thought she would never awake.

"You never did have much of a knack for speaking, truth be told," she said to him one evening. "Even before your... your horrid affliction. Even now, what you say doesn't make much sense. Had I only listened to my mother," she sighed. "She said you would never amount to much, no matter how hard you tried."

President Thorne would ignore these comments, though they hurt him deep inside. Quickly leaving the room, he would climb into his jeep, drive mindlessly around his ranch and, if he were lucky enough to find a tree that needed chopping, would take out his anger and frustration on the dead, gnarled piece of wasted wood. For it was one thing to be demonized by the press, to be drawn and quartered by the opposition, to be raked over the coals, as the expression goes, by the pundits and the people, but when your own wife took to disparaging you, it was bitter torture to bear.

Dolphin was his only comfort. He could ride her all day without one complaining neigh, take her through bush and bare field and she would obey just the same, would gallop and trot and prance at his command. Such is the difference between man and beast. The one enjoys your company on a whim, the other exhibits loyalty come day or darkness, calm or storm.

So on this day (it was a chilly, damp day on the endless Texas plains), as he was pitching wood into the fireplace, there came a loud pounding on the door and Mark Drove, who had remained loyal even after the fiasco he had caused, entered the room with a look on his face which President Thorne had not seen for quite some time.

"Mr. President," Drove said, ever composed, always the man to calm the rivers even as they raged out of control. "There's someone to see you, sir."

President Thorne tossed another piece of wood into the crackling fireplace and turned to Drove with a quizzical look on his face.

"It's rather urgent, I would say," Drove responded. "She requires your counsel."

President Thorne's face flashed with annoyance, and he turned and resumed feeding the fire, signaling his refusal to get involved.

"It's your duty, Mr. President," Drove said.

President Thorne tossed the last piece of wood into the fire and stood up. He walked slowly to his armchair and sat down. His face was worn, his eyes etched with heavy streaks of worry, his hair grayer than it had ever been. Even his mouth exhibited signs of anxiety which, just several years ago, had not been there. He gazed wearily at Drove, a look of resignation on his face and said,

"Very well. Show her in."

Several minutes later—several very long minutes, which President Thorne could hardly bear—the door opened and Bella Stromberg entered. She was dressed in a plain suit—a navy blue skirt with a matching jacket, a plain white blouse underneath—and her hair was ordinary and tired-looking with streaks of gray already fingering their way through her scalp. But the most noticeable thing about her was her face, which, once striking (President Thorne had to admit), was now drawn and heavy, and was conspicuous for its lack of what had become the most singularly important thing now to President Thorne: a mouth.

President Thorne suppressed a smile. He was not, after all, irreverent, no matter what else they said about him. And he completely understood what she was going through, understood thoroughly, now, why she had come to seek his advice.

He stood up and greeted her warmly. Silently commiserating, he put his arm around her shoulder as if they were old friends who had not seen each other for quite some time. Then, he beckoned for her to take a seat and, when she refused with a simple shake of her head, remained standing with her.

A long silence ensued as they stared at each other, the one understanding the trials of the other, the other in desperate need of counsel and comfort; the one humbled by experience, the other by the fires she was now being tested with on a daily basis.

"How can I be of help?" President Thorne said at last.

It was an honest, sincere question, completely devoid of malice for her or her party, and he took her hand in his and patted it gently.

Bella responded through her eyes—deep brown eyes which spoke volumes and revealed her appreciation for his kindness and understanding. She winced as she held back a tear. Then, she turned her back to him, bent way over, supporting herself by clutching her knees, and said, "Please tell me how to govern this ungrateful nation!"

Her words came out thick and raspy, and President Thorne stared at her in shock.

Having now broken the ice, the former president and the current one talked through the night, the one through a mouth which he was most grateful to have regained, the other through an orifice that we will simply not mention in polite company. They talked of policy and strategy and the direction the nation should follow. They talked of politicking and political intrigue. And they talked about the threats facing the country, threats from both inside and out. But mostly they talked about what it means to lose a mouth, how one's voice is, perhaps, the most important asset a person—any person, but especially a president—could ever have—how it defines one's life, and especially how, given President Thorne's invaluable experience, Bella might be able to recover hers.

Such are the ways our leaders sacrifice their lives in order to guide and protect us. Such are the iniquities they must endure so that we may lead free and peaceful lives. One may say whatever one wants about a particular individual or a particular president, but not until we fully understand what he or she has been through can we fully appreciate what it was that finally defined their tenure. One president loses a mouth while another gains an instrument with which to trumpet his or her ideas.

And that, my dear comrades, is the whole truth, such truth as there may be, as it is also the absolute end of our long and winding tale.

~ THE END ~

Acknowledgements

This novel began quite a number of years ago and, like many other projects, was put aside for what I perceived as more reachable goals. Then, during my MFA experience at George Mason University, I decided to revisit its possibilities and seek comments from my professors and colleagues.

The feedback I received was encouraging, and Susan Richards Shreve, my Fiction professor, convinced me the novel had much potential. Following her advice, I began waking up at four in the morning to work on it prior to going to my day job (a habit I still maintain) and finished it about two years later. Now, several years after that, it is finally ready to reach the public.

There are many people to thank for my being able to accomplish this achievement (for writing a novel is much different than putting together a collection of poetry, which is what I normally do). First, hearty thanks to those classmates who were truly anxious to see what would become of Choudry and the other characters they encountered in this story. Second to Susan Richards Shreve, immense gratitude; without her encouragement, this project would have never reached fruition. Special thanks go to Norah Vawter who spent time reading and critiquing some of the chapters. And an immeasurable amount of appreciation to my wife, Amal, who offered comments and support and came up with the title, and to my children—Fairuz, Yasmine and Karim—who allowed me the time to entertain my whims. And finally, a big thank you to the wonderful people at Little Feather Books— Katherine Boland and Cynthia Ceilán—who believed in this book and worked to make it happen.

And to you, the reader, very special appreciation for choosing this novel from the myriad number of books available in the marketplace. I hope you will find it entertaining, enlightening and worthy of your time.

About the Author

Mike Maggio was born in New York City, spent a great deal of time in Los Angeles and the Middle East, and now lives in Northern Virginia with his wife and family, including a green-cheeked conure named Zippy and three parakeets. He attended Queen's College (CUNY), where he studied Creative Writing and Literature, The New School, where he studied filmmaking, the University of Southern California, where he obtained a degree in Applied Linguistics, and George Mason University, where he received his MFA.

Mike's publications include fiction, poetry, travel and reviews in *The Montserrat Review, LA Weekly, The Washington CityPaper, The Washington Independent Review of Books,* and many others. He has instigated and realized collaborative performance projects with actors, artists and musicians, most notably *cloudism* and *Music for Mummies*. He is an assistant adjunct English professor at Northern Virginia Community College and an Associate Editor for *Potomac Review*.

Visit Mike Maggio's website at www.mikemaggio.net to learn about collaborative projects in which you could be involved.